Wyrd Of The Wolf

Wyrd Of The Wolf

Wyrd Of The Wolf Book I

John Broughton

Dedicated to Adam, Dylan and Jeanne

Special thanks go to my dear friend John Bentley for his steadfast and indefatigable support. His proofreading and suggestions have made an invaluable contribution to Wyrd.*of the* Wolf

Chapter 1

Aelfhere and Cynethryth

Steyning, West Sussex, January 685 AD

Aelfhere tugged at the thong at his neck causing the wizened ear of a wolf to prickle at his skin. The hidden amulet did not prevent his heart sinking when the aetheling of Kent downed more ale. The stripling drank fast, the flushed cheekbones, the sheen on his brow, the shrill voice over the oath-laden din, revealed as much. Did the fledgling ignore how much was at stake?

The smoky air caused Aelfhere to rub his smarting eyes before checking on the abiding frown of his daughter, Cynethryth, seated with other noblewomen at the end of the hall. She, who had more reason than anyone to appraise the young man, disapproved: an attitude that heightened his foreboding.

Strange table companions, the Suth Seaxe hosts and their guests. Nine years past, the Mercians — overlords to the Suth Seaxe — devastated Kent, and it rankled! The atmosphere, dense with mistrust, spread to the dogs; sensing the tension in the room, several left off chewing bones and stood, heckles rising. Some began to bark. Beside the aetheling sat King Aethelwahl. The old fox! Ruler owing to the support of the Mercians on his northern borders. Where lay the truth? Had he turned his back on the gods of his forefathers to embrace the milksop his neighbours worshipped: the so-called god who kissed his enemies instead of slaughtering them like swine or sending the *wæl-cyrge* to conduct the slain to the Hall of the Dead? Or, as Aelfhere suspected, did he enact a ploy to gain time before shaking off the alien yoke?

Staring upwards, Aelfhere's gaze roved along the rough-hewn tie beam, the oak from woodland covering the Downs. The same timber formed the palisade around the stronghold commanding the ford on the Adur. A flame flickered in a cresset, its light catching the image of the one-armed war god incised in the copper band at his wrist. The baleful likeness of Tīw glinted as he reached for his cup only for Baldwulf, his closest friend, to nudge him, causing his ale to spill and Aelfhere to curse. Pointing with a rib bone half-stripped of meat, the thegn indicated the refilling of the aetheling's drinking horn.

Once before in his life had Aelfhere seen Eadric, on Wiht, his island home: a babe in the arms of his mother, the sister of the king of the isle and wife to Ecgberht of Kent. The child had grown. His ten and eight years made him a man, but he must learn to pace his drink. No spearman would follow an exiled sop — not in the bloody matter of reclaiming a kingdom.

A cry of outrage disturbed his thoughts. Men leapt to their feet, horns, cups and food scattering on jostled tables as benches over-turned. Confused, Aelfhere too jumped up to see three warriors hang-ing on to a South Seaxe ealdorman — he who sat on the far side of Eadric. One man grasped his forearm with both hands to prevent the use of a seax. The other two struggled to pull the writhing assailant away from the aetheling while all around, men sniggered and pointed, stoking the fury of the outraged nobleman.

Eadric too held a knife but with his arm limp at his side as he rocked with merriment, his other hand clenching a long lock of hair.

"By the Giant Lord of Mischief," Aelfhere grinned at Baldwulf, "he's shorn him like a sheep!"

His thegn guffawed, "In the name of Lôgna, he has too!"

Shouts of applause at the aetheling's wit echoed from the rafters for these rude men understood this kind of humour.

Silence fell when Aethelwalh hammered with the pommel of his seax.

"Enough! It's poor sport when a man riles at a jest!" He turned to Eadric, "Brother, come now, hand back your prize to friend Fordraed."

The aetheling's smirk and the ill-concealed amusement in his eyes countered the malice in the expression of the other. An awed silence accompanied the younger man holding out a fistful of yellow hair; a huge hand dashed it to the ground.

"What use is it to me?"

The gesture and the pointless question led to more laughter but the wise ealdorman quelled his ire; too much ale and high temper are poor companions and worse counsellors. Servants bustled to right and replenish cups and nothing more fearsome than glares and scowls from the offended ealdorman pierced the blithe aetheling.

In vain, Aelfhere tried to sweep aside glum thoughts. This should be a joyous occasion but here he sat, a scarred warrior amid rowdy revellers with an old woman wittering in his head, vexing and nagging. Arwald of Wiht, his king, had ordered him here with a score of armed men. On the favourable outcome of their mission rode the safeguarding of the isle: a shield to their way of life. Wise advances, given the dying months of the year had brought a debilitating outbreak of the yellow illness after a poor harvest. In Aelfhere's lifetime, his homeland had never been so vulnerable. The Wihtwara must strengthen. No-one disputes the gods aid those who help themselves and, by Woden, no man would tell him who to serve and who to worship! Time to unite the Kenting with the Wihtwara and bind them with the people of the Suth Seaxe in a force to be reckoned with. Over the ages, Aethelwahl's folk had bred whelps with the Jutes! Enough blood in common flowed in their veins to weld a southern block capable of making an invader ponder long and hard before contemplating attack.

Ale and good food brightened his mood as the evening progressed, until the moon lighted the humped forms of men stupid with drink sprawled under the tables. Unsteady on his feet, Aelfhere braved the iron chill to regain his hut.

Cynethryth came to him in the morning. At her greeting, he ran his forefinger down the scar beside his nose over the thick moustache concealing the slash on his lip and down to his chin. This ritual, he enacted whenever forced to listen to what displeased him.

"Father, to insult and annoy one's guest in front of everyone is not the mark of a man but rather of an arrogant brat! I needn't tell *you* the importance of hair to a person of rank, an ealdorman no less."

Tongue like a skein of wool, head a smith's anvil, made discussion unwelcome.

"Only a jest," he managed.

"A jest! You men are so foolish! A prank like that can lead to bloodshed. I came to tell you, father, I like him not and will not take him for my spouse."

She crossed her arms and fixed him with a stare.

Fighting off the clenching of his stomach and the oath on his tongue, Aelfhere resorted to wiser tactics.

"Daughter, have pity on my poor skull! Steep me some of those dried flowers for the splitting head —"

"Feverfew?"

"Ay."

Busy about the fire, she prepared to boil water in a pot. Warmth suffused him for the girl he had cherished since his wife died in the throes of childbirth. If he were a scop, what verses he would chant to praise her beauty! A woman now, full ten and six years. Truth be told, her looks eclipsed even those of her mother, Elga, nicknamed 'elfin-grace' for her comeliness.

Ah, Cynethryth, joy of my life, changeable as the depths around our isle. One moment calm, the red-gold flood of hair like the sunset reflected on a creek; eyes the grey mist swirling on the morning shore — the surface ripple across the bay the smile on your lovely lips; the next, countenance pale as the wind-flung spume, a temper black and relentless as the endless waves.

A grating laugh at his own conceit caused his daughter to gaze at him.

"What?"

"Oh, nought. A fancy! I might take up the hearpe. Never know, if I spent the evening singing, there'd be less time for supping…"

Cynethryth smiled and tossed the dried flowers from her pouch in the water bubbling like fish eyes. "It'd serve for every last man of you. It'd stop the drinking, father… the hall'd empty faster than our Creek at low tide! There are rooks more tuneful than you!"

Blowing on the scalding liquid, he found consolation knowing other heads would be worse than his that morning.

How to broach it with her? Thunor hammering at my brain isn't helping.

Her dark grey eyes met his and he flinched at their piercing stare.

A finger dipped into his cup and withdrawn with a gasp produced the tinkling laugh that so pleased him. He had distracted her.

"He won't be a callow lad for ever, you know…"

"Uh?"

"Eadric. I said —"

"I hear you, father. My mind is made up. I shall not wed."

Aelfhere blew on his potion far harder than needed. A way had to be found, but how, with the girl as stubborn as the pot stones lining the fire? Also, he doubted his will to force her. Other men of Wiht treated their women as chattels, but he would not. This resolve shaped his approach.

Ennoble her, elevate her to the king's counsel.

"Daughter, let's set aside that you shall be the king's lady of a great folk and want for nought…" he held up an admonishing hand, "…hark! I love you and would chain you to my side, but My Life, there are circumstances that go beyond the wishes of a man. There is wyrd. The gods weave our destiny, Child."

Cynethryth, about to speak, halted when he shook his yellow locks and placed his finger beside his nose. In a voice of steel, he said, "At my birth, Wiht rankled under the yoke of the Seaxe from the West.

They sought to control our lives and force us to turn our backs on our gods. They destroyed our sacred groves and slaughtered our priests."

"Father, why are you telling me this?"

The herbal liquid now cooled, he took a long draught and wiped his mouth with the back of his hand.

"Patience! Heed my words! Wulfhere swept from Mercia and drove out the West Seaxe invader, making matters worse. Ten years ago, he died and Aethelred took the throne. See you, there's no love lost for him in Kent for he devastated their land to secure his borders. Then, when you were eleven, five winters past, he won a battle on the Trent against the men from north of the Humber and seized Lindesege from them."

"So, a most powerful king!"

Aelfhere bestowed on her a thin smile. In his mind, he had gained her attention and half-won the contest.

"Ay," he pressed on, "but the land he rules is vast and his grip on the southern kingdoms is weak. To the west, Centwine worships the new god...Christians...spine like jellyfish..!" he spat on the floor and swigged the last of his brew as if to wash away a bad taste, "...in the Andredes weald — the forest of Andred — roams a war-band of desperate men, West Seaxe and Meonwara, led by one who would be king hereabouts. These are turbulent, dangerous times, daughter. Because of this, Aethelred leaves the south to Aethelwalh who acknowledges him as overlord. In turn, he concedes Wiht to our own Arwald who is our lord. Understand?"

Her frown told him, *what has this to do with me?* In haste, he added, "The folk of Kent are our kin. They're from Jutish stock, as is half of the Suth Seaxe. United in arms, we can stand alone against all comers. In his heart, Aethelwalh worships the gods of our forefathers and he will leave us in peace. On this, we have his word. The aetheling is half-Wihtwara, you know? His mother is our king's sister. Cynethryth, will you not see? Our future lies with you, my wildcat. Eadric has eyes for you. Who would not? My task is to plight your troth and he will grow into a fine warrior and you will be the king's lady—"

She stepped up to him and placed a finger on his lips before throwing her arms around his neck. The cup slipped from his hand and clattered on the floor as he enfolded her. Breathing in the scent of apple blossom in her hair, his emotion overcame him and he vowed whatever her decision, he would abide by it.

"Father, I love you so," she murmured, "and I adore our island. We must do what we can to keep it safe. I obey father. Are you glad?"

He forced himself to say: "Are you sure, Child?"

Her oval countenance opened like sunlight from behind a cloud.

"I shall make him a man, father. Have no fear!"

At that, he laughed out loud.

"Rather him than me, wildcat!" and he kissed her on the forehead.

In the afternoon, a group of women came to prepare Cynethryth for betrothal. Washed and scented, she no longer should be seen 'in her hair'. Her handmaiden braided the flowing red-gold locks, the sign of her chastity, as a symbol of espousal. A summons came for Aelfhere and he led his daughter back into the hall, the scene of the previous night's revelry. Set to promise this blossom on his arm to another, he swelled with pride that she would be the king's lady if the gods so willed. The betrothal rested on one condition: Eadric should win back the throne of Kent from a usurper, his uncle, Hlothhere.

The hall, strewn with clean rushes, betrayed no sign of the previous night's roistering, the tables rearranged for the witnesses to sit with King Aethelwalh. Neither did Eadric show effects of overindulgence but for a noticeable pallor. The high set of his brow offset by the gold circlet around his head, bespoke nobility. So too did the pleasing jawline, the heavy gold bracelets at his wrists and his dress of the finest linen under a leathern tunic tooled in designs of biting beasts.

Drawing near the aetheling, Aelfhere admitted the splendour of the youth and, a good sign, the sharp intake of breath from the girl at his side confirmed as much. Eadric bowed to the lady and turned to the King of the Suth Seaxe.

"Before you today, I pledge a wedd of forty gold pieces to the trustees on my word to take as wife Cynethryth of Cerdicsford…"

With an offhand gesture, a bag dropped, thudding with dull heaviness.

"...and this," he said, opening a hand to reveal a gold ring adorned with a single ruby, "is the arrha, the earnest I bring from my mother's own hand." He slipped the band on Cynethryth's finger before reaching into his tunic to produce a jewel of threaded gold beads. A necklace interspersed with black, polished jet stones set in beaten gold, he clasped it around her throat. "And for last, *this*, my beloved," he bestowed a kiss, causing her to blush.

On the part of Cynethryth, Aelfhere addressed the King.

"My Lord, I swear before you and the trustees that I, Aelfhere of Cerdicsford, will make good any liability my daughter may incur in her married life. As representative of her family, I take responsibility on her behalf." From his belt, he pulled a purse, "Here is the fosterlean."

Aethelwalh raised a hand, "But, not all is stated," the murmurs among the assembled crowd hushed. What might hinder the espousal? The king gazed at Eadric with thoughtful mien and an expression of gloom, "should you within three seasons from this spring not be crowned in Kent, the betrothal is null."

The aetheling betrayed no surprise, "I accept."

"Well," Aethelwalh said, "the gathering is dismissed. Eadric, Aelfhere, my ealdormen, stay! It is of war we must speak."

While the thought of fighting did not trouble Aelfhere, he wished for the young man to be enthroned as soon as possible. Aelfhere and his score of Wihtwara would lend their arms to Eadric who would gather forces in West Kent and unite them to his bondsmen. Aethelwalh's pledge of two hundred men, led by the ealdorman of the shorn lock, also reassured him. The safety of his daughter concerned him but, as to that, the King meant to retreat to the stronghold of Kingsham with the women in safekeeping.

* * *

Two weeks had passed since the betrothal, fourteen days of marching, gathering men willing to throw in their lot with the aetheling for the promise of preference. Their numbers had swollen close to three hundred. The day before, their scouts found the foe led by Hlothhere heading south-east. They waited among the trees on a rise in the Ouse valley near the place known as Isefeld. Silent as wraiths, they slipped from cover and formed a shieldwall. The ground, a little higher to their advantage, favoured the use of throwing weapons. Unlike the Suth Seaxe and the Kenting, who carried a spear and several javelins, Aelfhere and his men had but the former and their axes.

In haste, the adversary, backs to the river, also formed a line of shields. The aetheling's uncle strode before his men and his voice drifted up the hill. In turn, Eadric stepped out before his warriors. Slightness of frame, piping voice and youth belied his pluck. Even though the Wihtwara did not hold with the weakling god the aetheling invoked, his words inspired him and, indeed, his men.

"Cantwara, here we fight to the last drop of blood in the name of the Father and to take back what is ours by right. The usurper, Hlothhere, must pay for his offence to the memory of King Ecgberht. Let he who lays down his life know his sacrifice is in a righteous cause and his soul will fly to heaven."

The aetheling turned and strode back, the metal whiskers wrought on the faceguard of his helm glinting in the sun.

Aelfhere besought his own god: *May Tīw be with us and give our sinews strength.*

Eadric went on, beating a fist against his chest, "Suth Seaxe and Wihtea friends, we are beholden and swear, a kingdom of brothers will ever be at your flank. Spare no foe! To the slaughter!"

A guttural roar and battering of weapons on shields drowned the shrill voice of the aetheling. Mid-speech, three hundred paces away, at the din, Hlothhere spun on his heel to stare at his enemy.

From the depths of his barrel chest, Aelfhere raised a battle cry and the host took up the blood-curdling howl. The Wihtwara rushed forward, the bannermen struggling to keep in the van. Thirty yards from the foe, men hurled the rocks they had garnered and their throwing axes spun through the air. Those with javelins flung some high, others flat, to confound the enemy shields; some buried into soft ground to be seized and hurled back, several transfixed the bodies of the luckless. The screams of the stricken echoed from the woodland behind.

Aelfhere stumbled as the body of the hapless man next to him dropped. No time to trouble over a soul plucked to Waelheal, instead, he adjusted his helm and lowered his spear. Those who bore shields crashed them into those held by the enemy and heaved. Those who, like Aelfhere, had but an iron-tipped ash pole, sought to impale a foeman. The resistance of a thighbone made the Wihtwara ealdorman release his grip on the weapon before unslinging his axe and evading a metal point aimed at his breast. Far better to swing his battle-axe, hard up to the foe, than to be impeded by an unwieldy spear.

The islanders followed his example. In a welter of red-spurting flesh, a clamour of shrieks, and the craze of bloodlust pounding in their veins, they scythed through the enemy ranks to reach the far side and open land. A press of men around a blue banner emblazoned with a white horse caught the eye of Aelfhere. He urged his men back into the thick of the fighting and after endless minutes of hacking and skipping, hewing and dodging, to a harsh roar they hauled down the trophy. The chase to the trees began.

His five and thirty years weighing on his aching limbs, Aelfhere leant on his battle-axe.. With the day won he would leave the chasing to younger legs. Shrieks from fleeing men meeting their end assailed his ears. Stood still, fatigued, soreness gripped him, but on inspection, he found no wounds under the spattered gore. All around sprawled the dead, tempting predators, kites, ravens and crows, to alight on the banquet of carrion. It sickened him.

His eyes roved over the carnage to where a warrior lay with a broken spear in his chest. He started: the object grasped in the man's hand — a sword! Aelfhere was about to fulfil a lifelong desire. Wiht boasted no smiths skilled in blade-making. By Tīw, elsewhere they cost the wergeld of an arm!

A glance warned him of comrades swarming back from the trees. Three bounds brought him to the fallen man. A red kite about to settle on the corpse flapped away with a screech of protest. The weapon wrenched from the lifeless grip, he stared at the blade with its snaking groove down the centre. The balance pleased him and he grunted, satisfied, gazing in awe at the bronze pommel shaped in the likeness of a wolf's head. How Tiw blessed him! Not only by the gift of a sword but by the richness of the helm, where the wrought figure of a gilded wolf ran about the rim. At the least, the dead man must be an eorl. Laying down his weapons, with trembling hand, Aelfhere unlaced the thongs under the man's chin to release the cheek-guards and ease off the helm. The sightless eyes, as unfeeling as the Wihtwara warrior, glared past him to the skies. His simple iron cap, he tossed to the ground, his brow slick with sweat from the leather inner cup and, weary, he hobbled with his spoils to greet his companions approaching.

The concern of Baldwulf gave way to a broad grin at seeing his friend exhausted but unhurt, "Aelfhere, old fox! Whilst we did the dirty work you helped yourself!"

Content, he beamed back, "By the gods, Baldwulf, these fox legs can scamper no more! Hunt around. You too might find a sword."

The thegn glanced round, "By the stars! they're worse than ravens!" And he plunged into the midst of his plundering comrades.

Startled, mid-laugh, by a hand clapped on his shoulder, Aelfhere turned to stare into the faceplate of the royal helm.

"The day is won. I struck down Hlothhere with my own hand. With my father's brother gone to Hell and my own father long passed over, there is call for another counsellor..." Behind the eyeholes, the pale blue irises shifted with anxiety.

Aelfhere sank down on one knee, "My lord —"

"Stand!" he dragged the Wihtwara to his feet, "I shall call you father," he said, "for they will crown me, then I shall wed my Cynethryth."

"With your own hands?" asked Aelfhere, unaware of the boyish grin hidden beneath the helm.

"Uh?"

"You slew Hlothhere with your own hands?"

Eadric grew grave.

"The traitor was stronger than I. But I am ten times faster and I sliced his throat."

The young man drew himself up, regal in appearance.

Aelfhere rejoiced.

"My lord, I am content you will wed my daughter! Her husband will be a worthy ruler and you may call me what you will."

In this season, the shadows grew long early in the day and the amber sun, sparkling on the river, modelled the land in rich, deep greens and ochre. A tranquil scene, made incongruous by the hideousness of the carnage and the squabbling of the warriors bickering over disputed trophies. The sky, thick with wheeling, screeching raptors, frustrated at the presence of human scavengers, made a stark contrast to the companionable silence of the two onlookers. Eadric broke the spell, slipping off a heavy gold ring and handing it to Aelfhere.

"A token of our gratitude," he said, "the Wihtwara fought well this day. How can we ever forget?"

Moved, he stared at the jewel and his eyes widened. Embossed on the golden band, nestling in his blood-encrusted palm, the maw of a beast gaped up at him — another wolf! What message eluded him? At the first opportunity, he would seek out a sorcerer to reveal the meaning of the gods.

A forced march took them to the small settlement of Uckefeld where they slaughtered two score sheep and goats and roasted them in the barn. Eadric, the king, pressed a purse of coins into the hands of the village elder. For the villagers, the worry of facing the rest of the winter without livestock was lost in exuberance. Once more, the aetheling drank hard but Aelfhere sized him with a different measure. Through no fault of his own, fate had hastened the youth into manhood, and by Thunor, the warrior was emerging!

In the morning, with an embrace, Aelfhere took his leave of Eadric: one directed to the land of the Cantwara and the other with his islanders and the men of the Suth Seaxe to join King Aethelwalh. The younger man parted with a promise on his lips to claim his bride before the spring bade farewell to summer.

Unscathed from battle, Aelfhere marched back to his daughter with joy-filled heart and counting but one Wihtwara dead, though two men had lost fingers in close fighting. Cynethryth would become lady of a great people and the husband he had feared a worthless sop proved to be a leader of men and stout-hearted warrior. Not least, he, Aelfhere, had entered the soon-to-be king's favour and, around the first night's campfire in the Weald, his wolf sword, helm and ring were sources of marvel. Life was good.

"You will have to change your name *Aelf*here to *Wulf*here," Baldwulf said.

"One mangy *bald* wulf is enough in this pack!" he said, to a roar of laughter, "besides Wulfhere is a name we curse on Wiht."

This led to a discussion about who they hated more, the West Seaxe or the Mercians. It lasted until one of the men called on him to recount how he had been gifted his ring and how he had found his weapon and helm. He passed the sword round to general wonder and Eadwin, one of Aelfhere's ceorls burst into improvised song:

'In this forest glade
In the oak's broad shade
In great Woden's name
Do I sing the fame
Of the arm that wields,
Till the foeman yields,
The finest blade
That e'er was made!'

No scop Eadwin, but wild applause and back-slapping greeted his offering and they pressed him to continue creating the saga of the battle. Eager voices called out contributions until the night grew older and the fires began to glow and smoulder and wise counsel prevailed, for the next day promised a wearisome march. They built up the flames against the February chill and drew lots for the watch. Before long, the men huddled tight in their cloaks to dream of exploits on the slaying field.

Aelfhere possessed the trait of the old warrior — of instant sleep and wakefulness. In the depths of the night, he leapt up, shed his cloak and brought down the shady figure of a thief making off with his sword. The ensuing scuffle was one-sided. The muscular frame of the islander soon overpowered the slighter build of a youth. The brawl roused the sleepers who thrust a torch to light up the struggling villain, rough hands dragging him to his feet. The face, eyes bulging with fear, showed one of the Suth Seaxe no more than ten and seven years old.

"Why the hue and cry?" called Fordraed, the ealdorman, hurrying over.

Several voices spoke at once but everyone recognised the rightful owner of the wolf-sword.

The gruff command came at once, "Fetch a log!"

A warrior hastened to do the ealdorman's bidding and returned with an oak branch thick as a man's thigh, which he dropped at the feet of the trembling scoundrel.

"Pin him down, his weapon-hand over the wood!"

In spite of his callowness, the youth lay still, eyes defiant, determined to accept punishment in a way befitting a warrior.

"An axe!" Fordraed waved an impatient hand for a cleaver and thrust it at Aelfhere, "Lop it off!" he pointed at the offending limb.

The Wihtwara rested the weapon against his right shoulder and it seemed, in the overwhelming hush, even the trees skirting the clearing leant in with expectancy.

"The other hand," he said, nodding toward the ground, "held a shield and parried an axe aimed at my throat a few hours ago." The onlookers did not notice the astonishment on the captive's face and relieved, Aelfhere went on, "His other drove a seax into the gut of my attacker." A growl of appreciation spread among the onlookers. Gazing around, with an air of unnecessary challenge, he added, "Let be the hand! Thus the score is settled! And you, *nithing*, swear an oath you take only what you gain by right, henceforth!"

* * *

On the fourth day since the battle, the gates of Kingsham swung open and the returning force trudged through. Tired but glad to share tidings of victory, they needed no excuse for another feast. Cynethryth sought out her father and rushed to embrace him, irking him with a flood of questions. He tried to be gruff, ordering her to wait for the evening when a scop would recount the tale of their deeds in song. In reality, he soon vaunted his new possessions: helm, ring and sword.

She marvelled and rejoiced at the good humour of the man who but a month past lived in sullen silence interspersed with irascibility. She needed no guile to coax forth the reason for his cheerfulness. Bursting to relate it, to her wonder he brushed aside any interest in the wolf-pommelled weapon and blurted, "Daughter, he's a warrior worthy of his forefathers!"

A love of riddles failed to serve her as Cynethryth struggled to grasp to whom her father referred. Had the sinews of one of the young Wihtwara ceorls wreaked destruction on the foe? About to enjoin him to make plain his thoughts, she halted when he added, "He slew the usurper with his own hands!"

She frowned, "*Who*, father?"

Aelfhere gazed at her in puzzlement. Was the girl slow-witted of a sudden?

"Eadric, of course! Ah, you should have seen him, Cynethryth! His shining helm, his vengeful blade and his noble bearing. *He* struck down a hardened warrior and a giant of a man!"

"Eadric?"

"Ay, Eadric! The rightful King of Kent and your husband-to-be. *He* gave me the wolf ring. Sweetness, this is a match made by the gods — I tell you, girl, never has life been so kind! Well, maybe when I wed your mother and the day you were born..."

15

"Oh, father, I'm *so* glad! Tonight we shall feast and hear the tale of your deeds."

"Ay, but first I must go and sacrifice to Woden lest these Saxons incur his wrath with the worship of yon timid god. They must thank the men of Wiht if they won the conflict. Thunor and Tiw strengthened our arms though they know it not. Stay! I shall go alone to find a sacred grove in the woodland. It is proper."

First, however, he had to seek out Fordraed. As he had guessed, the warrior of the Suth Seaxe had little time for the god of Aethelwalh. Under his breath, he confided the suspicion his king paid lip service to Christianity to sweeten their Mercian overlords. After his meeting with the ealdorman, Aelfhere, joyful, set out from the stronghold, spear in hand and sword at his side, to penetrate the dense woodland. Wiser to be well armed, given the wild beasts and the desperate men roaming the forests. Following directions, repeating them in his head, he came to a grove. The sight of a massive oak in the centre overawed him and he shuddered at the heaviness hanging in the air.

Weathered bones of various animals dangled on cords from the lower branches, among them three gaping skulls, one of them smaller — that of a child or woman. Below the overhanging boughs were charred patches of earth where the sacrifices had been burned after slaughter, the pale splintered fragments of bone contrasting with the blackness of the soil. High in the tree, interspersed among the bones swung offerings: necklaces, bracelets and the odd weapon, an inverted axe, a seax and hunting knives. Aelfhere prayed, thanking the gods for their gifts to him and determining to leave his own tribute. But what? Not his newfound sword! The wolf ring? An offence to the giver. Why had he not thought on it before setting out? What did he own, dear to him? It was obvious, but he did not want to leave his lucky wolf's ear. What else otherwise? With a heavy sigh, he drew the loop over his head, the familiar coarseness of the fur itching his skin and he strode over to the tree. One last glance at his talisman and the memory of the head of the beast, the pack leader, severed from its shoulders by his axe... and he hung the thong among the other offerings. Downcast at relinquishing his charm, he turned to leave, consoled by the thought that in combat Woden was sure to favour him.

Less than two hundred yards down the trail he halted, head cocked to one side. Imagination? Nay, the sound came again! Over to his left, disturbance, too much to be a bear or a boar. Shaking his head, he listened harder. No doubt in his mind, the sound of men — a considerable force moving forward in silence — still, he needed to be sure.

The scrub formed a barrier hard to penetrate and the long shaft of his spear hampered him. Leaning it against a tree, he moved with caution in the direction whence came the rustling undergrowth, crackling leaves and snapping twigs. He moved wary of outlying scouts. The woodland grew dense and once off the man-made track, he followed an animal trail to cut towards his quarry. Vulnerable without his spear, he hoped the way did not lead straight to the den of a beast. No need to worry, because as he went on, his hand-seax served to chop away the clinging hawthorn, briars and ferns, meaning no large animal had passed. Low voices murmured ahead; inching forward, he wormed his way over golden bracken and under a woody-stemmed shrub where, parting its branches, in spite of his wariness, he almost cried out in surprise. Before him stretched a clearing full of men armed with spears, axes and seaxes. Used to calculating the numbers of a massed foe, Aelfhere reckoned at ten score warriors, but were there more among the trees? His heart sank. This must be the war-band of the West Seaxe and Meonwara. They stood in groups but their attention was directed to three men who faced the rest.

The one in the centre, taller and broader in the shoulder, wore a loose leather tunic with steel rings sewn in overlaps. His long, curling blond hair bushed out from under a close-fitting cap protected by riveted plates and ornamented with a crest. From this distance, it looked like a hawk to the spying Wihtwara. His gaze dropped down to the tight leggings, bound with thongs, which disappeared into a pair of stout boots. A battle-axe hung from his belt, balanced on the other side by a long sword and like all the other men, he bore a spear. Aelfhere had no doubt, there stood one to be reckoned with, hostile to the settlement at his rear. The speech of the warrior was too distant but he managed to catch: "…here, now until twilight —"

These four words were enough to betray their plan, so forewarned, he crawled backwards with the utmost care. When he judged it safe to stand he picked his way back to where he had propped his spear, whence he hastened along the track, recalling all the turns taken before.

Why is it, at your happiest, life thrusts a knife betwixt the ribs?

No time to linger! Daylight was with him but fading and the half-light would bring an assault on the stronghold of Kingsham.

Chapter 2

Cynethryth

"Come, Nelda," Cynethryth said to her erstwhile nurse, now hand-maiden, voice muffled within the chest containing her clothing, "help me find a dress for tonight. Do you think the red one? Bright for a joyous feast!"

"Dear heart, choose the finer weave of the green and it better sets off your eyes. Why so troubled? Move aside, let me bring forth what you need else you will have everything in disorder! There, the grey mantle with the broidered hem and the white silk headdress." She spread her hand under the cloth. "See, as fine as the wing of a damselfly! Now, where is the green dress? Ah, now we have everything!"

The older woman bustled about arranging clothes on the bed before unbraiding and combing out her mistress' hair till it hung lustrous down her back.

"We must plait it again as befitting one betrothed."

"More's the pity!"

The servant halted her patient task, "How can you say such a thing? Is that what ails you? He's a fine young man, tall and blessed with fairness of brow, soon to be King of the Kenting and you his lady."

"Nelda, to be the king's lady I care not! What use is a fair countenance if the bearer pleases the eye but not the heart? He is given to base jests and supping ale."

"As are all men!"

The two women shared a reflective silence at last broken by a sigh from Cynethryth, followed by, "And yet I marry for love."

"Child, you bewilder me. First, you say —"

"Oh, Nelda, have no truck with a whimsical girl. Six and ten years make of me a woman. It's on duty I dwell." A toss of her blonde tresses elicited a growl of annoyance and a tug at the half-completed braid, making her wince. "Still," she flicked at a reed on the floor with the toe of her shoe, "I wish Eadric had not forsworn the gods of our forefathers." She ground the rush underfoot, "With the man, I shall not espouse the god..."

A knock disturbed them before she, hair braided, reached for her clothes on the bed. Peering past her handmaid she made out a girl of three and ten at most. Barefoot, she wore a coarse woven brown dress down to her ankles, tied at the waist by a length of string. This sparrow of a person wrung her hands and shifted from foot to foot.

"My Lady," she piped, her voice a-tremble, "they sent me to tell you to bring all your things at once to the hall. There's no time to lose!"

The girl turned to run off but Nelda grabbed her by the arm and hauled her back.

"They?" she said, "who are *they* to send orders to my Lady? What's the fuss about?"

Cynethryth drew near, smiled at the waif and noted the prettiness under the grime and short-hewn, unkempt hair.

"Child, be calm. Tell me now, what's amiss that we should flee to the hall?"

The girl rubbed her arm where the older woman had seized her. Eyes darting, she said, "Oh my Lady, he spied a host in the woods and they do be comin' to attack as when it gets dark. Soon, see?"

"*He?* Who?"

Impatient, the child-woman fair hopped on the spot and with an insolent roll of the eyes as if to attribute dullness of wit to the noblewoman, said, "Why, him as leads them there islanders. Hurry, Lady, them's goin' to bar the door!"

The messenger spun on her heel and dashed away.

Aghast, Cynethryth turned to her servant, "Father!" she said. "He sought a sacred grove in the woods and chanced on an enemy host! Quick! Throw those clothes into the chest and we'll carry it between us to the hall."

Not being a strongbox for money and jewels but a light softwood box, they made good progress. Still, they halted several times to avoid the headlong dash of men and boys heedless of aught but the need to seize weapons and reach the palisade. The confusion rendered hope of locating her father futile so Cynethryth, aware she, like the other women, would hinder the defence of the stronghold, obeyed her orders and entered the hall.

The dirty, ragged, half-starved women of Kingsham stood around in groups. Some sobbed while others comforted, all in stark contrast to the few South Seaxe noblewomen. These had accompanied their ealdormen husbands to the feast in the train of King Aethelwalh. Upon her entry, with dignified calm, they waved the betrothed maiden over to embrace her.

One of the double doors swung closed where stood Ealdorman Fordraed, battle-axe and spear in his hands, flanked by two guards.

"Wife!" he called, "See the entrance is barred. Fear not! The foe shall not pass!"

A warrior slammed the other half of the door shut.

Pale, one of the young noblewomen, her willowy figure enhanced by her close-fitting red gown, murmured, "Why must we bar it if they shall not pass?"

Anxious, they sought reassurance from one another. Warfare, a regular occurrence for these women, was conducted by men far from the hearth. The first cries and screams reached their ears and they began to tremble and weep. Cynethryth bit her lip and shook Nelda by the arm, "The beam, raise it into the brackets. You, you and you, help her!" She jabbed a finger at the cowering servants of the other noblewomen. "Now!" her eyes flashed. As if stung by a wasp, the women leapt forward and together attempted to lift the oaken bar. They struggled. "Two more!" she pointed and a young woman tugged a friend over to the others. "Mind your hands, now!" They heaved the stout wood and it thudded into position. The noise of battle reached them. The clash of steel and the screams of the wounded and dying.

Nelda remained at the doors with her eye to the narrow gap between them.

"What can you see?" Cynethryth breathed in her ear.

"Not much, for the light fades. I see men striking downwards, oh, one is hit! A spear — he falls!"

Cynethryth thrust her aside, impatient. Her servant spoke the truth. It was hard to discern the fighting. She peered into the gathering gloom. For the moment, at least, the defences held.

What numbers do they have? What will happen if they win the day?

She forced these thoughts out of her mind and with equal determination refused to worry about her father. Aelfhere had survived many a battle and there was no one in the world she would choose over him to defend her.

The fighting raged on but from within the hall, the din of combat made little sense. Now, nobody wept. As opposed to the chaos outside, inside the occasional whisper or a mother hushing her fretful babe disturbed the silence. Cynethryth counted the children. She did not know whether to be grateful or sad there were only eight because many starved or died of the yellow illness before the rigours of winter set in. She gazed with pity at the thin arms of the village women and hoped the defenders would repulse the attackers. If not, they and the children would become chattels of the foe.

May the gods save me! To think an hour ago I scorned Eadric! How I wish he and his men of Kent were here to protect me. He to wrap his strong arms around me.

"Hark, my Lady!" Nelda took her hand.

"What is it?"

Shouting reached her ears but no more the clash of steel, the screams and war cries. The fighting was over. The women clung together and wrapped the infants in their dresses. But who had won the day? Were they saved or was their situation hopeless? They would know all too soon.

Yet, long minutes passed. Nerves frayed, several of the women began to weep, setting off some of the children. A hammering came at the door accompanied by a loud voice ordering them to remove the bar. Cynethryth gasped.

The tang of a man from the country to the West.

She hurried over to the door and pressed an eye to the gap and almost sprang back in fright, but controlled her fear. Outside stood a group of men with torches. The flames flickered and lighted the steel of the rings of their mail, their helms and axes.

She gathered courage and shouted, "We are women and infants in here. There are no men. We have no arms. How can we unbar the door when you will harm us!"

There was a moment's silence. It lingered before a deep voice replied, "If you do not open the door we shall burn the hall to the ground and you will perish."

At these words, they began to wail and argue and a baby squalled. Cynethryth knew they had no choice.

"Hold," she called, "do not torch the hall. We will do as you command. The beam is heavy and we are weak. Give us time to lift it down."

The voice replied, "I am waiting."

She gave the order but only Nelda stepped forward.

"If you do not obey me, we shall die in flames — a cruel death." Her words sank home but nobody moved except a young boy aged five. "Craven curs!" Cynethryth hissed and pointed at the boy. "This little man has more courage in his forefinger than all of you put together. Have our men died to protect a nest of mice? You, you and you!" she spat out and this time, ashamed, the servants jumped to obey her command. Two or three other women helped raise the beam and it fell with a thud to the floor in a cloud of dust and scattered reeds.

"Stand back! I shall be first," she said, her tone peremptory. Cynethryth drew herself up, chin in the air and swung back the heavy door.

There he stood, torch in hand, the flames lighting his countenance to give him a more ferocious aspect. In the other, the leader of the exiled war-band of West Seaxe and Meonwara, held a bloodied battle-axe.

Her heart beat like a smith's hammer, her knees liable to betray her at any moment, but by Freya, she would not fail these women! Erect, she strode toward him halting close enough to reach out and touch his chest. Staring up into his face, the fineness of his features under a hawk-crested helm struck her. Startled by her boldness, his blue eyes even in this moment of bloodshed and triumph, revealed ill-concealed admiration.

"I am Cynethryth of Cerdicsford on Wiht, daughter of Aelfhere the ealdorman, betrothed to Eadric, King of Kent..." her jaw tightened, "...and your captive," she added in a bitter voice.

The warrior's steady gaze never wavered as he weighed her words with care. At last, he spoke, "I am Caedwalla, slayer of Aethelwalh and King of the South Seaxe." He handed the torch to the man next to him, "no harm will come to you, daughter of Aelfhere."

The gentleness of his tone came as a surprise and a relief.

"Lead the way into the hall."

She turned and did as ordered. The women retreated to the back of the room even as the warriors advanced with upraised torches. The victor raised his hand and the surge of men halted. He took in the situation at a glance and turning to a warrior with fine armour said, "Guthred, draw straws for them, first lots to my war-chiefs."

Cynethryth gasped and spun on the giant of a man, "For shame! See there are noblewomen here too. You cannot mean to sort for them as for common whores?"

The grin was wolfish. "Spoils of battle. My men have risked their lives this night. Those who were not carried off to Waelheal earned their pickings." Again he turned to the warrior he called Guthred, "See that no man quarrels over a woman else he will fight with me: enough blood has been let."

"A request, my Lord," Cynethryth said with calculated humility, "spare my handmaid. She served as my nurse." She indicated Nelda who put her hand to her mouth and opened her eyes wide.

The warrior nodded and gestured to the servant who came forward, "Aught else?" his tone mocking.

"Well, ay, my clothes," she gestured toward the chest.

He bellowed a laugh but called a torch-bearer and two other men. Drawing near to the ear of the former, he whispered orders and had Cynethryth, her handmaiden and the receptacle taken to the quarters formerly occupied by King Aethelwalh. Following the warriors, her mind raced. What fate awaited her at the hands of this huge bear? She shuddered. What death had her father endured? Her head began to spin and, faint, she clung tight in Nelda's reassuring embrace.

The men entered the building, not as sumptuous as a palace, for this was not a royal burh, but still more comfortable than the hut allocated to her father. In the main room stood a huge table and over it a wall hanging portrayed the emblem of the king of the Suth Seaxe. Six golden swallows swooped on a deep blue ground. The thread forming the birds shimmered in the torchlight. On either side hung a shield. She guessed they were trophies of war judging by their battered state. In one corner squatted a strongbox, the treasure of King Aethelwalh, now the loot of the West Seaxe leader. What little the room revealed, lighted by the flickering upraised flames, showed a scene of uninterrupted daily life where the embers of a fire still glowed in a floor pit.

It's as if nothing happened — how I wish it were so!

The men pushed aside a curtain screening off a large bed, covered by a blanket of wolf pelts. Cynethryth folded back one corner revealing the green linen lining matching a sheet covering the mattress filled with straw, across and over which stretched a down-stuffed bolster.

They deposited the chest at the foot of the bed and the torchbearer used his flames to light the torches in the wall cressets. One of them built up the fire in the centre of the room and another fetched a basin and a ewer of water. A curt command followed, "Await our lord!" Then they were alone.

The two women fell into each other's arms and stood for a while before Nelda took her hand and led her over to sit on the edge of the bed.

"Stay here, mistress. I shall hunt for a knife or other weapon to slay the ogre should he dare lay a hand on you."

"My brave and faithful nurse," she managed a sad smile, "do you hope to succeed where father and seasoned warriors failed?"

There was no time for an answer, because the door opened with a creak and footsteps crackled toward them across the reed-strewn floor. A hand swept the curtain aside, revealing their captor standing tall before them. Cynethryth leapt up from the edge of the bed to confront the stranger. Spear and axe, he had left elsewhere, but he exuded strength in his mail shirt with its truncated sleeves, showing bared muscles that gold armlets struggled to contain. Two swift steps and he stood, his body touching hers, but she did not flinch. A huge hand cupped her chin and the intense blue peered into the grey of her eyes.

"You too are the spoils of war, woodland flower...and I want you."

His voice was hoarse and heavy with longing and her cheeks flamed, but still she did not shy away from him. The warrior brought his head closer to hers and he repeated, "I want you for my own."

Now she pulled away and stepped back a pace, her gaze locked with his. She kept her voice level:

"I am betrothed to Eadric, King of the Kenting."

"And I am Caedwalla, son of King Coenberht and rightful King of the West Seaxe, now King of the Suth Seaxe and I take what I want."

She opened her mouth to reply but he went on, "Hold! Not a word! Hear me first!" He glanced at Nelda and waved her to leave their presence. "Daughter of Wiht, you are blessed with the beauty of Freya and I with the strength of Thunor. The south will be mine, Kent, too," he said in an even voice, "I will have a greater hall than Eadric and more men to sup there. With me, you will have the riches of three kingdoms." He held up a hand, forefinger pointing, "Never have I desired a woman as much as I yearn for you. Fear not, I shall be gentle and above all, *you* shall be the one to choose." He folded his arms, "A man can take what he wants but cannot command the heart of another. I shall not force you but remember, with me, you will lack for nothing…" his eyes softened and his voice lowered, "…most of all for love. Woman!" he bellowed and Nelda came running. "Prepare yourselves for the night. I will send a servant with food and drink. You sleep here," he pointed at the bed, "there will be a guard at the door and I shall slumber there," he tossed his head, "by the fire."

The warriors came with a meal, three of them, bearing platters of stuffed roast fowl with baked onions and turnips and toasted bread, a crock of dark ale and beakers. They had found the fare ready prepared in the kitchen for the feast. Instead of celebrating she would be dining as if on wormwood, mournful and melancholic. To her surprise, her stomach confuted her mind because she discovered she was hungry and though the food, tasty and wholesome, did not cheer her, it revived her spirits.

After the meal, she rinsed her hands and splashed her face from a basin of water as Nelda rummaged in the chest and pulled out her nightdress. While her servant helped her undress, she kept glancing at the curtain separating them from the rest of the room, aware of the nearness of their captor. Shivering, she was relieved to pull the heavy cover over her and when Nelda joined her in bed she clung on to her and relished the warmth and comfort.

They lay like this for a while before Cynethryth brought her mouth close to her servant's ear.

"How many springs do you give him?"

There was no need for the handmaid to ask who she referred to.

"At a guess, four and twenty, mistress."

"Do you think him handsome, Nelda?"

The pungent smell of smoke trapped in the handmaiden's hair made her recoil.

"Ay, in a brutish, savage sort of way."

"Nay, not the aspect of a brute! His features are fine and his eyes the colour of forget-me-nots, his hair and beard golden as a wheat field —"

The older woman mocked, "Lady, I'd say you are smitten! Need I remind you, you are betrothed?"

"He would take me for wife."

The servant's tone was bitter, the words bold as only a nursemaid dare, "The beast who slew your father?"

Cynethryth pushed away from her, "I told you before, he is no brute!" she hissed, "Has he not treated us with kindness and respect? How can you say he killed father? Where's the proof?"

"Hush, mistress! I meant no harm. All I'll say is, it's a pity he didn't show the same worthiness to the ealdormen's women in the hall."

She rolled over, her back to her handmaid, "Goodnight, Nelda." Her tone was as cold as the night air that held the settlement in its grip.

At dawn when she rose careful not to disturb her sleeping companion, it was even colder. In haste, she slipped off her nightdress and struggled into her clothes. Her feet were numb by the time she laced up her boots and her fingers near failed to buckle her belt. Drawing her heaviest mantle out of the chest, she flung it over her shoulders. On tiptoe, she ghosted beyond the curtain and paused only to gaze upon the profile of the warrior curled up in his cloak by the spent ashes in the fire pit. She stared on the countenance of her captor and the hint of a smile quavered on her lips.

Tugging back the heavy door, she startled a guard sat with his knees drawn up, tight-wrapped in a blanket and with a spear in the crook of his arm. Before he leapt up, she put a finger to her lips, "Hush! Do not wake your lord!" She bent down until the ale on his breath wafted in her face. "I seek the body of my father among the corpses. See, the gate is shut, I cannot take flight."

Doubtful, the watchman nodded his head, "Who's to say you won't disappear?"

"May Freya strike me dead as I stand here..." she spat out the words with such venom the man widened his eyes in awe, "...I give you my word I shall not hide or flee."

He waved consent with his free hand.

In disbelief, she gazed around at the intact buildings. No plundering and destruction to be seen and this, she chose to opine, was down to Caedwalla. She began her gruesome task. In truth, her gaze needed not linger on the scuttling rats on the gory, hacked and maimed corpses for a glance was enough to recognise the colour of her father's hair, his build and what he wore. She tried to be thorough but when she reached the wall by the gate where the bodies heaped from the most relentless fighting, bile rose in her gorge.

"Lady, what are you about? This is no sight for your eyes."

Startled, she spun round. How did this well-built man move silent as a lynx? The expression of Caedwalla was full of concern.

"The guard tells me you seek your father."

"I know not whether he be alive or dead."

"Dead, Lady. How can he live? His battle is lost. As we speak, he sups in Waelheal with Woden under a roof of golden shields. Be not sorrow-filled for such a man! Come!" He held out his arm, assuming she would take it. Cynethryth hesitated long enough for him to raise an eyebrow, but linked hers through his and a shudder of pleasure coursed through her at the touch of the iron-hard muscles. She shivered.

"You are chilled." His voice tender, he added, "I shall have the guard bring you broth."

He held the door for her and gave orders to the watchman. In moments, two warriors came one with an armful of twigs and branches and the other with flints and straw to strike up a fire. Caedwalla hoisted the huge oak bench from beside the table as if it were a weightless trinket and placed it next to the hearth.

"Ah, here is the broth!"

He took the steaming bowl and a wooden spoon from the guard and passed them to her with a boyish smile. Nelda's guess at four and twenty years was likely true to the mark but sitting next to her now, he looked younger. Cynethryth smiled at him for the first time. Yet, this was a trick of the moment. The gentle gestures, effected with the calmness of the summer sea, came from a man as changeable, as capable of wreaking destruction, as the tempest-driven breakers. She ought to hate him.

This war chieftain, leader of West Seaxe exiles, unaccustomed King of the Suth Seaxe, gave a snicker of pleasure at her smile but then looked abashed. She smiled again, blew on her broth and sipped at her spoon while the flames rose in a merry dance and the warriors bowed their way unheeded from their presence. Caedwalla sat in silence, eyes never leaving hers for an instant, his cheek on the side exposed to the fire reddening, his visage taking on a brindled aspect. She stood, "It might be wise to move the bench back a pace or two," she smiled and moved aside not to hamper his careless hoist. Once more impressed by his strength, she tried not to reveal her thoughts.

Wrap those arms around me!

Supping, she studied the lines of his face: the noble brow under two golden waves of hair falling over his ears, the nose straight with a curve at the bridge, enough to lend character. Emotion stirred in the depths of her soul, a wild impulse, blind desire to possess this man of destiny. His cheekbones, well-sculpted, cradled deep-set eyes sparkling with mirth at her so-serious study of his features. Imperturbable, her gaze passed to the firm, bearded jaw and the sensuous lips. She longed to press hers against them as they curled upwards at awareness her stare had lingered an unconscionable time. She stared into the fire and was lost.

Her mind advised her to resist, her burning heart ordered her to assent, to succumb. Wicked betrayal in less than a day! To break a solemn oath and endure shame and wrath. What of the safety of their island home? She was pledged to wed Eadric — a mere boy. Next to her sat a warrior, a man with a deep voice that resonated to the core of her being. Why not sway this man to protect Wiht?

Why not? — Forgive me father — and with this unremitting indulgence, she yielded to fate.

The Uurdi weave as they will!

30

Her wyrd was irrepressible. No dam she constructed would hold back the flood. It overwhelmed her. In full spate, her words breached the silence, "The offer of last night, does it stand?"

Is he still of that mind?

One time as a girl, in a creek near home, a drowning playmate clung to her. Cynethryth hesitated to rescue her but feared her friend in panic might submerge her. Up to now, that moment of decision, to save or doom her, had been the most interminable. This was longer.

At last, he grinned, rose and raised her chin for a long-tarrying kiss.

"You taste of gruel!"

"Would that be an 'ay'?"

The warrior kissed her again, "What do you think?"

"I'd say you can't resist broth!"

They laughed together but he grew grave and his eyes were as far off as the sky.

"There is much to be done. This is a momentous but contrary day. Before noon, we must honour and bury the dead. We'll raise a mound for the fallen. How shall my men know your father?"

The question surprised, saddened and gratified her. "On his hand a wolf ring and..." her voice faltered, "...if he be not maimed, a scar here..." she drew a line down beside her nose across her lips, "...and if they have not been taken, a sword and a helm both with the form of a wolf — he won them in battle," she added with pride.

"Then he was a warrior as fierce as the creature he sired and worthy of Woden's hall."

She was grateful for his words and tears brimmed over.

"He was a good father," she said and hung her head.

He sat next to her and drew her to his shoulder.

"After noon, the day will brighten. No betrothal! We two shall wed and there will be such a feast as scops will sing about for years to come. Hark! The day is young. You and your servant go gather all the women in the place and set them about organising the festivities. Here, take this ring!"

He slipped a gold band with a dragon writhing around its centre on her finger but it was far too big for her delicate hand. "Wear it on your thumb," he laughed, "show this and my men, however high in rank, will obey your command." He leant over and kissed her again, "Now go, wake up your handmaiden and make the joyous preparations. I, instead, shall set about my doleful task."

The argument with Nelda was short and sharp. Cynethryth, empowered by love brought all the authority of a noblewoman to bear on her servant, whose faithfulness overcame her resentment when confronted with the evident joy of her mistress. They went from door to door rousing those who were still not afoot. The ring worked its power on those warriors who chose to be truculent meaning the task of assembling the womenfolk was soon completed. Some of them were tearful, others resigned and an unexpected few contented with their lot. Among the latter, the noblewoman, Rowena, she of the red dress, keen to vaunt the heavy gold pendant adorning her breast.

"The war chiefs drew straws for first," she confided to Cynethryth and Nelda, "Guthred picked the longest and chose me straight away! He gave me this," she lifted the weighty jewel, "isn't it a wonder! He's taken me for wife…" she lowered her voice, "…this is for your ears only…he's twice the man my husband was and much gentler."

The women assembled in the hall where Cynethryth announced her wedding to a mixed reception. Some scowled and glared, others clapped and cheered while Rowena hurried forward and embraced her. She had gained a new friend.

After giving instructions to the women and setting them about their allotted tasks she drew Rowena aside.

"What am I to do, Lady?"

"Be my companion and adviser, will you do that?"

The almond-shaped eyes creased at the corners with pleasure, "My Lady," she took her friend's hand, "you do me great honour."

"You must call me Cynethryth if we are to be friends."

Her eyes, alight with joy, were green, like fresh leaves of sage and her pale copper-gold hair gleamed even in the dim light of the hall.

She hugged the Wihtwara once more and kissed her on the cheek. Cynethryth did the same to seal the friendship.

They were sitting in intimate talk when Caedwalla strode with distracted air into the room.

Cynethryth interpreted his expression as one of bewilderment. She rose and said, "Lord, this is Lady Rowena, my friend."

The warrior favoured the woman in red with a fleeting glance and a hint of a smile, soon replaced with a frown and a look of concern. He wandered off a few paces and returned, cupping his chin between thumb and forefinger."

"What ails you, heart of mine?"

Not even the endearment elicited a smile, "My men are filling the graves with soil. Over them will rise a mound in a circle."

Cynethryth's chest tightened and she swallowed hard, "Father?"

"They found no ring with a wolf, nor sword nor helm such as you described."

Hope sprang in her breast, "Can it be he's alive?"

Caedwalla shrugged, "Not unless he has wings like the *waelcyrge*."

Now it was her turn to be confused, "…and yet they did not find his body…"

"They did not. I gave orders —"

"I know, I know. Can it be he's still alive?" she repeated.

Chapter 3

Wilfrith

The Abbey of Selsea, West Sussex — three years before — 682 AD

The rhythmic striking of an iron mallet against a soft-tempered chisel came to an abrupt halt. Humbert, the mason, laid down his tools, reached for the leather bottle and poured water over his head washing away the sandstone dust gathered at eyebrows and moustache. The fine powder caused a sore throat and itching skin. All told, a trifling price in exchange for the ten-and-six-foot masterpiece emerging from the engrossment of a year and a half, lying longwise on the ground. The sculpting nigh on ended, he glanced at Erbin, his underling, and nodded in silent approbation. The last leaf in the vine scroll framing the bottom panel on the west side of the cross was taking shape under the youngster's blows. Wiping his brow with his forearm, Humbert selected a tool from several at his belt. He proceeded to punch a pupil in the eye of a basilisk — ugly beast — positioned under the foot of Christ.

His workmate coughed. Nothing untoward, given these particles in the air, except Humbert knew a warning when he heard one and sure enough, from under his bowed forehead, he spied his master approaching: the bishop who had set him to this task on the same day the quarrymen had trundled the huge stone block to the abbey gates.

The mason straightened up, only to bow at once in reverence to the newcomer.

The prelate spread his hands in wonder at the malign basilisk staring back at him.

"The Heavens be praised, Humbert!"

The cleric ran his hand over the flowing mane of the lion, carved between a dragon and an asp, companions of the reptile trodden under the feet of the Son of God.

"What art! Our Father has guided your hand."

"Nay Lord," Humbert scooped up a handful of sandstone dust and let it trickle through his fingers, "here be the art, not yon," he gestured toward the sculpture with his other hand.

The long, thin countenance of Wilfrith seamed with furrows, his mouth also defined at each edge by deep lines, lit up at the remark.

"I take your meaning, Master Humbert. Bless the day I chanced upon you whittling wood! But, it is not what the eye sees, rather that which makes the eye see, that is the Holy Spirit."

The mason looked at the exiled Bishop of York with fondness. The prelate wore a long, adorned cloak of sumptuous purple, held below the neck by a gem-studded clasp, over a white linen robe. A leather cord bound it at the waist. The richness of his dress belied the disarming blend of powerful intelligence and sweetness and — above all — unchallengeable authority.

The mason gathered his courage, "Lord, may I ask a question?"

The broad brow of the clergyman wrinkled and he nodded.

"Beggin' your pardon, Lord, them runes you had me copy and hollow out on this side," Humbert pointed with his punch, "what do they say, what meaning have they?"

The bishop sauntered to the top end of the stone cross and ran his finger in the groove of the first rune and began to read: "This slender pillar," his hand moved with his words, "Wilfrith set up at the behest of Aethelwalh, King, and his queen, Eafe." He had reached the mason and the figure of Christ on the skyward side of the pillar, "Pray for their sins, their souls." His forefinger traced the last rune at the end of the shaft.

"The King, Aethelwalh?"

"Ay, Humbert. The King: he who gave us these eighty-seven hides of land at Selsea to build the abbey to the glory of God."

"Bless the king, eh Erbin? We'd still be slaves along with the others if it weren't for his gift and the goodness of our Lord Bishop. Them were hard times."

The countenance of the mason took on a faraway and pained expression, "Three years of drought and the yellow sickness. You remember, Erbin?" He ignored the Briton's shrug and went on, "I'll never rid it from my memory. At least fifty of them, men, women and children, so starved and desperate they flung themselves off the point yonder and drowned."

Wilfrith frowned, "Despair is a sin."

"Ay, but back then we worshipped the false gods. Then you came, Lord, and began to baptise the men you freed — twelve score and more…remember…? On that day…the first day, it rained! Rain, for the first time in three years — a miracle! God sent you to save us, body and soul."

The bishop smiled, "The soul is the prime concern. But hark, when will the cross be ready?"

"Ay, the soul, it's true, but the body has its needs too." Imperturbable, the mason continued, "It wasn't the rain alone, you taught us how to make nets and how to fish. We've never lacked for aught since you came, Lord."

"Remember to pray and thank our Heavenly Father for his blessings. Now, tell me, when will the cross be ready?"

"Not like 'em monks over at Boseam —"

"Humbert!"

The mason looked sheepish, "Beg pardon, Lord. Erbin here has only to finish this vine scroll and I got to put scales on this here lizard —"

"Basilisk."

"Eh?"

"It's a basilisk, hatched a serpent by a cockerel from a snake's egg. Kills with a glance. Psalm Ninety-One, 'The asp and the basilisk you will trample underfoot.' See, there's Our Saviour treading on the beasts."

"'Orrible. Kill with a glance, eh?"

"The power of the Evil One. Now, you were saying," the bishop directed a sour glance of his own in the direction of the mason, "once you've finished the scales..."

"Ay, some men will come and paint the scenes here," he screwed up his eyes into an inquisitive expression. He paused as if wishing to ask a question, thought better of it and added, "when the paint's dry, we'll roll it on logs to the base yonder and lever it into the hole. It's exact yon is, twenty-two by twenty-two inches. Measured it myself a dozen times. Three days, no more."

"Green, most likely."

"Eh?"

The bishop turned and began to stroll away, "The basilisk, you wished to know its colour," he called over his shoulder.

The mason's jaw dropped and he turned to Erbin, "How by Thunor's —"

"Hush!" the Briton hissed, "Don't let him hear yon name or you'll be for it!"

* * *

The Abbey of Selsea — three years later — February, 685 AD

Wilfrith stamped chilled feet on the iron-hard ground and stared at the grey sky extending as flat as beaten tin. Beyond the bare trees lay mudflats dotted with lagoons edged with desolate reed beds. The bishop drew his cloak tighter and sighed. Where was the sun? An absent friend, mourning for this world leached of colour? Bleakness in its severity offered its own beauty, he reflected. He shivered and crossed his arms over his chest for warmth.

"I've been staring at the scenery, unaware I'm a part of the land-scape," he murmured, "the cold morning distracts me."

The sound of breaking waves spoke to him and he sought them out. Slate grey breakers marched like an invading host to dash on the pebble beach, a splash of silver in a world of pewter, exacting the hiss of tumbling shingle upon its ebb.

God gave me the ear that sees and the eye that hears. What happens outside occurs in me — they are one...

A sharp cry cut across the prelate's musings. A lad of no more than four and ten years hurtled toward him.

"My Lord! My Lord Bishop! A messenger's come — he be up at the abbey!"

The youngster halted before the clergyman, keen, nigh on bursting to blurt out the rest of his news but overawed by the presence of the personage before him.

Wilfrith looked at the shivering urchin, less concerned with the forthcoming communication than troubled by the child's threadbare tunic affording no protection from the icy teeth of the north-easterly wind. How must it be to stand barefoot on this frozen ground? Ashamed at the weakness of his own flesh, the bishop bent forward over the boy."

"What is your name, little brother?"

Eyes wide, the stripling gaped at the exalted figure who deigned to speak with him.

"You do have a name?"

The tone was gentle.

"Beg pardon, my Lord, it be Osric."

"Well, Osric, you run straight back to the abbey and go to Brother Byrnstan. He's the monk with white hair and the withered hand. Do you know where to find him?"

The tousled blond head nodded.

"Tell him the bishop beseeches a pair of leathern shoes and a woollen cloak be bestowed on you. Say I shall seek him out later."

Disquieted, Wilfrith had no time to react as the boy dropped to his knees and kissed his shoe. Just as fast, the lad bounded to his feet and set off for the abbey at full tilt.

"Wait! The rest of your message?"

"Abbot Eappa says the news-bearer is with him and you've to come at once!" Osric shouted before turning and haring off along the trail, the words of his thin voice, snatched by the wind, hard for the prelate to distinguish.

Wilfrith smiled. No doubt he would have to soothe the almoner later. Indeed, a worse choice of alms-giver was difficult to imagine, the tightfistedness of Brother Byrnstan being famed well beyond the marshlands. The bishop hastened along the trail to the religious house he had founded.

What can be so urgent in this forlorn and uneventful season?

Once through the gate, he approached the colourful palm cross and, as ever, paused to marvel at the chequers and interlace knots surrounding the panel he liked best. The Virgin with the Child in her lap stared down at him. Wilfrith's gaze shifted to the sundial above the scene and he repressed a sigh. The shrouded sun lay like Christ at Golgotha — oh what joy he would feel at its resurrection!

Aware more pressing matters called for his presence, he strode beyond the stone church to the quarters of the abbot.

Abbot Eappa, too fond of his cup and therefore rubicund, wore a troubled expression that sat ill on his genial countenance. The aspect of the messenger came as the second surprise to the bishop. Whatever he expected, it did not resemble the man who towered over the rotund monk. From his bearing, a warrior — his visage revealed his unease in the company of an abbot and a bishop.

Wilfrith took charge, "Tell me, son, what brings you to this humble place of worship?" The efficient, authoritative tone of the prelate lacked any trace of the humility implicit in his words.

The messenger bowed, "Lord, I come from Boseam," Wilfrith did not fail to catch the twang of West Seaxe speech, "or rather first from Kingsham…" said the man.

"Dire tidings!" Abbot Eappa intervened, "The King is dead! Aethel-walh is slain at the hands of Caedwalla."

"Aethelwalh, dead?" The brow of the bishop furrowed.

"Ay Lord," the warrior said, "we took Kingsham and the monk speaks true —"

"The 'monk' is an abbot, show respect, man!"

Wilfrith glared at the messenger.

"Beggin' pardon, Lord. Fact is, we know little of your ways and there's the problem. Our King, Caedwalla, sent us with the body of Aethelwalh to be brought to Selsea for burial. Not knowing the way, we sought directions to the monks' abode and they directed us to Boseam —"

"The Irishmen have the body!" the abbot interrupted. "Those way-farers with their skew-shaven heads! We must act at once!"

Florid by nature, he grew ruddier and rubbed the back of his neck.

"Patience, Father!" Wilfrith turned to the warrior, "Why, once aware you had the wrong monks, did you not bring the body here?"

The messenger frowned, "Well, their leader, they call him Dicuill, said it was God's will the mortal remains of Aethelwalh had come to them. He wants to bury the King at Boseam."

"And you let him?"

"Nay," our commander, Ealdorman Guthred, delays. The monk threatened us with his God's wrath if we dared move the body thence. Guthred sent me here to fetch you, Lord. He says you Christians can sort it out among yourselves. He will not offend any god."

"We shall come, anon. First, I must ask you to await us outdoors, for I must speak in confidence with my Abbot."

As soon as the door closed behind the messenger, Wilfrith said, "The death of Aethelwalh is, of course, regrettable. Yet, it may benefit us. I have an understanding with Caedwalla —"

The troubled features of the abbot cleared a little. "With the war-lord?"

"Ay, we met in the Andredes weald. The man is a pagan, but I have hopes the Spirit will move him to baptism. He is young with a yearning for power, but in him, I see a rare intelligence and determination. In his turn, he sees me not as a Man of Christ, but as a wise man who has seen much of the world…as one who possesses potent talismans and charms, a giver of sound advice…"

"But this understanding?"

"His fortune will be mine, and mine his."

The Abbot pressed his hands together, "The Almighty moves in mysterious ways. But now we must make haste." The bishop found it hard to repress a smile at the incongruity of the troubled expression and the benign face.

"I shall send for ten strong men to accompany you, there are full four leagues to Boseam."

Leaving the abbot instructions to deal with the almoner, Wilfrith set off with his band of men. It was mid-afternoon when they, at last, sighted the few roofs nestling among the trees at the edge of the great Andredes weald. Close to the banks of a creek ran a crude quay, made of logs stacked lengthways one on top of the other and held in place by piles driven into the silt. Boseam with the tide out bespoke solitude: a moored boat lay on its side in the company of a few waders pecking the mud in a desultory manner. Wilfrith sniffed and looked down his nose at the group of huts.

"The remoteness these Irishmen seek in their *peregrinatio*," he murmured.

The bishop's resolve not to leave this forsaken inlet without the corpse of King Aethelwalh redoubled.

A wain stood before the simple dwellings. Wilfrith strolled over to it made the sign of the cross and prayed over the body of the king. It lay bound in a winding sheet on the rough boards of the cart. Nearby, a tethered ox stared with stolid impassivity at the arrival of the others. Not so a group of warriors who leapt to their feet from the various objects adapted as temporary seats. They jested and mouthed oaths at their companion, the returning messenger, who grinned back at them. At this commotion, five monks with the crowns of their heads shaven, wearing coarse undyed woollen habits, appeared from one of the huts.

The leader of the Irish monks, Dicuill, cast a sour glance at Wilfrith, frowned and said, "Do you come to defy the will of God?"

"It's a bold claim to know the will of God," the bishop said. "In simple error, the mortal remains of Aethelwalh arrived here and not in Selsea."

The Irishman turned to his fellow monks as if for sustainment.

"He stands there, dressed in rich attire and speaks of error when Our Lord was born in a manger amid the beasts of the field."

The bishop reddened, his voice tight with ill-concealed ire.

"In an age when the Church seeks visible unity, it is pernicious and obstinate to cling to a bygone manner of shaving the head. Worse, you scorn the will of the Bishop of Rome as to when you should keep the holy feast of Easter and induce poor folk into unwitting fault."

Dicuill stabbed a finger toward the prelate, "We follow the precepts of our founder, Columba, a martyr to the faith long before you Saxons left your swamps to infest these shores. When Rome was overrun by barbarism, humble men kept the light of the Gospel shining in the Western Isles. Why must we change our customs at the bidding of an erring man sent by the Bishop of Rome?"

Wilfrith took a step forward. Sensing the danger of protracted, irreconcilable debate, Guthred intervened. "Winter days are short! Set aside your wrangling and settle on what to do with the corpse or by Woden we'll lay him in yon boat and burn him on the sea."

Aghast, united in vexation, the antagonists turned on the ealdorman.

"Pagan!"

"Idolater!"

"Aethelwalh, baptised in the true faith, will have a Christian burial," Wilfrith said, and Dicuill nodded in agreement. "Not in this forlorn wilderness, cast in the earth to fatten worms, but sealed in the crypt of the abbey church in Selsea. It will be a fitting resting place for such a man, where hereafter the faithful —"

" 'As he had come naked from his mother's womb, so will he return as he came. He will take nothing from the fruit of his labour that he can carry in his hand,' " Dicuill said. "The soil of Boseam is the same for king or slave."

Exasperated, Wilfrith turned to Guthred, "Caedwalla commanded you to bring the body to Selsea and you will answer to him alone. Let be the threats of the monks from the Isles. Their God is my God so His wrath shall not be directed at you. These are worthy men, blessed in their simplicity and humility. Let us leave them to their lives of self-denial…"

Reassured, the ealdorman shouted orders. The warriors backed the ox into its traces and soon the cart rumbled along the trail into the woods above the creek.

The discomfort of a night spent in a woodland camp was not new to Wilfrith. Indeed, since his exile by King Ecgfrith from Northumbria, there were few places safe for him. The Queen of Mercia was sister to that king; the Queen of the West Seaxe, sister to Ecgfrith's queen, so the forest of Andred had served him as a refuge. There he had met Caedwalla where they sealed their pact.

Sleepless, Wilfrith tugged his cloak tighter and rolled on his side toward the fire. With his eight and forty winters, he had hoped not to endure this particular hardship again. But in the words of the Apostle Paul, *Who has known the mind of the Lord? Or who has been his counsellor?* He dwelled on the obdurate Irish monks. True, they were holy men, but their failure to convert the South Seaxe did not surprise him. Why should the conquerors embrace the faith of the conquered Britons they so despised? The grand ideal of Christian unity he so cared for heartened him. One day all England would obey the Holy Father in Rome.

At last, comforted by such thoughts, the bishop slumbered.

When they entered the abbey the next morning, a monk came running to meet them.

"My Lord Bishop, a band of men arrived last eve with a communication for the ealdorman."

"For me?" Guthred cried, "Where are they? Take me to them!"

The monk bowed and turned on his heel. Wilfrith accompanied Guthred. What urgent news from one day to another? It whetted his curiosity.

The brother led them to the refectory where they found ten warriors. Their leader sat with his back to them, one hand around a cup of ale while tearing at a strip of dried meat with his teeth.

"Werhard! What brings you here?" the ealdorman cried.

The warrior threw down his food, leapt to his feet and spun round.

"Grave news! Our scouts report the duces of the South Seaxe unite and seek vengeance on our King for the death of Aethelwalh. Their numbers are far greater than ours. Soon they march for Kingsham. Lord, King Caedwalla bids you make haste, for — his words, not mine — he is in need of his cunning fox…"

Chapter 4

Aelfhere

Two narrow slits opened for eyes, head pounding, his jaw throbbed: swollen, even broken. This must be Niflheim, the world of darkness. Why was he here and not in Waelheal? Had he not died a warrior's death? He peered up through the treetops and started: the Dog Star! What? Here in Hel's domain?

"At last! The winter bear wakes!"

Thunor's hammer struck his skull and his stomach clenched to fight back the sickness rising in his gorge when Aelfhere tried to sit up.

Baldwulf! Here in the mist-home? Why?

His words forced through an immobile jaw sounded like a growling hound. "Old friend, is that you? Dead?"

What he did not expect in the dark and shadowy realm was the bellow of laughter that greeted his utterance.

"Dead! Not likely, but we will be if we stay here much longer. I thought you'd never wake up! Mind, it was a mighty blow you took —"

Aelfhere raised himself on one elbow and gazed at his thegn. "Where are we?"

"As far as I carried you from yon gate —"

"Gate?"

"Ay, where the fray raged thickest. Remember? The foe forced entry and pushed us back. You drove your seax into a West Seaxe gut but it left you open to a strike. Yon tried to break his shield against your chin and he'd have finished you, but I took him out with my axe and pulled you behind the gate. It was nigh on dark and in the havoc, we went unseen as the slaughtering pressed farther from us —"

"We lost the day?"

"Ay, many a brave man —"

The ealdorman sat up and groaned. There was accusation in his voice. "They're dead and we are alive?"

"I...I thought it best. Under the cover of darkness, I carried you on my back into the weald. Better to live and fight another day..."

Aelfhere laid a hand on the shoulder of the thegn. "Right enough! I should thank you, brother," his eyes clouded, "but what of Cynethryth?"

Futile question: she was taken — the spoils of war. Fury surged in his breast; he stared into the night sky and swore to Woden he would not rest until the last of the West Seaxe scum lay bloodied at his feet.

Baldwulf hauled him upright.

"We must be leagues away before daybreak! Can you run?"

Every time his foot hit the ground a mallet struck his head and his teeth ached and throbbed. In spite of the pain, Aelfhere pursued his thegn along the woodland trail, marvelling how Baldwulf picked his way at speed with so little light.

The man must have the sight of an owl — I'll wager he can find a dormouse in a cornfield by the glow of a candle!'

They ran for what seemed forever before Baldwulf called a halt. Chest heaving and gasping to force out the words, he pointed to a stream.

"We should follow it," he put his hands on his knees and bent over, struggling for breath, "chances are it'll lead to the sea."

Too breathless to speak, Aelfhere nodded in agreement.

Far enough from danger now, they eased their pace. Soon the dawn would reveal their whereabouts. The gods were with them because, curious for the season, the ground lay hard through lack of rain, making the going easier. Following the turbulent stream proved to be an inspired choice; although, at times, they had to hack at vegetation or skirt a gorge before thrusting back toward the water course. When the sky, lightening to grey, became tinted with the rosy hues of the rising sun, Aelfhere stopped and sniffed the air.

"Smell it?"

Baldwulf breathed in, "Ay, sea air. The coast isn't far off."

To the accompaniment of mewling gulls swooping over a deserted marshy plain, they left the forest. The stream emptied into a tidal creek edged by eight-foot cliffs of friable brown brick-earth, which Baldwulf scrambled down, dislodging white flint pebbles with his boots.

"Here! Sea kale!"

Munching on the light green leaves, his words became indistinct.

By Woden, if Baldwulf were an ox, I'd roast him! That's how hungry I am!

Aelfhere had fought a battle, lost consciousness and run through a forest: no wonder his stomach complained. Two bounds brought him to his friend but he found eating and chewing painful activities; the bruising and swelling would take days to pass. While he ate, he tried to work out their position.

In the distance to the west, the outline of their isle was visible. Given this, likely they were on the seal island, Seals-ey, not a true island but a promontory.

He joined Baldwulf, who had strayed down the shingle beach and was staring toward Wiht.

"Home," said the ealdorman. "Time presses." He grasped his thegn by the arm. "Arwald must hear of the death of Aethelwalh. We must beseech a war-band to unite with our Suth Seaxe friends to kill the usurper..." he pointed westward, "...if we head that way we should find the abbey at Selsea. The Christians can help us find a boat."

* * *

Not only that, they also ate a meal, received a bed for the night and made arrangements for the vessel. A monk accompanied them next morning to a creek, where a ship with furled sail was moored to a jetty. A man stood waiting with muscular arms crossed over his chest. Having established what coin the boatman wanted to take them across to Wiht, an honest price agreed, they clasped hands.

"There's a contrary wind," the sailor said, "can you handle an oar?"

"We're Wihtwara born and bred," Aelfhere smiled.

"As well, for once out of the creek, the waves will test your mettle."

The ealdorman studied the grinning weather-beaten face, noting the white lines of deep wrinkles beside the eyes contrasting with the wind-tanned skin. The furrows caused by the fellow's cheerful nature, by laughter and smiles, made Aelfhere warm to him at once.

The three men pulled on the oars and, his back to the bows, Aelfhere studied the lone figure of the monk on the jetty. Dwindling in size before his eyes, the cowled shape did not move.

As though he wants to make sure we're gone.

Experienced oarsmen all three, they made swift progress along the creek but the ealdorman was under no illusions. The tide rushing out through the entrance to the inlet swirled and eddied causing small white-crested waves. To the west side of the mouth, breakers crashed over a sand bank.

The boatman caught the direction of his gaze. "Ay, we have to steer wide of yon else our boat will serve for nought but firewood." They pulled out into the open sea, "Here comes a long wave," he said, "haul hard and we'll keep her head into it."

A wall of water towered above them and loomed over the bows of the vessel, threatening to swamp them. The boat rose in a smooth arc and plunged down on the other side, while the huge wave rolled on and crashed behind them on the shore.

"We're clear of all the banks," the boatman said, dragging in his oars and grasping the steer-board. "Nothing but open sea from now on."

The muscles of the two Wihtwara were afire, so it came as a relief when the steersman shouted, "Another two minutes and we'll have enough offing to raise the sail!" The gurgling sound under the bows told them they were moving fast. They rowed farther from the land and the sea got up more. This caused the boat to surge wildly ahead, sink down in the trough between waves, to rise, raising her stern before careering forward until the prow rose in the air and the wave curled over before them.

"In with your oars and unfurl the sail!"

Aelfhere and Baldwulf leapt to obey and their boatman struggled with the steer-board to keep the vessel from broaching-to. When the canvas filled, they made headway at twice their rowing speed and the men of Wiht grinned at the Suth Seaxe sailor as they anticipated the air of home.

Impossible to judge the time of day, with the compact February clouds leaching the light from the world and masking the sun. Past noon, Aelfhere guessed as the isle filled their horizon and he staggered aft to the steersman.

"Know you the isle, friend?"

"Ay, would I had a hide of land for every time I crossed these waters!"

"Then you'll know Odeton Creek?"

"Tell me you wish me to take you there!"

The weather-beaten creases deepened in a smile.

"Ay, for we're bound for Wihtgarabyrig to the hall of the king."

"So much the better! No need to sail across the heavy swell. We can hold this course."

They lowered sail as they entered a creek fringed by dense woodland and once more took up the oars. For a league, they rowed until it was too shallow to go farther.

"Will I wait for your return?" the boatman asked.

"No need, friend." Aelfhere shook his head, "By the one-armed god, it will be with a fleet when we sail back!"

They clasped hands and jumped ashore. The bearded sailor poled the boat around, positioned two oars and bent his back to row away from them, aided by the current of the Odeton Creek.

"He has a following wind, "Baldwulf said, "it will speed him to Selsea. But what of us? I know not the isle but for the hides of Cerdicsford. I have never gone round the sandbanks and over the marsh to where the sun rises."

"Your own island you know not, but you've been to the land of the Suth Seaxe."

"Ay, and a lot of good it did me!"

Aelfhere clapped his friend on the back. "Fear not, we shall not go astray! I know these woods like the band on my wrist," he held out the copper likeness of the war god to his friend's gaze.

"How so?"

"Mother was a woman of Wihtgarabyrig and many's the time she brought me as a child to gather mushrooms, herbs and blackberries. I still have family in the burh. Come, no time to lose!"

They hurried in among the oaks bearded with lungwort, following a trail through the hazel. A startled lone squirrel scrabbled up an aspen to stare down in accusation as they hastened ahead to the calls of indignant redwings, their feast of holly berries interrupted.

After little more than a league, they came to the edge of the forest where the trees had been cleared to leave open ground surrounding the foot of a hill. The rise was heightened by a steep embankment crowned by a wooden palisade — the fortress of Wihtgarabyrig, dominating the centre of the isle.

Purpose stated at the gate, they entered the stronghold where the main street led to the hall of the king. After only a few yards, a shovelful of steaming dung splattered at the feet of Baldwulf, who cursed and skipped over it. He spun round, glaring into the dim interior of a stable.

"Hey! Watch where you fling muck!"

"Next time, I'll aim better! *Ow...!*"

"Welcome to Wihtgarabyrig!" Aelfhere muttered.

They peered into the gloom, where a man in a leather apron pointed at a cowering youth rubbing his ear, a spade dropped at his feet.

"'Old your tongue, clot! An' I'll not tell you agin, you chuck yon muck in yon muck cart an' if you don't, I'll bash yer bloody 'ead against yon wall! Sorry abaht that, sirs," he said, casting a wary glance at the sword at Aelfhere's belt. "Get shovelling, little turd!"

He turned to them with an apologetic expression and the urchin, picking up the shovel, stuck his tongue out behind the stableman's back.

"Yer'd think yer'd get decent 'elp when times're 'ard, but it's like —"

"Just the two of you for all these horses?" Aelfhere interrupted.

"There be anither back there," the barrel-chested fellow jerked a thumb over his shoulder into the darkness.

"We'll be on our way," the ealdorman nodded and grinned as a kick found the arse of the bending urchin to send him sprawling in the muck.

Their laughter at the expense of the ragamuffin gave way to anxiety at the doorway to the king's hall. Two guards barred their way. One, with the teeth in the left side of his mouth missing, sauntered off to inform the king's advisers of the urgency of their mission. Before long, he returned to tell them the king would receive them the next morning. All protests in vain, Aelfhere dragged his thegn, flushed with rage, away from the heavy-set guard whose hand hovered over his seax and whose scowl did not bode well.

"Come, brother, bite back your words. Ill temper gains us nought. One more day...one more day."

"Ay," Baldwulf said, through clenched teeth, "we lose twenty men and that useless oaf keeps us from meeting with Arwald. Why, I have half a mind —"

Aelfhere hauled on the thegn's arm.

"I have no wish to lose another brave man. Come, we must seek a roof over our heads."

"No easy task in this cesspit of a —"

"Wrong again..." he led his friend down a side lane flanked by huts. Grimy, half-naked toddlers stopped their games to gape in curiosity, their stares outdone by those of a skinny woman carrying a pail of water. Another was sweeping filthy rushes out of the door to add to the rubbish and droppings befouling the street. Starving, spiritless dogs, more bone than flesh, slunk by as they passed. Foraging kites flapped off screeching and rats scampered, long tails vanishing into holes at the base of the daubed walls. Baldwulf wrinkled his nose at the stink.

"Told you it was a cesspit. Give me the open sea any day, what —"

He cut off his planned discourse and raised an eyebrow as the ealdorman knocked on the door of a hut.

It opened a fraction and a middle-aged woman stared out at them, her expression uncomprehending and suspicious.

"Don't you know me, Leofe?" Aelfhere grinned at her.

She squinted at him with no sign of recognition, but her frown cleared and with a broad smile, she said, "Cousin! It *is* you! After all this time, well, well!"

"This is Baldwulf, my thegn and trusted comrade."

Baldwulf placed his hand over his heart and nodded. The door inched wider.

"Will you not ask us in?" the ealdorman smiled. At which, she blushed and threw open the door.

"Of course, come in do! And right welcome you are!"

The aroma of bay and rosemary, wafting from a pot suspended from an iron frame over embers, replaced the vile reek of the lane. Leofe fussed around pulling chairs and then, grasping a jug with two ear-like handles, asked, "Will you sup some ale?"

Baldwulf grinned at Aelfhere, who replied, "Right glad to, but tell me, where's Siferth?"

She reached for a leathern flask, pulled a stopper and poured amber liquid into the ewer.

"Out in the fields," she said, "preparing the ground for spring sowing. He'll be back soon. Will you eat with us?"

"Cousin, you do us honour. And the girls?"

Leofe's eyes filled with tears, "The younger died in childbirth two winters past and as to the other, better I say nought."

Nor did she, instead she busied herself adding herbs to the pot and the rapid drying of her eyes with a sleeve did not escape the ealdorman. The two men drank ale in silence; it was weak with a pleasant taste of malt. Aelfhere and Leofe resumed talking about relatives and changes to the burh until the door opened and a sturdy dark-haired man came in. Hands begrimed by toil, he halted in surprise as the two visitors rose in greeting.

"Aelfhere! Your beard is grey!"

"Ay, and you've got a bald patch big as the moon!"

The two men embraced, laughing, and the ealdorman introduced his thegn. Over a stew of beans and chopped pigeon breast, Siferth questioned his wife's cousin to learn the reason for their visit. Aelfhere explained but finished by revealing his perplexity at their failure to gain admittance to Arwald.

"Like the guards to the hall didn't want us to see the king. Though what it mattered—"

"Was one of them a heavy-set fellow with half his teeth gone?"

"Ay," Aelfhere stiffened in his chair, "the ugly brute."

"Yon's our Eabbe's husband."

"I meant no offence."

"And none taken, cousin Aelfhere. Harder words serve for yon. He beats our Eabbe and forbids her from seeing us —"

"I — I haven't seen other than a glimpse of my grandson for four winters since he was a babe in arms," Leofe said, her eyes filling once more.

"I'd slay him with my own hands, but the lout's a giant and even if I managed somehow, the king'd dangle me by the neck from the Dancing Tree —"

"The *what?*" Baldwulf asked.

"The Dancing Tree. What Arwald calls the oak he uses to hang men from. His jest, see, 'dancing'…because the doomed man jerks and kicks when his life ends. There's no justice for the likes of us plain folk here on Wiht. Siferth shook his head. "Now, you being an ealdor-man, it might be different, but I wouldn't be sure. Arwald thrives on power…but I've said more than's wise!"

When pressed further, the ceorl gave a stubborn shake of his head — the subject was closed.

The next morning, Aelfhere with Baldwulf at his side, entered the hall of Arwald. The narrow doorway, no more than a yard wide, was flanked by impressive posts carved in images of coiled serpents. Two rows of wooden columns ran down the centre but they had no time to take in more of their surroundings. The guard they recognised as Eabbe's husband shoved Baldwulf into a line of petitioners.

"Wait your turn!"

He was spoiling for a fight but, all the way to the hall, Aelfhere had impressed upon his thegn to keep his temper. Baldwulf contented himself with a baleful glare, bowed his head and shuffled his feet on the reeds strewn over the river-pebble floor. The king sat behind the long feasting table, a counsellor on either side of him, dealing with each man in turn. The two guards positioned themselves near those approaching the ruler. Questions of wergild, disputes over animals and land, none given sufficient consideration, grim dissatisfaction among petitioners dismissed summarily, left Aelfhere uneasy. On the other hand, the colourful hangings on the oak-planked walls impressed him. Behind the table, between two doors leading to other quarters, hung the emblem of the Wihtwara, a rampant white dragon on a red ground. Arwald slept in one of those rooms.

The last man before their turn presented his case to the king, who was more interested in drinking from the horn in front of him. An object crafted with exquisite workmanship, rimmed with bronze, the mouth of the vessel — continuing for four inches as a sleeve — was overlaid by beaten gold petals and swirls. The length of the horn curved away in an s-shape to end in a ringed tube, decorated in gold leaf and capped by a flattened curl. The ealdorman's admiration ended when the petitioner in front of him protested in a loud voice, "...but I am the dead man's next of kin..." For his effrontery, he received a violent blow to the side of the head from the guard, sending him staggering into Aelfhere, who pushed him away. Both guards pounced on the man, throwing him to the ground and kicking him until he lay groaning, bloodied and still.

The king sat back in his chair, a sneer twitched under his bushy whiskers. "Out of my sight! Thrash the impudent nithing some more!"

They dragged the limp protester out of the hall.

Arwald turned his coarse features toward Aelfhere and forced his brutal expression into a smile.

Across the broad forehead, the russet inked hawk with outspread wings heightened the roundness of the face and the blondness of the matted hair. In spite of the smile, the ealdorman found no welcome in the narrowed eyes.

"Tell me your mission to Aethelwalh was a success!"

The command rumbled, threatening, deep and heavy as the king shifted his thick-set form to lean forward over the table.

"Lord," Aelfhere bowed, "the betrothal of my daughter to Eadric of Kent is well done as you charged me." He indicated Baldwulf with a wave of his hand, "Afterwards, we fought alongside the aetheling and defeated the usurper Hlothhere. Eadric slew him with his own hand before returning to his kingdom to take the throne."

Arwald's gaze, rather than linger on Aelfhere's face, fixed upon the sword hanging at his side. This did not escape the ealdorman's notice. The grunt that met his words, he took to be one of approbation — but he still had to deliver the bad news.

"Aethelwalh is dead, lord."

"What!"

At last, the close-set eyes detached themselves from the wolf pommel to glower at him. Muscular, ink-patterned arm raised, Arwald formed a fist and brought it crashing down on the table. Both counsellors and Aelfhere winced at the might of the man.

"How? In battle against the usurper?"

"Nay, lord, in a night attack on Kingsham. A score of my men died there."

Arwald taunted, "And yet you live to tell the tale?"

"Lord, I lost my senses in the fight and my thegn carried me thence under cover of darkness."

Turning his head slowly, Arwald fixed his gaze on Baldwulf, menace conveyed in the deliberateness of the motion, his words scornful, "You serve your lord *well*, thegn."

Pale, Baldwulf bowed and stayed silent.

"So, the usurper slew Aethelwalh —"

"Forgive me, lord, he did not." Once more the king's eyes dwelled on his sword. "The war-band infesting the Andredes weald took the burh and their leader claimed the throne —"

"What!" The roar reverberated through the hall. "Another upstart! Name him!"

Aelfhere half-turned at a movement beside him. The two guards had returned. The king glared at Eabbe's husband.

"Did you beat the nithing?"

"Ay, lord. I fear he's dead."

"Good!"

The expression of the ruler was impassive, only the eyes moved back to the ealdorman. "I asked you a question," he said.

"Lord, his name I know not, but from his accent, he's of the West Seaxe like most of his men; but Meonwara fight beside them." Aelfhere stumbled over his words, "Th-they took my daughter in the raid, Cynethryth, betrothed to Eadric. I come to plead for warriors. I can lead them to the Suth Seaxe, together we shall slay the upstart, regain my child and restore the alliance."

He waited, aware of the fascination his sword exerted over Arwald. Was it of more interest to the King of Wiht than the fate of the isle?

Arwald shifted his stare elsewhere and leant, his mane of hair nigh on touching the head of the counsellor at his side, their murmured exchange inaudible. When the king looked up, the malice in his eyes shocked Aelfhere.

"Leave our presence and wait for our decision," he said. Then ordered the guards, "Clear out these folk. They'll return when next I hear petitions."

Aelfhere bowed and backed away. Baldwulf, following his example, left on the heels of several frustrated petitioners who were muttering words of disapproval into their beards not to be overheard by the vengeful sentinels.

Outside the hall, the thegn frowned and shook his head, "I don't like the way Arwald stared at us."

The ealdorman grimaced, "Indeed! Make haste, we must flee!"

"What...!"

The ealdorman lowered his voice, "Arwald means us harm. As I speak, he is taking advice from his counsellors. Already he seeks to turn events to his advantage, to treat with the West Seaxe in Kingsham — and he covets my weapon. Come! We must away."

They hurried down the lane with backward glances, but the door to the hall stayed shut. When they neared the gate to the burh Aelfhere said, "The stable... we'll take two horses, by force if need be."

They entered the building and stated their purpose. The stableman frowned, his face a mask of suspicion. "On the king's business, you say, but who's to —"

"Friend, would you enrage the king? There is no time to lose! Take these coins as a warrant of good faith." Aelfhere held out three silver pieces and waited, ready to draw his sword. The stableman then scrutinised the ealdorman, reluctance fighting with greed, before grasping the money.

"I suppose..." he called over his shoulder, "...hey, lumpen lout! Get o'er 'ere! 'Elp me saddle up two 'orses!"

No sign of the urchin of the previous day, instead a squat, bandy-legged character appeared from one of the stalls.

"Saddle up yon bay in the fourth stall an' make 'aste!" the stableman said, thrusting the coins into the pocket of his leather apron. Good as his word, he hurried over to a dappled grey mare and in little time led her, saddled, to the ealdorman. "She's a steady 'un, nice-natured. Treat her well, mind."

The guards at the gate, caring nought for those leaving rather than entering the burh, let them pass without a glance.

Leading his mount by the reins to the foot of the steep embankment, Aelfhere drew close to Baldwulf.

"At a lope till we're out of sight not to arouse suspicion, then it's at speed toward Cerdicsford."

* * *

They galloped the horses for two miles, helped by the firm going and the slope of the chalk downs in their favour. A stiff wind from the south-west swept the high white clouds overhead so the weak sun came and went as they rode. Aelfhere reined in to a halt, their mares snorting and breathing fast. He dared not push them harder with another three leagues ahead of them to reach his homestead. Yet, time was against them. Patting the dappled mare and soothing her with gentle words, he turned to survey his surroundings. To his right, in a patchwork of light and shadow, the land undulated down into dense woodland of stunted oak and ash trees; to his left, the ridge gave way to heathland of impenetrable gorse and scrub.

"We should walk the beasts for a while. Let them get their wind. There's a way to go yet."

The ealdorman twisted in his saddle and squinted back toward Wihtgarabyrig. His voice betrayed tension. "By now, Arwald will have learned of our flight and our king is as tenacious as rough- coated hounds from Gwent, he loves nothing more than a manhunt."

They went on at a slow pace. Baldwulf wondered at the silence of his comrade, but knowing his lord well, he let him be. When Aelfhere spoke, at last, the thegn marvelled the more.

"The call of the curlew...can you mimic it?"

Baldwulf grinned, "The times I heard yon! I'd be a dullard otherwise!" He let out a shrill '*coo-leee*'.

The ealdorman nodded, "Hark!" Then, '*Coo-leee*', he imitated the sound.

"But why —"

"Do you have your fire-steel and flint?"

"Ay, but —"

"The tide was high when the boatman left us, right?"

"True, but —"

"By mid-afternoon, it'll be on the ebb…" Aelfhere murmured. "*Yee-ah!*" He urged the mare to a lope and Baldwulf did the same, reckoning his lord would tell him the meaning of his questions when he was ready. Meanwhile, he loved a riddle so he creased his brow to find a link between the bird call, the flint and the tide, but failed.

The ealdorman left the chalk ridge near the coast, urging his horse along a narrow trail into the heathland. Baldwulf made no sense of this either, sure that if pursued, the gorse would be their undoing. The maze-like paths, created at random by nature, designed as fine a trap as Arwald might wish for. Still, with unwavering trust, he followed his friend up a humped knoll covered in scrub until Aelfhere halted and dismounted.

"Come," he said, drawing his sword, "help me clear this brushwood." The ealdorman slashed and heaved the vegetation into piles as he cleared a swathe at the foot of the rise.

"My axe is no use," Baldwulf said, taking it from its harness on his back and laying it on the ground. He pulled his seax from his belt, "Thanks for not choosing the gorse," he pointed to his right, " …yon's a tougher nut to crack…" and he began to hack and tear at the plants. They made rapid progress clearing up to the top of the knoll. Below them, the cut scrub lay in heaps.

"Now what?" Baldwulf asked.

"Now…here's my plan…" The thegn listened, at first unconvinced, but given the direction and strength of the wind, the plan of the ealdorman might work. In any case, they needed to gain time and no other way came to mind.

They set to, dragging the heaps of brushwood where possible in among the gorse on the windward side of the track. At last, ready, they remounted and scouted the land behind the hillock. An escape route found, Aelfhere, satisfied, headed back to the knoll with its clear view of the ridge they had ridden along. The ealdorman sat motionless on horseback, holding the reins of the dun mare alongside his own mount.

"Remember," he said to Baldwulf, "on the first curlew call, only one! On the second, the rest as fast as you can!"

The thegn nodded and grinned, "I'll go bind a tight bundle."

As expected, not much time passed before the ealdorman spotted movement in the distance. A couple of minutes went by until he was sure ten or a dozen riders were approaching. Before long, the sounds of hounds baying and of hoof beats reached him — so he imitated the shrill call of a curlew.

A thin grey plume of smoke rose into the air and Aelfhere grunted in approval.

That'll draw them. They'll think we're cooking!

The leading hound swerved into the heathland trail the two men had followed, while the following hounds ran no more than two abreast, owing to the narrowness of the track. Sitting still as a rock on the hilltop, the ealdorman was by now visible to the first rider. The husband of Eabbe led the charge. Preferring to send his minions, Arwald had renounced the chase. Unmoved, Aelfhere waited for the headlong gallop to approach. At what he judged to be the right distance, he whistled a second bird call.

As anticipated, the stiff wind and uncommon dryness of the season served his purpose. Sharp crackling and a black billowing cloud disturbed the clean silence of the heathland. Torch ablaze, Baldwulf sprinted from one heap of tinder-dry brushwood to the next, setting the gorse alight. Flames surrounded the track and a smothering fog blinded the riders, hounds and horses. The fire spread faster, fanned and driven by the wind, the smoke denser, more stifling. Where the bushes were not on fire it was impenetrable. Backwards was the only escape but the horses reared in panic, their bestial screams united to those of the hounds and men. The fierce blaze swept on along its swift course of destruction; in its trail, smouldering charred limbs of gorse twisted like the tortuous serpents carved into the doorposts of Arwald's hall.

The acrid air began to clear at the foot of the knoll as the wind drove the fire and smoke farther along the track to the edge of the heathland. Baldwulf reached his lord in time to see the first terrible effects of their deed. Nearest them a frightful figure writhed and rolled on the ground, gibbering, hair and clothing burned away, the flesh a waxy, white colour, a hideous, contorted bloody mess.

Aelfhere looked on in a dispassionate way as the once mighty warrior twitched and lay still.

Eabbe's husband will beat her no more!

The fire had spared none of their pursuers. There was no sign of the hounds among the carnage. Being closer to the ground, he guessed, they had forced their way under the gorse. In the distance, two or three horses galloped free but others added their tortured cries to those of the dying men. Two figures rose as ghastly forms to run a few paces before dropping in a shower of sparks, groaning among the smouldering embers on the trail.

Sickened, but safe for the moment, Aelfhere and Baldwulf turned their horses to the north-east along the route they had scouted before the blaze.

"The king will suspect nought before nightfall. At that hour we must be in the land of the Suth Seaxe with our folk, since few are the warriors able to resist the malevolence of Arwald."

* * *

Their ride took them to the coast where a great wall of chalk fell three hundred feet down to the sea. Here, Aelfhere recalled, an uncle had lost an eye as a boy to a vindictive gull for the sake of collecting eggs from one of the almost unapproachable ledges: a high price to pay for staving off hunger. Their horses carried them westward down to what appeared an impassable marshy valley, but as foreseen, low tide made the ford across the Creek crossable. They dismounted and led their unwilling beasts through the river on to Freshwater Island.

Early afternoon, the ceorls of his estate gathered before the hall eager to know what was so pressing they should leave the fields and gather here with wife and children.

The ealdorman gazed around at the expectant folk. Among the score of ceorls, only two or three ranked as warriors. There was no time to avert those on outlying settlements to the west, who would have to take their chance. For sure the king would wreak vengeance on his hall and barn and on these poor huts.

"Not a man or woman of you ever left this isle. In Wihtgarabyrig, beyond the marshlands, resides the warlord, Arwald. The grain we send there and the arms we lend when called upon means we live and work in peace. The king protects us — unless he directs his ire against us..."

Aelfhere paused to let his words drive home. As their lord, he cared for every last one of them. He had shared in the joys and sorrows of their existence from an early age and now he must wrench them from their homes.

"The wrath of Arwald turns on us through no fault of my own. These matters I cannot explain." He shook his head, the weight of sadness sagging his shoulders. "I scarce understand them myself. What I am sure of is this — we are defenceless against him and must flee across the sea."

Women gasped and grabbed at their husbands, men stared from one to another then at Aelfhere, everyone shouting, questions lost in the outcry. The ealdorman stretched out an arm, palm raised.

"This is what we must do. Each man will take one sack of grain from the barn down to the boats, the women a bag of dried beans and one of winter apples. Return and gather what clothes and belongings you can carry. Within an hour we sail for Selsea. It is a place where men worship a strange god, but they welcome all who come in peace. In this way, we protect the children — I can think of nought else," he ended lamely.

Two hours later, three boats laden with supplies and a score of men with their families set sail for Selsea.

At the stern of the leading boat, Aelfhere stared at the buildings above Cerdicsford harbour, dwindling before his gaze. Would they ever see home again? What of the two stubborn ceorls who had remained behind? How were they to survive the wrath of the king?

Bereft of his overlord's support and deprived of the warriors he sought, Aelfhere despaired. Arwald must not treat with the West Seaxe dragon for fire was a perilous element as he and Baldwulf knew well.

Chapter 5

Cynethryth and Caedwalla

West Sussex, March 685 AD

The golden-hued rind of bacon smoked over a hickory fire hanging from a rafter in the food store appealed to Cynethryth's eye. Next to the cured meat, a row of birds dangled from the beam by their trussed legs.

"What fowl are these?" she asked, pointing with the iron key of the storeroom.

"Plover, lady. An' they need eatin' right away afore they spoil. We can lard 'em an' roast 'em over a brisk fire. There's enough for the lord's table, anyhow."

Cynethryth smiled at her new helper. Cook to the late King Aethelwalh, true, but her loyalty was sworn to her pots and pans. It mattered not whether the stomach of the ruler originated in Suth or West Seaxe — suffice it appreciate her offerings. Of course, sensible lordship, to the cook's way of thinking, also meant a full larder. The sacks raised on a wooden dais in the corner drew her attention. Cynethryth followed her gaze.

"What's in the bags?"

"Barley, lady. What say you to bacon barley? We can chop yon and some onion into pieces and chuck in some rosemary and sage." She scratched her short grey hair. "We ought to soak the grain right away, mind..."

On they went, choosing from the store and planning for the feast, Cynethryth pleased to wield authority. As they emerged blinking from the hut into the stronger light, she spotted the waif who had warned them of the attack the day before. The child, slight of frame, struggled to carry a pail brim-full of water toward the kitchen.

"Stop!" Cynethryth called.

The girl halted and set down her burden before drawing her sleeve across her brow. Through the open gate, two hundred yards from the palisade loured the mound of earth and the sorrowful gaze of the bride-to-be lingered on it. Their toil ended, the diggers stood or sat around in small groups.

And what of father?

She dragged herself back to the present.

"Child, run and fetch the nearest man! Tell him the lady has need of his muscles."

Puzzled, the girl glanced at the cook, who urged her into action with a swift nod. As soon as the girl returned with a warrior, Cynethryth gave out her instructions.

"Go with the cook to the kitchen. Carry this pail and empty the water. Return to the well and draw the water they need. As for you, little sparrow, make haste, find a basket and go down to the brook. Gather all the cress you can find and bring it to the women. It's work more suited to those frail wings. Away! Off you fly!"

A deep full-throated laugh made her spin round. Caedwalla, amused by her manner, said, "So, soon you order everyone around!" He folded his arms over his chest and grinned at her dismayed expression, which lighted up at the reappearance of the girl, a trug on her arm.

Shaking off her distraction once more, "Fish!" she said. "My love, can you spare three men to go to the river? Chub, lamprey and rudd, whatever they can net —"

The warrior seized her and sought to steal a kiss but she beat his chest with her fists. He held her at arm's length, frowning in surprise.

"There'll be time later," she mumbled, "we've so much to prepare —"

Without a word, he turned away and she gazed in anxiety at his back as he strode toward his men. Had she annoyed him on this of all days? To her relief, he barked orders to three men. They rose and hastened into a hut to re-emerge, one with nets slung over his shoulder and the other two each carrying a pair of creels; she hoped they would fill them.

To talk with Rowena, she hurried to the hall, where her friend was overseeing the preparations. Outside the entrance, children gathered up armfuls of filthy rushes and dashed away with them to the midden. Inside, three women with brooms were sweeping gnawed bones, shards of pottery, eggshell, fruit stones and other droppings into dusty piles. Later, these would be cleared for the spreading of the fresh river sedge and dried lavender flowers. Two others removed torches in need of replacement from their cressets. As Cynethryth approached, Rowena ceased discussing the arrangement of side tables and greeted her with a smile.

"I must take you away from your task for a while," she said. Drawing her aside, she lowered her voice. "Come, I would speak with you away from prying ears."

In a quiet corner, she stared into the green eyes of her friend.

"It is the ardour of Caedwalla disturbs me," she whispered, "I — I never had a man," she reddened.

Rowena laughed and embraced her. Stepping back, she smiled, "Be not afraid, it is a natural thing you will come to enjoy. Think of being wrapped in those strong arms and his heart beating over yours! Why you're a fine healthy woman and will soon bear a child. Then he will love you the more." She caressed Cynethryth's cheek. "Imagine the joy when you stare at the little one for the first time!"

In truth, a child tugging at her skirt appealed to her.

"Rowena, dear friend, you will think me a foolish girl but I must ask you this. There's no use talking to Nelda, she's an old maid as dry as a kindling stick..." After a hesitation, her words came in a flood,

"...shall I undress tonight and be ready for him in bed? Shall I douse the candles?"

Rowena's teeth flashed white in the darkness of the hall and her tinkling laugh soothed Cynethryth's worries.

"My, my, how you fret! Would you deny him the pleasure of undressing you by candlelight and discovering your charms? Now come! There is much to be done. You are to wed this afternoon."

The organisation went on apace under the guidance of Caedwalla, Rowena and the cook. Cynethryth consigned herself to the ministrations of Nelda, who dressed her in a pale blue gown and undid her plaits, making her hair long, wild and dishevelled over her shoulders. As custom demanded, everyone should know she was a noble-born virgin. Midway through these preparations came a knock at the door and Nelda admitted Rowena.

"Lady," she said, in formal tone for the benefit of the maid, "my lord sends me for the ring he entrusted to you this morning for the wedding. He also demands one of your shoes."

"A shoe, whatever for?" she asked.

"I know not, he says any old shoe will do."

Cynethryth gasped and put her hand to her mouth. "I forgot! An earnest! What have I that will serve? Nothing!"

Her servant calmed her, "You have something for an arrha, my sweet," and she whispered into her lady's ear causing Rowena to frown.

"Oh!" she sighed, her hands went to her cheeks and her eyes widened, "But he must never know whence it came!"

In the fading light of late-afternoon, Cynethryth strolled arm in arm with Rowena into the hubbub of the horseshoe-shaped gathering before the hall. What mixed emotions tore at her heart: joy, for she was to wed the man she loved; sorrow, for her father, not her friend, ought to be giving her away; guilt, for her father would never have blessed this union.

Every living soul in Kingsham had assembled in the yard. When the bride arrived the crowd fell silent. Feeling all eyes on her, she blushed and lowered her head. A waiflike form broke away from the throng and thrust a tightly-bound bundle of snowdrops into her hand. When in gratitude she bent to kiss the child a cheer burst from the throng.

Caedwalla, in a clean tunic, with no weapon or armour on his person, greeted her with a warm smile.

"My lady, more comely than her wild flowers!"

Rowena took her hand and placed it into the groom's. The hand-fast began the ceremony before the bride spoke her ritual words. "I take you Caedwalla," her voice firm and even, "to be my wedded husband, to have and to hold, from this day forward, for better for worse, for richer for poorer, in sickness and health, to be bonny and buxom, in bed and at board, for fairer for fouler till death do us part."

The West Seaxe warrior made his solemn pledge in a deep assured tone and a mighty roar and clapping signalled the binding.

He fumbled in his clothing and pulled forth the arrha — the gold ring she had worn earlier.

"Let this band be an earnest to seal our love," he said and kissed her to further acclamation. Forgetful, he pushed the ring on her fourth finger, such was the usage but overlarge, it did not fit; laughing, he slid it on her thumb.

When Cynethryth nudged her Rowena drew forth a gold object, passing it to her friend.

"Let this ring be an earnest to seal our love," she repeated and craned up to kiss his mouth to the clamour and banter of the people. Never had such happiness existed. Distracted, she tried to slip the band on his fourth finger, but too small, it did not pass the first joint. This time, the surrounding throng shared their laughter when the nearest onlookers explained the reason for their mirth to those who did not understand. The bride slipped the gold band on the groom's little finger with a silent prayer to Freya he would never link it to her betrothal to Eadric of Kent.

What happened next shocked her. Caedwalla reached into his tunic once more and pulled out her shoe. Before she blinked he struck her on the head with it.

"Wha — ?"

"A sign," he said, his voice loud for all to hear, "of your husband's authority." He handed it to Rowena, "Place it at the head of the bed. On my side. Now, at the sounding of the horn, the feast will begin!"

On his side of the bed. We'll see about that!

Caedwalla swept her into his arms and gave her such a kiss she forgot rebellion for the moment. To satisfy tradition, she flung the bundle of snowdrops into the gathering for a maid to catch.

The crowd dispersed but well before dusk, the men made their way into the hall to the sound of the horn blast. A scop began to play the lyre and promised the tale of the glorious victory over Aethelwalh, in exchange for yarrow-flavoured ale. Some of the women looked after the children while in the kitchen the rest worked the fires and ovens. From the latter, wafted a mouth-watering aroma as they drew forth loaves half the size of cartwheels on wooden shovels. In clouds of steam, others drained vegetables while some sliced meat dripping juices or filled bowls with bacon barley. Another used a willow switch to whip out salivating dogs and prowling cats. Amid the bustle, the voices of the cook and Rowena issuing orders rang out over the din of clattering pots and light-hearted chatter.

In the hall, the king's lady, hair raised in a crown of honour, bore a cup to her husband in the manner of her folk. An evening of serving him at table awaited her, but his high good temper and loving glances made her consider it worthwhile. Cynethryth lost count of the trips the women made to the kitchen. Bowls of bacon barley preceded the boiled goose eggs, baked pike fillet, roasted plover and smew, and grilled cow steaks with vegetables. These, they consigned to her and she set them before her lord. All this time, she filled the drinking horn with ale and wondered whether her man would survive the evening sober enough to fulfil his night-time duty. Either the drink was weak or his resistance was stiffer than Eadric's for he showed no sign of the drunkenness she had witnessed with distaste some days — a lifetime — ago. When he wiped his mouth with relish after the griddle cakes dribbling with honey, Caedwalla caught her by the arm, "Send for your maid when you are ready, wife."

In the calmness of her quarters, her servant bathed and dried Cynethryth before seeking a vial of precious elderflower oil to scent her skin. "Best to dress in a linen slip, joy of my heart," said Nelda with surprising practicality for an old maid. Down came her mistress' hair and she combed it into a red-gold cascade to her waist.

"Go and inform the king of my readiness."

Nelda hastened to the hall and strode to the long table where she curtseyed before Caedwalla.

"My lady awaits you, lord."

The servant, who had never lain with a man, blushed to the roots of her grey hair at the bawdy advice and suggestions from warriors besotted with cider and mead. As she resisted the urge to flee from the building in favour of a more dignified gait, she prayed to the Earth Mother, may the warlord be gentle with the maiden.

Outside, Caedwalla breathed the crisp air and sought inspiration in the stars, his eye passing from Woden's Wain, low in the sky, to the pulsing Herd of Boar. His mind somewhat clouded by drink, he shook his head to clear his thoughts. True, he had experience of women, but never had he lain with one he loved. Cynethryth, fierce as a lynx, hair as the saxifrage in bloom, must have a magnificent morning gift as tradition demanded. But what? He scanned the firmament but found it lacking in suggestions: what was missing?

That's it! The Mearh! The foal — it shines in the December sky. Now it's February. It's galloped off!

Pleased at his unshared joke he chortled and entered the bedchamber where his smile died. The ceremonial shoe issued its silent challenge from his wife's side of the bed.

"Ah, vixen!" he cried. "Not content to command my men, is it?"

"A real man has no need of a shoe!" she said, defiant.

* * *

When she woke in the morning, her body sore but her heart full of joy, she found at first only the hollow in the mattress where he had slept. When she rose, she discovered the shoe, impaled by a knife driven so deep into her bedhead all her might could not draw it out.

"Nelda!" she called.

The servant entered and Cynethryth did not fail to note the ill-concealed merriment in the woman's eyes. "Braid up my hair! I shall bathe."

Contentedness made the intended severity of her tone ring false. Nobody understood Cynethryth so well as her old nurse. By the time her lady stepped out on the morning dew, the maid was privy to the secrets of her mistress' soul.

Outside, Cynethryth found her husband sat on an upturned pail running a whetstone along the cutting edge of his sword.

"There you are, wife! Nought would wake you. See, I risk this blade wearing so thin I'd be better off wielding a spike of grass!"

At his roguish grin, a never-experienced warmth suffused her.

I'm a woman in love!

For once she found no words, but the gaiety of her smile brought him to her side.

"Come! Time for your morning gift."

Not a calculating woman, she had forgotten this custom, so she followed him in surprise. As they approached a stable, a youth dashed inside to reappear a moment later leading a white foal and reassuring the timid creature with soft words.

"What think you, wife? The filly has five moons and is weaned."

"Oh, she's a wonder! What's her name?"

"That is for you to decide."

Cynethryth strode over to stroke the velvety muzzle and received a gratifying whinny and a toss of the head.

"I shall think on it." Her dark grey eyes flashed love and gratitude for the generous bestowal.

"Think thrice, wife. Your mount comes with two other fillies — bays — a few weeks older. A horse must be a horse, not a spoilt plaything and together they will rear well under the guidance of this youth. He's a patient fellow." Caedwalla rested a hand on the young man's shoulder. "When they are mares, he will be your horse thegn."

"She's as white as the spume cast upon the rocks — I shall call her *Foam*."

"Spoken like a true Wihtwara!"

At the end of the morning, she revelled in the intimacy of eating alone with her husband. His every gesture, each curl of his mouth, gave her an inkling of the man she had wed. The illusion that Time might be cosseted like a gem, a precious object turned in the hand to reveal all its facets, was shattered as she poured cider into his cup. Contentment revealed its fleeting nature when Caedwalla admitted a messenger, a scout, into their presence.

The man bowed, hair matted and clothing grey with dust. "Lord, the duces of the South Seaxe have raised a host to avenge the slaying of their king. Forgive me, lord, I err. To be exact, they have mustered two hosts and have sent emissaries to Eadric of Kent for more men."

If Cynethryth needed more insight into the nature of her man, his reaction to the news provided it. The fierce light in the blue eyes, the set of the jaw, the clenching of the fist, all spoke of one who gloried in combat. Death, destruction, sacrifice meant nothing to him — power, everything. Another aspect of his character lay unveiled before her, but tyrannous Time now cast a shroud over the brief glimpse it had conceded.

"The nearest force, what is its size? Who leads it and how many leagues lie between us?"

"The first alone outnumbers us, lord, two to one. The dux, Beorhthun, is at their head. He who holds the hidage from Wlensing on the coast to the Arun river in the north. They are at two day's march from here. I know not whether he means to move or await the men of the other dux, Andhun, farther east. I reckoned it best to ride here at once."

Caedwalla stroked his beard, "A wise decision. I thank you. Either way, we cannot meet them in open battle." His eyes lingered an instant on the emblem of the South Seaxe hanging on the wall. "I shall not give *you* up without a fight," he muttered. He spoke to the messenger again, "Go to the kitchen, seek refreshment and rest for soon we move." Then he summoned a servant with a wave of his hand. "Send for my thegns, Maldred and Werhard, bid them come with all haste."

* * *

The two thegns bowed before their lord, their frames in marked contrast. Werhard, a wiry blond warrior of the Meonwara, stood head and shoulders above Maldred of the West Seaxe, a squat, dark-haired individual so brutal in appearance that he brought an involuntary shiver from Cynethryth.

With interest she listened as her husband broke the news of their foe, but grew pale and tense at his next words.

"Werhard, yon waggon with the tarred linen covering, double-yoke it with oxen. See the servants prepare it with benches and cushions and with all my lady and her companions will need on their journey." He paused for a moment to smile at her, which wrenched at her heart, for they must separate after but one night together. "Choose ten warriors and with them escort my wife to the Abbey at Selsea. Find he who goes by the name of Wilfrith."

Hard and determined, his eyes met hers and held them, "It is for the best, my love. The cross-bearer will hold you safe until I come for you. Never fear, I shall come. No man will keep us apart!"

Every fibre of her body ached to argue, to scream her refusal, but she would not contradict him in front of his men. Nor would she allow a tear to fill her eye. She would not displease him here. Instead, she nodded and held her head high.

He addressed Werhard once more, "There you will find Guthred. He set off yesterday with the body of Aethelwalh. Tell him to make haste, for I have need of my cunning fox." He proceeded to give instructions on where to re-join his war-band, somewhere in the weald unknown to Cynethryth, before he said, "… and take the foals and the youth who looks after them to Selsea."

Again, he turned to smile at her but this time she would not meet his eye. Instead, he offered Maldred a mirthless grin, more like the snarl of a wolf, "Gather the men. Have them hone their blades; on the horses pack food and drink. We leave in an hour. The women, children and servants who wish to stay in Kingsham may do so. They will come to no harm from their own kinsfolk when the enemy arrives. Go now!"

Alone, at last, she turned to Caedwalla, her voice no more than a hiss, "I swore to remain by your side...for fairer for fouler...till death us do part."

"Wife, you leave with Werhard."

Dashing the cup of cider from his grasp, she struck two feeble blows on his upper arm.

"See," he taunted, "what use are you in combat? A man might lose his life to save yours."

"I *will* come with you!" She stamped her foot.

He rose from the table and towered over her, his face was a mask of fury and she quailed before him. Of a sudden, a sly expression replaced the rage.

"It is true," he said, "we swore death would us part. By rights, the gods must decide. What say you? Come, a handclasp on it!"

Long and hard she stared at him, but he met her scrutiny without a qualm. She feared a trick but placed her trust in Freya. Not even Caedwalla could beckon Lôgna, the mischief maker, to his will. Her tiny hand, she lost in his.

Oh, I never want to let go!

He grinned at her.

"Well, wife. May the gods give you strength." He led her into the bed-chamber. "There!" he pointed to the weapon embedded in the wood. "Release the shoe and you shall come into the weald; fail, and you go to Selsea."

"A vile ploy! Oh, why did I put my faith in you?"

Feigning hurt, Caedwalla said, "Do you doubt the gods, my love? If it be their will the knife will slide out as from cream cheese. Go on! See what is their wish for you."

Cynethryth glared at him, pursed her mouth and strode over to the bedhead. With a swift prayer to Freya, she grasped the hilt and hauled with all her might. The weapon did not budge. Red with effort, she tried again, to no avail. He did not mock, instead, in a gentle voice, he said, "Wife, it grieves me to leave you. I swear I will come for you soon. Now, call your servant and have her prepare your belongings."

He strode over to the knife and before her disbelieving eyes, pulled it free without effort, tossed the shoe to the floor and returned the weapon to his belt.

"One day," she said, "sooner or later, I will make you pay for this!"

But her actions betrayed her words, for they fell into each other's arms and the kiss was long — sweet and sorrowful.

* * *

Overnight in the forest, while grateful not to be lying on the hard ground like her escort, even so, Cynethryth did not sleep. Unlike for Rowena and Nelda, the hours of darkness passed in sufferance. Although good sense told her Caedwalla had survived thus far without her prayers, worry and guilt over the breaking of her betrothal tormented her.

Mid-morning the next day, the oxen plodded into the abbey at Selsea where the youth in charge of the foals led the animals to the stables. A wimpled nun in a grey dress, with a large wooden cross dangling over her breast, conducted the women to their austere quarters. Testing the thin straw mattress on her pallet with the flat of her hand, Cynethryth confirmed its lack of comfort. A knock at the door meant she was not granted the time to appreciate her surroundings. Rowena! How could she refuse her friend's urgent plea to help her find Guthred when she too had spent little time with her new husband?

Intercepting a reluctant woman clothed in a habit, they coerced her to lead them to the warriors. They met them outside the refectory where the grim expression of the ealdorman softened at the sight of his woman.

About to withdraw a discreet distance as the couple embraced, Cynethryth instead hesitated. A monk caught her attention by dashing toward a distinguished and splendidly attired man with a thin furrowed countenance, to one side of the West Seaxe warriors. The brother addressed the man in the sumptuous purple cloak. "Lord Bishop, Wihtwara at the gate seek sanctuary: men, women and children. There must be two score of them. What am I to tell them?"

"Admit them! We are overstretched but God will provide. I will meet with their leader."

The prelate turned, and said something to Werhard that Cynethryth failed to catch, before hastening off after the monk. Guthred detached himself from Rowena, approached Cynethryth and bowed. "My lady, time presses, we must take our leave. The king awaits us in the weald."

Taking her glum companion by the arm, Cynethryth smiled. "Come, we'll accompany them to the gate," she turned to the ealdorman, "we shall sacrifice to the gods for your swift return."

They strode past a wooden building with a straw roof and a cross above the door, beyond the well, where a monk was drawing water near the impressive stone column with its bright-coloured carved beasts. Another time, Cynethryth mused, she would study the scenes portrayed in the panels.

Her reflections gave way to astonishment as they neared the gate. From the group of people gathered around two men, familiar faces grinned at her and children pointed. She had known these people all her young life.

In the centre she made out the purple-cloaked figure of the bishop talking to — her heart missed a beat — her father!

As if in a dream, she looked on as Aelfhere broke off his conversation to gape in her direction before the encircling Wihtwara opened a gap to let him pass.

"Cynethryth! Wherefore are you here?"

"Father, you are alive!" she said, and at once regretted the pointlessness of her words.

He took her in his strong arms and held her tight before slackening his embrace to kiss her forehead. As he did so, his eyes narrowed in confusion when they settled on the West Seaxe warriors behind her. His body tensed, and at the same moment, her stomach clenched. Deep down she had believed him dead. His survival was inconceivable. In a fight, he would be the last man to lay down his weapon or to flee. She had no doubt either, he was not for persuading: but neither was she. How come he was alive? What unexpected fate! The reckoning was upon her. In desperation, Cynethryth thought of her husband and found strength. Before her father uttered a word, she transfixed him with a voice as hard as the graven sandstone column at her back.

"Aelfhere of Cerdicsford, know this, your daughter is wed to the King of the Suth Seaxe."

May love for me quell your rage!

This thought and the pleading in her eyes was in vain.

With utter disdain, he said, "The King is dead — the betrothal betrayed! I must right these wrongs."

Untold sorrow filled her. How bitter the cup the Uurdi had drawn from the Well of Fate — she must drink it to the dregs!

"My heart is not yours to command. It belongs to another."

Even the children stood in silence, not understanding, but conscious of the tension in the air.

"Since the raising of the great pillar connecting the nine worlds, daughters have obeyed their fathers. You will come with me!"

Cynethryth glared at him. "Wives obey their husbands. I stay here!"

The hand of Aelfhere flew to the pommel of his sword, "Betrayal! You —"

"Hold!" Wilfrith stepped forward, voice laden with authority. "This is a house of peace. No blood will be spilt on this sacred ground." He scowled around the West Seaxe warriors, their weapons drawn.

"My Lady," Guthred glanced at Cynethryth, "your command?"

"The Lord Bishop is right. We are his guests. There will be no fighting." She turned toward Aelfhere once more, "Father, as you see, my men outnumber yours. There is no point in conflict. Go back home!

Inform Arwald your daughter has wed the King of the Suth Seaxe. Tell him he has nothing to fear from Caedwalla. Indeed, the king's lady, being of the isle, offers protection to Wiht."

Her fervent wish was she had not overstepped the mark. Why did the Bishop look askance? After all, might not her husband provide such a shield? Must he not contend with dire peril himself? Had she convinced her father?

His harsh response came as unforeseen as his laugh was bitter, "Return! To the treacherous dog, Arwald?" his words came as shocking as the glare he darted her. "Eadric will slay him along with the upstart who has taken you for his whore!"

He spat on the ground and spun, as though she did not exist, to plead with Wilfrith. "Bishop, I have few warriors with me. We leave for the land of the Suth Seaxe, but the isle is no longer safe for these other men and their families and I have nought left to offer them. I beg you, take them under your protection. They have willing hands and can work the fields and the women know how to spin..."

The bishop smiled. "Abbot Eappa is absent and while the decision belongs to him, I know he will be pleased to see the village grow. I give my assent on his behalf. There are conditions, of course. Until the men have built homes outside the abbey walls where the houses stand, the women and children will quarter with the nuns. Instead, the men will sleep in the monks' dormitory and everyone must consent to be instructed in the true faith."

Aelfhere had discussed this possibility with his bondsmen on the crossing. "I thank you. We have spoken of this and they accept your terms."

"And will you not make peace with your daughter?" the bishop asked.

"Ay, when she's a widow ready to wed Eadric."

Cynethryth took one step forward. "Father..." she said, stretching out a hand.

But the ealdorman did not deign to bestow her a glance, instead, he strode over to the Wihtwara. "Baldwulf, Wulflaf, Ewald, Hynsige, say your farewells! We leave!"

Determined to be strong, Cynethryth fought the lump in her throat and shut her eyes tight. Rowena drew close and took her hand, "Be brave," she whispered, "the Uurdi weave, but at times they unpick the threads."

Grateful to her friend, she nodded, fixing Guthred with a fierce stare. "Ealdorman, give me your word you will let them go unharmed and unhindered." She pointed at the backs of the Wihtwara warriors as they passed through the abbey gates.

"We will follow them until we are sure they do not mean to return. When we are satisfied, we will hasten to our King, your husband." He caught Rowena by the arm. "Wife, I charge you to watch over the king's lady — no harm must come to her."

Chapter 6

Aelfhere

Kingsham, West Sussex, March 685 AD

"How vast this cursed Andredes weald!"

The fingers of the dux, Beorhthun, drummed on the map and the edge to his voice betrayed his annoyance. "One hundred and fifty miles from the eastern marshes to the western limit and thirty-five in width. It's like —"

The wandering attention of his ealdormen lost, he followed their stares to the guard hastening down the hall.

"What is it, man?"

"Lord, the chieftain who led the Wihtwara against the usurper Hlothhere is at the door and begs leave to enter."

Beorhthun straightened to his full, imposing height. "Bring him to me!"

Aelfhere did not recall the dux from the battle near Isefeld, but the Suth Seaxe nobleman remembered the ealdorman's prowess and greeted him with warmth, not destined to last.

"Lord, I am fresh come from Wiht whence I bear grave news. Arwald intends to throw in his lot with the king slayer, Caedwalla, who it is said can rely on the Meonwara for support. Time is vital! We must snare and destroy this upstart before he can gather more men from the west."

"Arwald breaks his bond with the Suth Seaxe?"

In an instant Beorhthun had grasped the peril but to Aelfhere's dismay said, "Snare him? Easier to find a shrew in an acre of scrub!" He jabbed at the parchment. "Apart from the drove roads and a few scattered steadings, we know nought of the forest." A fist smashed into the palm of his hand, "I sent scouts in all directions but they returned with no sighting... except for two." He tapped the chart. "They travelled west three days hence in this direction... but did not return." His expression thoughtful, he looked up at Aelfhere. "How many men do you bring from Wiht?"

"Four, lord, but —"

"Four!" the scornful tone matched the mockery in the blue eyes while the bushy blond eyebrows met in a frown as the ealdorman from Wiht bent over the map.

"We should move here," he ran his finger from Kingsham along the South Downs to the west, "to cut Caedwalla off from the West Seaxe and —"

"Tell me," the dux said with a sneer, his tone more sardonic than ever as he gazed around the other ealdormen, "why heed the counsel of one who brings a mighty force of *four* warriors to the table?"

With a provocative chortle, he grinned around the moot to muttered approval and nodded heads.

Aelfhere flushed, but kept his voice even. "I repeat, time presses. We must move before our foe strengthens —"

"We?" Beorhthun brushed back his long hair as he stood straight and folded his arms.

From his arrogant tone, the it was clear the Wihtwara's opinion counted not at all, but he determined not to be made a fool of in the presence of his peers. "*We*," the dux stressed the word, "deliberated to await the arrival of Andhun and his host from the Kent borderlands."

"A five-day march —"

"Five days that you, my friend, and your warriors" — there followed a mirthless smirk, and the dux jabbed a finger on the area where the scouts disappeared — "may use to locate the war-band. Should you find them, whereon your ferreting will amaze us, report back here! Not till we know their whereabouts for sure shall we move."

Aelfhere stared at the Suth Seaxe dux, careful to show ire in neither his gaze nor his voice, "Better an owl than a ferret to spot a shrew, lord. And the bird is known for its wisdom." Daring to say no more, he inclined his head in deference, adding, "We will return within five days with the news you seek."

Outside, he stared up at the sky and sniffed the air. Heavy grey clouds in the distance towards the coast threatened rain.

"Weather's changing," Baldwulf said, pausing to assess the expression of the other man. "Another storm in the offing?"

The ealdorman sighed and shrugged, "Old friend, what would I do without you? The vixen betrayed me and runs with the fox. Why is it, no-one heeds the danger? Yon dux will make us all pay for his haughtiness unless…ah well, where are the others? Best not delay, we take the road until dusk. I'll explain on the way."

* * *

Bears, packs of wolves, boars and outlaws frequented the Andredes weald, all dangerous beyond doubt, but the five men of Wiht wished to remain unseen by scouts of the war-band. They avoided the first steading on their way out of Kingsham. Rain began to fall as the daylight faded, so when they came to the second, they asked to lodge in the barn. Their spirits raised by the safety and comfort of their shelter, they fell into an easy sleep.

Of the five of them, Ewald best understood woodland. Back on Wiht, he was used to driving his grey pigs deep among the trees to forage for acorns. The next day, before they left the road and plunged into the forest, the ealdorman confided the supposed whereabouts of the foe and entrusted progress to the swineherd's sense of direction. With only a vague idea of the enemy position, obtained by a glance at a map back at the hall, the enormity of what he had undertaken dawned on Aelfhere. The sun, hidden behind a grey mantle of cloud, would not appear to help orient them. The rain relented to a drizzle, but the wet vegetation made their march uncomfortable and the prospect of a campfire at night negligible. The chances of aimless wandering, indeed, of returning to the same spot were considerable.

And yet, what choice did he have? Reckless impulse had not spurred him into this situation, but rather a combination of circumstances. Prime among these, an acute awareness of going unheeded regarding the menace of the West Seaxe war-band. By killing Aethelwalh and seizing Kingsham, Caedwalla had made his ambitions clear. Not only the Suth Seaxe but their own isle, and even the Cantwara, were at risk. The consciousness of this increasing threat urged him on.

Mid-afternoon, they halted to build a palisade where they endured a miserable night before rising early to press on. The sky was dull but the rain held off, which encouraged them to march for many hours. At last, they came to a burbling brook where they stopped for rest and refreshment.

"Hush!" Ewald raised a finger to his lips. Each man strained to catch the slightest sound other than the frightened calls of birds that had alerted the swineherd. Without a word, the ealdorman gestured, directing them to spread out in a wide circle. In a few moments, they were invisible and silent.

A ragged figure, staff in hand, approached the small waterfall in the brook where the Wihtwara had paused and where Aelfhere still crouched, hidden in the undergrowth. The fellow wore leggings the worse for holes and a threadbare tunic tied at the waist with woven grasses. Tucked into this belt was a flint blade knife, bound into a rough wooden haft. Despite his dishevelled appearance, under the thin cloth the form of his hard muscles, worthy of a warrior, impressed Aelfhere as the man lay his staff beside him and knelt to drink. By the unkempt black hair and length of face, the ealdorman judged him to be a Briton.

When the vagrant cupped his hands into the water, Aelfhere, sword drawn, stepped out to pin the stave to the ground with his boot. Their quarry leapt to his feet and made to flee, but on seeing the four warriors emerge, blocking his escape, his shoulders sagged and, fearful, he dropped to his knees.

"What are you? A thief on the run?"

The brown eyes darted from one man to another, "Nay, lord." The lilt to his accent was of the folk from the long western coast. "On the run is true, but I never stole in my life."

"Yet, the law commands anyone roaming the forest to blow a horn to announce his presence, else he's an outlaw and can be killed," Aelfhere said.

The man bowed his head and spoke to the ground, his voice bitter. "No man should be the slave of another. Far better to die." In spite of the silence of the woodland, the Wihtwara barely heard the next words. "Make an end to it, then!"

The ealdorman exchanged glances with Baldwulf and shook his head, a shrewd gleam in his eye.

"What say you, my thegn? Shall we put a stop to this wretch's outlawry?"

"Ay, no life for a man. Let's do him a favour!"

Aelfhere lifted the man's chin.

"What say you, Briton? Throw in your lot with us. Be a free man, with a lord to protect you. Fight by our side."

Not daring to comprehend, the fugitive sought the trickery beneath the offer. Yet, the countenance of the man bent over him read true enough.

".Come, sit with us, eat and drink. There's no haste for a decision. Do you have a name?"

"Cadan." He took the proffered strip of dried salted meat, scarce believing the luck befallen him — if indeed, the need to fight was good fortune. He listened to the explanation for the presence of men of Wiht deep in the Andredes weald, and having slaked the thirst induced by the salt, sat again cross-legged.

"If it's the Gewissa you combat, I'm your man," he said, using the name the Britons gave the West Seaxe. "Their king, Centwine, seized the land of the Defnas and there they torched my homestead, leaving it in ashes..." He paused and stared into the distance, as gloomy as the sky above them, "They caught us along the coast from two directions and enslaved those of us captured. At the end of the campaign, an ealdorman brought me in chains to a village called Cealc tun, it stands three leagues north-west of here."

"Why did you flee?" Baldwulf asked.

"I couldn't bear another winter. One was enough. They worked me like a beast but the food was scarce and the blows plentiful. Tales of hunting in the great forest a few miles away reached my ears. So one night, I upped and fled. There's trout in this brook, you know?" He jerked a thumb at the stream. "Anyhow, I built a hut, high in a tree, in a dense part of the woods, over yonder," he repeated the gesture, "not easy to find and it serves to keep me safe from wolves and other prowling beasts."

"Hence, you know the forest well," Aelfhere said.

The Briton nodded.

"Then you know why I ask..."

"Ay, I can lead you to them. But beware their scouts. I brushed with them more than once. This is the first time...but I didn't expect —"

"Cadan of the Defnas, swear to be my man and to do my bidding." He held out his hand. The Briton clasped it but the ealdorman did not release his grip. "Back on Wiht, you will be a free ceorl, on my oath."

They followed their guide for a league or more till, of a sudden, he halted.

"Over there," he indicated to his left, "is the river. They call it the Aemele because it flows down to a fortified village on the coast named Aemeles worth. Thing is, the ground is clay here and the drainage is bad. We have to skirt the swamp." He turned to Aelfhere, "They chose their base well. It's a patch of heathland, swamp on one side, forest on the other. I can get you close enough to see it, but we must have a care, there are lookouts in all directions. We move forward without a sound and in short stages. One at a time. From cover to cover. Clear?"

Cadan dashed ahead, swift and silent as a deer, before vanishing into dense undergrowth. In a moment or two he reappeared, beckoning with his hand. Aelfhere set off with all haste and squatted down beside the Briton.

"You'll have to try harder," the guide hissed, "don't tread on dead branches!"

Intent on hearing the slightest sound, he poked his head out from the vegetation and stared around. Satisfied, he signed to the next man, Wulflaf.

"Better, see! *He* didn't make any noise," he said to the ealdorman, who sniffed.

In this way, they made tedious but safe progress until the six of them lay prone, side by side, in the grass at the confines of the forest. Without raising his arm above the ground, Cadan pointed to a gorse-flanked rise. "The encampment," he mouthed soundless words.

On the heath, Aelfhere made out the tents, guards patrolling the edge of the knoll and the thin plumes of smoke from their fires. He had seen enough. They must hasten to Kingsham without delay. This time, he would stand before Beorhthun with the invaluable Briton as living testimony.

Retreating, they left the enemy camp behind them until, when Aelfhere began to feel they were clean away, their guide waved them down behind a thicket of buckthorn. Through the trees, he gestured to the solitary figure of a West Seaxe warrior armed with spear and shield, seax at his side. Cadan waited till the man turned his back before dashing behind another clump of alders five yards away. In spite of the silence and swiftness of his movement, it set off the alarm call of a redpoll resulting in a number of finches flocking. Alert to any such disturbance, the lookout readied his shield and with caution approached the Briton's hiding place. Fearing his guide would be discovered Aelfhere stepped out and charged the foe, heedless of noise. The Wihtwara rushed after him and although their long strides ate up the ground between them and the watchman, they did not close fast enough to prevent him from putting a horn to his mouth and blowing a shrill blast, ended by a violent blow to the back of the head from Cadan's staff.

They glared down at the fallen man, sharing the thought that the sound had reached enemy ears. Baldwulf bent down and placed his fingers on the neck of the scout.

"He lives. What now?"

They looked to the ealdorman for directions but the Briton took charge, "The warning will have alerted them. Once before, I fled hereabouts. Our only chance is the swamp but we cannot leave him here," he pointed at the unconscious lookout and indicated Wulflaf and Hynsige, the sturdiest of the band, "hoist him up and follow me."

He picked up the spear and flinging his staff into the undergrowth, led them down through the alders into a shallow valley. At first the ground was slippery, then their feet began to sink into the cloying earth that sucked at their boots. With their burden, the two warriors slithered and cursed, earning reproval and admonishment to silence from Aelfhere. Soon, the wetness seeped over their footwear, still Cadan led on till they were wading knee deep through murky water that at last became the River Aemele. There, it reached their waists before becoming shallower and they slid, exhausted, among alder buckthorn fringing a sandy knoll.

Wulflaf and Hynsige lowered their captive to the ground while Baldwulf scowled down at him. "We should slit his throat and bury him."

Aghast, the ealdorman said, "This fellow's more use to us alive. The dux will thank us for delivering him to Kingsham," he frowned, "but there is no rope to bind him."

"The thongs of his boots…" the thegn grinned at Cadan. "Help me strip him, Briton. He's about your size. You've gained yourself some decent clothes and a weapon."

Respect won already, in his new garments the aspect of their guide and comrade met general approval. Baldwulf glanced up from tying the wrists of the lookout behind his back.

"As well I didn't meet you dressed that way…you look threatening…I'd have had no choice but to slaughter you —"

"As well, it is! Without me as a guide, *he*'d be the one binding you!"

Aelfhere hushed them once more. "This hillock has much that pleases me. It's dry, sheltered and the swamp deters beasts. True, time is precious but the West Seaxe will be out scouring the forest for him and us." The bound man began to groan. "Pity we can't light a fire for these damp clothes."

"After dark, it won't harm, though we ought to keep it small," Cadan said.

* * *

Three days later, without further mishap in the woodlands, Aelfhere stood in the hall at Kingsham with the Briton and their captive. Dux Beorhthun, together with his counsellors, his expression sour, studied the West Seaxe warrior with disdain as the ealdorman ended his explanation.

Tone condescending, the Suth Seaxe leader addressed the Wihtwara. "You have done well." His gaze shifted to the Briton. "How many men does this war-band number?"

"I can't be sure, lord, I didn't get too close."

Beorhthun looked down his nose at the captive standing with bowed head before him, "Only a treacherous assault by night can explain the defeat of our king at the hands of these wretches. Look at the rat trembling in his filth!" he mocked, "it will be a simple affair to rid our lands of the vermin." This time addressing the captive directly, he repeated his question. "How many men in your band?"

Sullen silence met his demand.

With an impatient gesture of his hand, the dux summoned two warriors standing near the wall under the emblem of the Suth Seaxe.

"I wish to learn the numbers of the foe and about their defences. Find out the plans of this Caedwalla that we may thwart them…" He pointed at the man in bonds. "Take him outside. Bind him to stakes and flay him until he reveals what I seek to know."

Sickened at his part in delivering his prisoner to this fate, Aelfhere said, "Lord, this is not necessary. I can supply sufficient answer to your questions."

Indifferent, in a condescending tone, the dux said, "Ealdorman, I'm after facts, not the opinion of an island dweller." A wave of the hand as if swatting a wasp, then "Take him away!" Attention back on the map, he said to the pallid ealdorman, "Now, show us where the rodent wove its nest."

Skinning alive a hapless man disgusted the Wihtwara, in spite of their being inured to butchery on the battlefield. Cadan, careless of the screams from outside, indicated the best route to reach the enemy in the shortest time. This, explained the Briton to the attentive dux, meant following the line of the downs as far as Aemeles worth, skirting the swamp, swinging round from the north and trapping Caedwalla on the stretch of heathland, turning the strength of his position into a weakness.

An ominous silence from outside matched the quiet concentration of the counsellors as they pored over the parchment. All of them were hardened warriors who recognised at once the merits of the manoeuvre.

One of the men who had hauled out the wretch returned to the long table and bowed to the dux.

"Well? Spit it out, man!"

"Lord, the fellow revealed the band is made up of West Seaxe and Meonwara and numbers around one hundred and fifty." The dux raised an eyebrow, "The encampment is on a heath, edged by swamp and forest —"

"We know that!" Beorhthun said.

The warrior hesitated, searching for the words not to offend his lord. "Their leader, he called him 'king', Caedwalla, is in agreement with the Meonwara. Through his brother, he is in contact with two underkings, one in the land of the Sumerseate and the other in that of the Wilsaete. He means to unite with them, overthrow Centwine and seize the throne of the West Seaxe..." He hesitated again, looking uncomfortable.

"Go on! What else?"

"Forgive me, lord, he said their leader plans to right the wrongs inflicted by the Mercians...for giving us...he hates us...for having taken the —"

"Enough! Kill the cur!"

"Pardon, lord, he died..."

"Throw the body in the cesspit!"

Impassive, the dux turned to his ealdormen. "One hundred and fifty of them — we are twice their number. Ready your men to march at first light. Andhun ought to be here by now but I'll wait for him no longer."

Aelfhere left the hall with mixed sentiments. At last, to his relief and satisfaction, the dux would move against Caedwalla, but the captured scout had met an atrocious end. The ealdorman shrugged, not only the West Seaxe would perish in the forthcoming clash, he might die himself in the slaughter. The manner of death was what mattered. In his opinion, arrogance and savagery did not make for wise leadership, but what could go wrong? They had adopted the Briton's plan. It was time to whet their blades and put an end to this warlord and his ravaging ways.

* * *

On the second day out of Kingsham, with the Suth Seaxe host proceeding with stealth through the forest, at less than a league from the enemy base and due to veer to the north-west, an alarm sounded. Cursing his advance guards who had failed to find and finish off the lookout, Beorhthun drew near the ealdorman chosen to lead the left flank of the host.

"We cannot lose time by changing direction. Ahead at a trot!"

Ordered to stay close to the dux, Cadan overheard this command. Appalled, he hastened over to Aelfhere to inform him of this decision. Even as he did so, more blasts of enemy horns reached them from afar.

"The fool is leading us to disaster," he whispered, "urge him to revert to the original plan, before it's too late!"

The Wihtwara ealdorman hurried abreast of Beorhthun. "Lord, beg pardon," he said, "the approach is wrong. This way leads into quag. We should swing round as planned, to the north-west."

"Islander, do not presume to tell me what to do! Lost the advantage of surprise, it is perilous to waste time. Our greater numbers will prevail in a frontward assault."

"But lord —"

"Enough! Save your wind for the fight!"

The menace in the tone of the dux was clear enough, so with sinking heart Aelfhere managed a polite, "As you command, lord," before withdrawing to join the Briton. "It's no use, he pays no heed."

"Let me try to persuade him," Cadan said.

"By Tiw, he'll have you flayed! Let it be!"

Even as he uttered this advice the ground began to squelch under their stride. A few moments later the first men started to slip and curse and soon afterwards the soil became waterlogged. Perplexed, the leaders, among them Beorhthun, slithered to a halt. Through the trees, they glimpsed thinner woodland with occasional clumps of downy birch, their trunks emerging from the water.

Furious, the dux waved the Briton over, "Why did you lead us into the swamp? You will pay for this!"

Pale, but without quavering, Cadan met his eye, "Lord, I sent the ealdorman, Aelfhere, to you, with the message to stick to the agreed plan. We must go back to skirt this mire and skew to the north-west —"

"We go back!" Beorhthun shouted the counter-order.

Aelfhere muttered a silent oath. Surprise thwarted, strategy nullified, in reality now they must rely on greater numbers. But even this proved useless. Caedwalla did not mean to risk men in open conflict. A hail of spears and flying axes cut swathes in the ranks of the Suth Seaxe. Warriors struggled to find a footing in the cloying mud, made more slippery by the previous passage of hundreds of boots. Agility impeded, as they slid about unable to manage their shields, cold steel mowed down the men closest to the foe like stalks of grain before a sickle. On firmer ground, the West Seaxe warriors interchanged with deadly swiftness so men with throwing weapons replaced those with empty hands. Few of Beorhthun's men hurled their javelins, for they had no purchase on the treacherous earth. The slaughter ceased when the attackers exhausted their missiles. Damage inflicted, they melted away to the jeers and impotent rage of the Suth Seaxe struggling toward firmer footing.

The left flank of the Suth Seaxe host lay dead or wounded in the mud. From the centre of the stricken force, Aelfhere and his men, with their wrathful leaders, slithered and stumbled while picking their way over fallen comrades.

They lost time regaining solid ground. Scouts sent in the wake of the war-band returned to report sighting them heading westward. The ealdorman approached the dux.

"Lord," his tone beseeching, "we should follow and attack them at night otherwise, the scourge will return more powerful than ever."

Beorhthun raised his chin and looked down on the Wihtwara, "And we shall be ready for him. This day, we achieved our purpose. We expelled the ravagers from our lands."

The dispiriting task of raising a mound over the dead completed, the march back to Kingsham hauling rough-hewn litters bearing the wounded began. In the overnight camp, sat around a fire, the Wihtwara and Cadan discussed the happenings in low voices.

"Trust a cur like Beorhthun to pretend success from carnage," Baldwulf said.

The Briton nodded. "He reckons himself too lofty to heed another..."

"I fear his faults will cost us dear," Aelfhere said, "the southern lands must find a cure for this scourge — the spear of Caedwalla, the war-wolf, never rests."

Chapter 7

Wilfrith and Cynethryth

Hunched over, her knees drawn up to her chin, Cynethryth sat on the wooden floor in the corner of her cell. Since the departure of her father three days ago she had been inconsolable, upsetting Rowena with her unresponsiveness and weeping.

The Suth Seaxe woman paced to and fro across the small room, her arms crossed over her chest. For a moment she hesitated, before sliding down against the wall beside the Wihtwara. Wary and gentle, she squeezed the limp hand of her friend.

"Do you care to know my secret?"

Sure to have pricked the curiosity of her companion, she waited. Wordless, listless, Cynethryth turned red-rimmed eyes toward her and nodded.

"Well," she said, "in my village, everybody went down to the river with a priest and he poured water on our heads and told us after death we would live for ever —"

The younger woman sat up, "You're a Christian, like them?"

"I suppose so," Rowena said, puzzled, "understand, the king wished for all his folk to be baptised — the name they use when they drench you with water. To wash away your sins, they say..."

"And does it?"

"I don't think so," she lowered her voice, "when Guthred drew lots and chose me, I couldn't wait to make love." She giggled, "These Christians say lust is wicked but where's the harm in pleasing a man, what say you?"

Cynethryth managed a wan smile, shook her head and asked, "Do you no longer follow the customs of our forefathers?"

"This is what I wished to share with you…to unburden…" She paused, and released the hand to stroke the young woman's hair instead. "I cannot bear it when you're so glum. There is a way. Trust me. Let's leave this grim room…" she cast a baleful glance at the wooden cross hanging from a nail on the wall, "…and go to the village —"

"The village?"

"There is a remedy for what ails you. But come, the sun may yet break through the clouds."

Cynethryth did not doubt that her words bore double meaning and together with the weariness of confinement, her persuasion swayed her. Outside the walls of the abbey, certain no-one should overhear, Rowena confided in her.

"These priests and nuns believe in an unseen God, but look around you! The sun, moon, earth, stars, the springs refresh us, trees give us shelter and food, plants supply balm and potions…" She took Cynethryth by the arm as though contact might sustain her argument, "The Christians refute the old ways but…but can't you sense the spirits in the wind, the stream, the oak…?"

The sun shone forth in brief moments of brightness conceded by the scudding clouds. The bracing nip in the air invigorated Cynethryth and she patted the hand on her arm, "All around us, it's true, good spirits and bad —"

"Ay, and elves. And there's the point: elf envy. They've pierced you with their invisible arrows! They made you pay thrice over in sorrow for your joy when you wed. On the coastal side of the village," she said, pointing at the first of the reed-thatched huts, "lives one steeped in

ancient lore, a *haegtesse.* It's what mother used to call the wise woman
in our town — she awaits you, for I spoke with her yester morn."

* * *

The settlement struck them as lifeless but for a toothless old man, sitting on a log, baring his gums in a grin. Two crows on a roof cawed
down on the street and a dog, more interested in sniffing at a wall
than in their hasty passage, snubbed them. No doubt the women and
children kept indoors sheltered from the biting wind off the sea while
the men of the village were toiling in the fields, the abbey or the forest.
Three hens pecked in a desultory manner in the grass beside the last
of the huts, from whose doorframe hung dried agrimony.

Before knocking, Rowena pointed to the cluster of stems fastened to
the entrance. "This," she said in hushed tones, "drives bad spirits away."

A wizened, weather-beaten old woman opened the door and gestured to them to enter. In awe, Cynethryth stared at a room that to
her fanciful mind appeared to be a field turned upside down. From all
the roof trusses dangled bunches of herbs, plants, seaweed, porcupine
quills, feathers and straw woven into a variety of animal and human
forms. Below, bottles and flasks covered the table and bench positioned
against a wall. Out of one of these vials, the woman poured a few
drops of liquid into an earthenware cup. Then she dipped a ladle into
a tub to pour water over the contents of the drinking vessel. The gap-
toothed crone shuffled over to the Wihtwara, handed over the potion
and urged her to sup.

"Root of setwall wards off the envy of the elves," she said, and to
the amazement of Cynethryth, her incongruous laugh rang sweet and
kind. "But it bain't no cure. Not for the weeping. There're those as say
elfin folk make 'emselves unseen to gather tears of sorrow." She shook
her head at the puzzlement of her refined visitor. "Pure water, see, it
keeps 'em young forever —"

Rowena interrupted to avoid a lengthy explanation, "But yesterday,
you told me there was a remedy —"

"So I did." She swept her long grey hair behind an ear. "For a cure she'll need the Ring Stone."

Taking down a mantle from a hook by the door, she flung it around her skinny shoulders and tied it over her chest. The haegtesse led them outdoors and across the rough grassland separating her hut from the gorse- and broom-covered coastal heathland, pausing only to bend down and pick up a stick.

Rowena shrugged and took Cynethryth by the hand, "Trust her," she purred.

Showing no sign of frailty, the old woman strode along a narrow pathway winding through the gorse. In places, white tufts of wool, waving in the wind like tiny banners, showed where the thorns had snagged a goat or a sheep as the animal brushed past. Indeed, it grasped at the women's clothes, causing Cynethryth to wonder about the malignity of the spirit in the plant.

Not far away, the waves broke with a crash on the shore and gave a tang to the salt air. The wind flattened their dresses tight to their legs and all three pulled their cloaks close. Their guide halted and pointed with the stick to a clearing in the broom.

"There!" she said. "The Ring Stone."

In the middle of the break, stood a solitary boulder, squat, waist-high to the Wihtwara, its base buried in the ground. The peculiar feature of the rock was the gap at its centre. Four hand spans across, the round hole, five inches above the earth, was large enough for a child to crawl through. Orange and green patches of lichen clung to the leeward side while on its opposite, smooth, surface the grey stone glimmered yellow-tinged in the fleeting sunlight.

"Take this stick," the haegtesse said, holding it out to Cynethryth. "In the other hand! Good. Kneel! Pass it through the rock — good, right! Put your head in the hole up to your shoulders, ay, now tell your worries to the wood. Every one of them mind — don't leave a thing unsaid."

The old woman seized Rowena by the arm. "Come! We may not hear these things!"

They moved away a short distance and the Suth Seaxe woman caught the odd word: "…father…dead…widow ready to wed…forgive myself…ever have children…"

The voice droned on. The Suth Seaxe woman stared at the grey-haired woman in astonishment. The haegtesse nodded, her mouth pursed. "The poor child is full of anguish," she said, "the once is not enough. For the cure to take effect, you must come here tomorrow and for two more days. Mind, there'll be no need for another branch."

Cynethryth's cheek pressed against the smooth surface of the stone and a sensation of calmness soothed her. An increasing numbness made her eyelids droop until the weariness born of wakeful nights threatened to overwhelm her.

The wise woman tugged at Rowena's sleeve. "It is time! Hark, she recites no more," before hastening over, where she slapped the kneeling woman a stinging blow across the buttocks. "Come, child, do not doze. Be swift! Hurl the stick over your left shoulder. Go on! Good! It has taken your troubles. We are done here," the crone said. "The worry spirit no longer knows where they dwell. Do you not feel lighter, better?"

"But for my bottom," Cynethryth said, rubbing her rear and, to Rowena's relief, joining in their laughter. As if to mark the occasion, the sun slid from behind a cloud to brighten the heath.

On the path through the gorse, the haegtesse slipped her arm under the young woman's and pressed close.

"Put your head in the Ring Stone and, without moving, count ten hundreds for the cure to take effect. Do this for three days! But when you think on your worries, drive them away. Thus are the elves confounded. As to men's wyrd, your dreads work no change, my dear."

On the way back to the abbey, Rowena urged Cynethryth to relate her experience at the boulder — but how can one describe nothingness? What words could express such a void? One certainty, she had: it appeared to be no more than a lump of rock, yet the Ring Stone held the power to free the mind. Was not the mind meant to soar above the fields rather than plod along a furrow in a mire of sorrow?

This sureness led her back the next two mornings, and the impassible sandstone induced the same effect. Each time, she failed to share her impression with her companion, but Rowena needed no other persuasion than to witness the change in mood and spirit of her friend.

On the third morning, the last for the definitive cure according to the haegtesse, strolling past the spiny shrubbery, the hair of the Suth Seaxe woman prickled at the neck. This tingle happened when anyone, unbeknown to her, stared at her back. In time, she spun round to glimpse a figure in grey crouching down behind the gorse.

"Someone spies on us!" she whispered to Cynethryth, who halted.

"What of it? We have nothing to hide."

Rowena sighed at the ingenuity of her friend. "Indeed we do. Don't you see? For the Christians back at the abbey, you are practising the old magic. They say it is the way of the Devil."

"The what?"

"The Devil. It is he who causes all the evil and troubles in the world."

"Like Lôgna?"

"Worse! The Tempter steals away the soul to burn it in eternal fire!"

Shuddering at the image, in vain Cynethryth scanned the heath over her shoulder.

"No-one!" she said, "Are you sure?"

"Someone dressed in grey. Likely one of the nuns."

They set off again.

"I shall not renounce my time at the stone," the Wihtwara said, pursing her mouth. "I mean to complete the cure."

"They will accuse you of sorcery."

"I do not share or care for their beliefs."

They reached the Ring Stone. Without hesitation, Cynethryth spread her arms about it and began to count. Uneasy, Rowena stared back down the path, but for all her searching did not catch a glimpse of a living creature, except a tern gliding overhead.

Afterwards, passing through the village, she glanced back where a nun in grey habit followed them, with a wicker basket on her arm. Determined to confront the woman, she slowed down, but to what purpose? She would deny spying and invent the gathering of wild herbs or some other credible tale. An accusation on their part might imply an admission of wrongdoing — better to let it be.

The matter, however, did not rest there. Later in the day, Bishop Wilfrith summoned them to his residence. Two nuns awaiting them led them indoors without knocking. Cynethryth and Rowena gazed in wonder at the sumptuousness of the prelate's dwelling. The colourful hangings, the ornate caskets and embroidered cushions proclaimed the bishop's taste for finery. At their footsteps, he rose from a kneeler positioned under the wooden cross on the wall, and turned to stand. An icon hung glistening beside him as if vying to outdo the opulent drapery. Out of the gilded panel stared a bearded man with a golden disc around his head and a book clasped to his chest.

No less splendid than his surroundings, Wilfrith, in his white robe fastened at the waist by a silken cord, studied the women in front of him. At a glance, the older woman betrayed more nervousness in his presence than the king's lady. The latter exuded an air of calm curiosity that extended to a scrutiny of his own person, from the domed cap with its gold-stitched cross, down past the wide wrinkled brow to meet, unabashed, his dark deep-set eyes.

A winsome smile bestowed on them and he said to Cynethryth, "I hope you are comfortable and settled here in our abbey." The flash of suspicion in her eyes did not escape him. His plans for her would need patience and subtlety, for this was not the hoped-for malleable young woman that best served his purpose.

Her biting words confirmed as much. "Not as comfortable as you, it appears."

"Do not judge a man by the objects he possesses, but by his possession of the Holy Spirit, which no human power can grant." He waved a hand. "These are mere trifles. All a man wants in this world are food and warm clothing. The Tempter offered the world to our Lord but he chose to wander in poverty and preach the love of God."

"And yet you own all this —"

"Of no import. Take what you want!"

Cynethryth gazed around the room, her expression like a satisfied cat. "I'll take two cushions to help my friend and I sleep better."

"They are yours but you have chosen badly," the bishop said.

"How so?"

"Objects, as I said, have no value unless they feed the soul." He pointed to the cross on the wall.

"It's a piece of wood," the Wihtwara said.

"One reason why I called you here is because you do not share our beliefs." The furrows of his face deepened with a frown. "I wish you...to let me talk each day about our faith. I shall not weary you and there will be no insistence or pretence."

The bishop caught the swift glance the young woman exchanged with her friend, but Rowena stood expressionless. The beauty of the Wihtwara's features, Wilfrith observed, matched their strength. They revealed no loss of confidence but of course, as a non-Christian, why should she hold him in reverence? In the long moments before her reply, he offered up a silent prayer. So many of his hopes rode on her answer. When it came, he suppressed a sigh of relief — far better she did not realise the full importance of her consent.

Cynethryth assented. "Understand, I will not forsake the customs of our forefathers but I will hear your words. It would be ill-mannered to repay your kindness in any other way."

The thin, firm mouth of the bishop smiled for the first time, forming deep lines at each corner. "Agreed then, I shall send for you both in the morning. We can converse here."

"I'll take the cushions," she said, thrusting one at Rowena who, shamefaced, took it.

The prelate's piercing eyes followed their backs out of the room but his plans roamed much farther afield.

A small price for so great a conquest.'

* * *

A nun came to fetch them the next day. Following her, they passed a group of men at a shed delivering spades and pickaxes to a monk. At that moment, Cynethryth ignored them, unaware *she* was the cause of the activity.

Wilfrith admitted them to his presence with careful politeness, the same two nuns as the day before stood by the door as minders. The Wihtwara listened with attention to the bishop's exposition about turning the other cheek, but impatient, intervened, "Why then do men sing the fame of warrior heroes? Is it not a noble thing to smite plunderers and ravagers to protect the weak or to use the seax in a just quarrel?"

The aquiline features of Wilfrith softened. "And yet, herein lies the mystery. It may seem as you say, but more is achieved in this world by following the example of Christ's meekness and divine wisdom than by all the blows struck by earthbound sinews. Did not the Lord say, '*Put your sword back in its place, for all who draw the sword will die by the sword*'?" The prelate smiled and shook his head. "For nine lifetimes, unbelievers tried to destroy our beliefs with weapons, but Christianity grew not through wielding power and flaunting magnificence, but by the blood of the blessed martyrs. Killing did not stop the faith. They died one after the other — but from each death, a thousand new believers sprang forth."

Cynethryth, not by nature mild and accepting, found counterarguments and so the discussion wound on, eddying around Rowena, who finding herself wanting, shook or nodded her head from time to time.

Back in her cell, away from the eloquence of the bishop, Cynethryth turned to her friend.

"The man confounds me!" she said. "Part of me wishes to believe his message of love. What do you think?"

The Suth Seaxe woman shrugged, "He spoke of the greatest hero being one who does simple deeds for the sake of others, no matter the cost in suffering. I don't know. It's all back to front to me…"

"In fact! Where was this new god when Cerdric took Wiht from the Britons? The gods were faithful to our forefathers and received mighty rewards for sacrificing to them."

In spite of her stubborn assertion, on her pallet that night, Cynethryth mulled over her exchanges with Wilfrith. A remarkable man who had travelled far, the prelate combined in his manner a self-asserting gentleness with a power of persuasion. The meeting with him had unsettled her. What hitherto were certainties now wavered before his logic. She must resist, for they were to meet for the second time the next day. She yawned into her cushion with a sleepiness that in no way foreshadowed the outrage that would make her want to abandon the encounter.

The clatter caused by loading tools and the shrillness of raised voices under the window of her cell woke her at first light. Curious, she peered out on an ox cart laden with slender tree trunks, blocks of wood and ropes, while men were tossing pickaxes, spades and shovels. Her inquisitiveness sated, she would have returned to bed but then Wilfrith, wrapped in his purple mantle, arrived. He spoke with the villagers in a low voice, making it difficult for Cynethryth to catch his words. Drawn to the down-filled cushion on her pallet she turned away from the aperture but caught, '...the Ring Stone...' uttered by the prelate. She peered out again to where Wilfrith was strolling toward his residence while the men urged the oxen forward.

By Thunor! I must stop this!

Dressing in haste, Cynethryth did not wake Rowena, deciding the loss of time waiting for her to be ready outweighed the need for support. Hastening through the abbey gates, in the village she caught up with the plodding beasts and the band of eight men. She hung back a moment to form a plan.

Should I alert the haegtesse?

What served her purpose, however, was persuasion, not confrontation. Better to create no disturbance and to follow the men to the heath in order not to arouse the curiosity of the villagers.

The creaking cart ground to a halt in the Ring Stone clearing, where Cynethryth spoke to the tallest of the men.

"Who's in charge here?" she asked in a peremptory tone.

"Suppose I am..." said a burly fellow stepping forward. "Who wants to know?"

"The king's lady."

The man was surprised — but not as amazed as she at his reply.

"Sorry for your loss, lady."

"My loss?"

"Ay, sealed the tomb in the crypt myself —"

The young woman laughed, "Not Aethelwalh! The *new* king."

The man frowned, "Beg pardon, fact is, we know nought of these matters. Live in the village." A thumb jerked over his shoulder. "What is it you want of me?"

Pity she hadn't paused back at the abbey to pin her brooch to her cloak. There was no outward sign of rank and these simple folk had never set eyes on Caedwalla, else they would leap to obey her commands. As things stood, she would have to tread with care.

"The bishop sent you to remove the Ring Stone, is it not so?"

The man agreed.

"You must not, lest you offend the gods."

The man scratched his head and glanced at his fellow villagers. Frowning, he folded his hands across his chest.

"See here, lady, we've no quarrel with you, but Bishop Wilfrith was clear. 'Get rid of the boulder,' says he, so that's what we'll do."

Her heart sank. How dare he interfere with the sacred stone?

"There is older knowledge than that of the Christians. The Ring Stone has healing powers. Molest at your peril the spirit that dwells inside the rock!"

"Lady, we are all baptised and believe in the one God. There bain't no other gods. A stone's a stone. When Wilfrith came there'd been no water for months, but when he wetted us all straight away it rained. The Lord smiled on our baptism, He refreshed the land. We were slaves and the bishop freed us, gave us food and gave us work. There's nought we won't do for him!"

"Ay!" The others nodded in agreement, their expressions truculent.

Cynethryth had no means of convincing them.

They unloaded the cart under her sorrowful gaze, seized picks and spades and began removing the earth at the base of the rock. Soon, it stood like the tooth of an elder with shrunken gums. Would the smooth mass be too heavy? Cynethryth hoped in vain. The combined efforts of eight men using rope, block and levers, extracted the monolith from the ground. After standing there for time immemorial the Ring Stone, with agonising slowness, toppled onto its side. Once more their efforts raised the stone, to inch it down with care on a simple oak sled.

"Where are you taking the boulder?"

"To the quag, as our bishop ordered," said the burly ceorl.

"If you take it to the abbey, I will give you coins...each of you."

"Nowt personal. We can't take your money. Our lord is Wilfrith and we obey him...yah!" he slapped the rump of the nearest ox.

The men forced the unwilling beasts into the marsh until the bog reached their knees. Using the tree trunks as a pier, eight men squelched into the mud to slide the sled bearing the stone along the submerged, tilting, trunks.

The rock slipped off and vanished forever into the mire.

Cynethryth scowled. The nails of her right hand dug into her folded arm and her eyes narrowed. Wilfrith would pay for this.

If his God is the Lord of Creation did he not, therefore, create the Ring Stone?

Sorrowful, she turned her back on the desecrators. For entire lifetimes folk had come to seek a cure at the monolith. They would come no more. Her anger made her stride so fast, she arrived breathless in the abbey yard. The more she thought about what Wilfrith had done, the less was she inclined to meet to discuss his religion.

Determined to refuse his invitation, when later the nun knocked on her door, Cynethryth was surprised the summons was not from the bishop but from Abbot Eappa. She and Rowena followed the sister to the abbot's quarter where for propriety, two other nuns were stationed inside the door.

Simpler than the bishop's residence, the rooms boasted no trace of luxury to compromise the simple monastic life the abbot avowed. The benign nature of the monk contrasted with the stern intellect and assertiveness of Wilfrith. The bishop stood tall, lean and austere, but the plump, rubicund and mellow abbot had a manner that put them both at their ease. Reassured, the Wihtwara set aside her outrage for the moment and gave in to her curiosity.

"The Bishop sends his regrets…" Eappa began at once, causing the young woman to stiffen with indignation. Too late for remorse, the stone was irretrievable. "He had to leave this morning for Cantwaraburh, where he meets with Bishop Theodore. Aah…" sighed the abbot, his glance and tone confidential, "…he's not like us. Wilfrith is one who troubles himself over much service, the affairs of the world concern him. The doings of powerful men are his delight." The monk shook his head, "A simple life far from the entanglements of the world suits me…"

The ruddy cheeks dimpled as he beamed at the two women, and his bald pate shone in the light from the window. An uncomfortable silence followed his words, one in which he waited in vain for a reaction. It did not come.

"Anyway," he resumed, "I asked you here because the Bishop wishes me to explain our faith to you —"

"I told him I'd not forsake the customs of our forefathers," Cynethryth said, "and regarding that, do you know what he had his men do this morning?"

Eappa frowned and shook his head. The young woman's voice cut as cold as the midwinter wind.

"He cast the Ring Stone into the mire."

"Why on earth — ?"

"Because it cured me of my worries and it's part of the old lore. Bishop Wilfrith will not accept that there are powers other than those of your God."

"How can a rock cure?"

The Wihtwara stepped towards the abbot who shrank before her icy onslaught.

"The spirit of the stone heals those who believe," she said, "just as the gods favour those who sacrifice to them."

Abbot Eappa, hitherto so docile, with unexpected firmness asked, "How is this done?"

As though explaining to a slow child, Cynethryth said," The priest takes the captive, the slave or an animal and slits its throat. Then he sprinkles the blood in the sacred grove and burns the entrails to send up the smoke to please the deity. Next, he throws the bones with runes and reads them to know the mood of the god. If he is not satisfied, we make another offering."

The monk smiled and spoke in a gentle tone. "There, lady, is the difference. Jesus Christ offered *Himself* as the sacrifice and God showed he had accepted it by raising Jesus from the dead. The Father let his Son walk and talk among us, sharing food and drink for forty days before granting Him life eternal." The monk beamed. "God sacrificed for *us* — not us for Him...but these things need time to make clear. Come, sit with me!"

"I don't know," said Rowena taking the proffered seat, "it's like I said before, this religion is back to front..."

Abbot Eappa began to explain how the murder of God — seemingly the most abject failure ever — became the greatest success. With an awkward proselyte such as Cynethryth, it needed all the mild forbearance of the monk to achieve the task.

Apart from their conversations with the abbot, Cynethryth and Rowena filled their time learning from the nuns how to read. Sometimes they used a needle for fine work or visited the ponies in the stables. Russet and golden leaves dropped from the trees and still the two women had no news of their men. The Wihtwara came to think of her wedding as a distant dream. Every day she brooded on her father's fate until toward the end of the year she found herself praying to the Virgin to keep him safe.

The perseverance of Abbot Eappa had borne fruit.

On the fifth day of March, an hour before their usual encounter — by now she looked forward to the occasion with eagerness — a novice knocked on Cynethryth's door.

"Forgive the disturbance, lady, Father Abbot wishes to speak with you."

"Is it not early for our meeting?"

The messenger made to share a confidence but thought better of it.

"He says to come alone and at once."

Intrigued, she took down her cloak, wrapped it around her and followed the young woman to Eappa.

The reason for the summons became clear the moment she crossed the threshold. Were the furrows in the stern countenance more graven after a year or was she being fanciful? On seeing her, however, Bishop Wilfrith bestowed such a smile as to disarm her utterly. "My lady, I did not imagine such high praise from Father Abbot."

Turning, he inclined his head to the monk in acknowledgement, "You exceed all my expectations and how we are in need of you now!" He indicated a chair, "Please sit, I have news of your husband."

"News?"

The bishop picked up on the anxiety in the single word.

"Do not worry, dear lady," he said glancing again toward the abbot, "even though the events I have to impart to you are destined to change the land." His tone, merging excitement with foreboding, matched the weight of his statement.

Cynethryth, unsettled, dug her nails into her palm, "How so? What news is there of Caedwalla?"

"Your consort united with the underkings of Sumerseate and Wilsaete, together they marched on Centwine and forced his abdication. The old king is now in a monastery and your husband is King of all the West Seaxe. Of course," Wilfrith added in haste, "he is a direct descendant of Cerdric, the first king of those folk and as such, has a legitimate claim to the throne. But what I want to tell you most of all…" he stepped across to rest his hand on her shoulder, "…is…"

A thought struck Cynethryth: *Like prey under the falcon's talons.*

"…that storm clouds are gathering. Caedwalla musters a host and swears to destroy the Suth Seaxe. He intends to create a strong kingdom in the south. Think of it…from the ocean far in the west to Kent in the east! Divine providence sent you to us, Cynethryth..." She noted the use of her name for the first time. "Should this kingdom come into being, God willing, then it must be a Christian one if it is to survive. Its neighbour, Mercia and beyond, the powerful kingdom of Northumbria, will not tolerate pagans to the south. You *do* see? The Lord chose you to bring your husband to serve Him. However, the time is not propitious."

He released his grip on her shoulder and straightened. "Meanwhile, as we await the outcome of the inevitable conflict, I implore you to ponder this matter — prepare your arguments. We will help you." He waved at the abbot, who nodded his consent. "The destiny of the south may lie in your gentle hands and sweet words."

Chapter 8

Aelfhere

The Andredes weald, West Sussex, March 686 AD

"A captive has no choice. Are you sure of what she said?"

"The decision is hers Baldwulf, and she chooses to betray her father."

Aelfhere stabbed his seax to the hilt in the soft earth of the forest bed with such venom that his companion thanked the gods Cynethryth was safe back in Selsea.

"Disloyal, deceitful — I did not raise her to... she swore an oath and broke it—"

"She thought you were dead."

Silence.

The flickering light of the camp fire enhanced the expression in the haggard features of the ealdorman.

The thegn sighed. Images of Cynethryth's girlhood came to mind: she laughing on her father's shoulders, clinging to his hair or sitting on his knee as he carved a wooden doll for her. Again, of late, as a young woman on Aelfhere's arm, he so proud at her betrothal to Eadric. No wonder he was inconsolable.

"And when she saw I was alive? Baldwulf, you ought to have seen the coldness in her eyes."

He pulled the knife out of the ground and thrust it back with the same ferocity, "Lost to me, old friend, my girl is changed: in her stead is a spitting wildcat. By Thunor, I'll clip her claws if it's the last thing I do! When the force of Beorhthun unites with the hosts of Andhun and Eadric and we slaughter the West Seaxe..." he slid the blade out once more and studied it in meditative silence, before adding, "...and when my sword plunges into the bowels of Caedwalla —"

"Aren't you forgetting something?"

"What?"

"We have to find him. We're five days out of Kingsham and not even he..." the thegn peered at the sleeping Cadan, "...can pick up the wolf spoor."

"Time we can ill afford when the pack grows in number. The dux awaits our news. Let's sleep and see what the morrow brings."

* * *

The next morning at the stream where they had made camp, the Briton wiped droplets from his forehead and beard. He stood, weighing possibilities before replying to Aelfhere.

"No sign they returned to the encampment near the swamp and no settlement ravaged on the way to the coast means either Caedwalla pushes deep into the weald to the east or he heads for the valley of the Meon."

"The latter more likely." Aelfhere dried his neck with his sleeve. "The men there chafe under the Mercian yoke and, true to the old gods, seek to shake off the Christian overlord. I reckon he will add their numbers to his host before driving toward Kingsham." Through clenched teeth he said, "I understand the Meonwara but the wolf may devour the hand that strokes its muzzle. Come, Cadan, remove the hobbles from the horses. What do you know of the Meon? Can you lead us there?"

Taking a stick, the Briton traced a route in the damp soil by the stream.

"Along the old way on the chalk hills there are settlements where the first men built forts and raised mounds over the dead. Striking to the north, after four leagues the land drops down to Wernæforda where the watercress grows and where, with care, a man can cross the river on foot —"

"Now you mention care. We must move with stealth," Baldwulf said. "Caedwalla has the cunning of a grey wolf. Scouts will guard his tail!"

Since the dense forest cloaking them served also as a mantle for the foe, they shared the fear of stumbling upon them unexpectedly. And if that happened, well, better not to think of the cruel fate awaiting a captive spy.

An hour into their stalking they came to a wider track and Baldwulf, ever alert, spotted footprints in the soft earth of the verge. He dismounted to bend down, with his nose all but touching the ground.

"The prints are fresh," he said. "No more than a day."

"This is the old road from Kingsham to Wintanceastre I sketched back there," Cadan said, "but I doubt they mean to take it far west if their aim is to rouse the Meonwara. They must leave it and head into the forest back to the Meon again. We have a problem..."

"How so?" Aelfhere asked.

The Briton ran his hand through his hair, "Uh, we should take the road well beyond Wicham. There's a problem though. Once over the river, broom grass covering the open land makes it easy for a watchman to spot us."

"What shall we do?" Baldwulf murmured.

Cadan stared into the distance and spoke as if to himself. "If we follow the dirty brook and cross the beam bridge, the forest will hide us as far as the Great Tree in Thunor's Clearing —"

"Ay, whatever!" Aelfhere said, impatient to move on, "We're closing on them — let's not lose them again!|"

Along the dell to the river they rode, in plain sight and risking all, across a ford to follow ploughed land skirting the valley bottom stream. In the forest fringe, they came to the head of the slade. From time to time, Cadan pointed out a landmark; a willow stump or a small thorn tree, until they reached the ridgeway running down the western side of the Meon, bringing them to a break in the woodland.

The Briton leapt off his horse, tied it to an ash trunk and signalled to his comrades to do likewise. With caution they approached the edge of the leaf cover to squat and peer across grassland sloping down to a plain dotted with tents where thin spirals of smoke rose in the still air.

"Rocga's Open Country," Cadan said in a hushed voice. "I guessed they might be here."

Aelfhere laid a hand on his shoulder. "Well done." But instead of satisfaction his tone betrayed unease. "How many?"

A long moment passed while each calculated the number of the host.

Baldwulf whispered first, "Eight hundred?"

Cadan shook his head, "More."

The ealdorman pursed his lips. "With or without the Meonwara? There's no way of knowing."

"What do we tell the dux?" his thegn asked.

"Twelve hundred," Aelfhere said with decision, "best not to underestimate the size of the foe, especially with Beorhthun to lead us. Let's go!"

Silent as three wraiths, they slipped through the woodland and their quietness paid off near the glade. Baldwulf held up a hand, putting a finger to his lips before pointing through the trees. A warrior, they assumed a West Seaxe sentry, was inspecting their horses.

"Get behind him," the thegn said. "I'll distract him from this side. The dux will welcome another scout to interrogate."

"Flay, more like…" Aelfhere muttered; nonetheless, he and Cadan crept through the trees and bushes to the back of the intruder.

One horse neighed, causing the lookout to stroke its muzzle and speak low in its ear to quieten it, not to reveal his presence.

When Baldwulf entered the clearing, unslinging his battle-axe from its harness, his comrades were in position. The thegn took three steps forward when a spear thudded between his shoulder blades, the iron point emerging from his chest.

For the rest of his days, Aelfhere would not forget the horror on the face of his friend as he toppled to the ground. A red mist passed before the ealdorman's eyes and heedless of how many foes might lurk in the undergrowth, with a war cry he hurled himself at the scout near the horses. The fury of the assault overwhelmed his adversary, the blade of the Wihtwara's sword biting into his neck. The ealdorman spun round. Another West Seaxe warrior, he who had launched the death spear, had shattered Cadan's shield with an axe blow and threatened to sever the limbs of the nimble Briton with the scything swings of his weapon.

Cold, calculating hatred replaced Aelfhere's rage. Dropping his shield and scooping a handful of soil, he charged into the fray and on the downward swing of the enemy's axe hurled earth into his face. Momentarily blinded, the West Seaxe warrior shook his head to regain his sight. Too late. Cadan's seax buried into his stomach and Aelfhere's sword plunged into his throat.

Freeing their weapons, both men stood panting, concerned at the whinnying of the horses tugging at their reins. The Briton hurried over to calm them while the ealdorman cursed the ill chance that had led to an encounter with enemy scouts. Withdrawing the spear from the body of Baldwulf, he rolled him over and closed his eyes. A warrior such as he deserved a better end — not to be struck down from behind. With infinite sorrow, Aelfhere stared at the body of his friend.

Tonight he sups in Waelheal.

Cadan helped him hoist the corpse of the thegn onto the back of a horse. After pulling the axe harness from the dead man, the ealdorman slung it across his own body and put the weapon into place. In Kingsham he would ensure Baldwulf a decent burial, battle-axe beside him — the earth of his beloved isle would not embrace his remains but he would not go weaponless to the Hall of the Gods.

Morose thoughts occupied his mind as they rode in silence: the death of Baldwulf's father at the hands of the Mercians when Wulfhere forced Christianity on Wiht; how he had taken the orphan into his service and the times spent at Cerdicsford as Baldwulf grew into a man; the goat they sacrificed to Woden when the Mercians left the isle; how a few weeks ago his thegn had saved his life — and how, in the end, he had failed to do as much for his friend.

Deep in gloom, he rode into Kingsham, the bloated face of the thegn too ghastly for even he to look upon. Summoning his three Wihtwara, they dug into the mound and saluted their comrade for the last time, the ealdorman drawing slight consolation that his thegn lay in repose with the warriors of the isle fallen when defending King Aethelwalh.

With a backwards glance at the brown scar in the side of the green barrow, Aelfhere headed for the hall to report to the dux.

Hands spread apart and flat on the chart, Beorhthun stood in deep discussion surrounded by his chief ealdormen. One of his them drew his attention to the presence of the islander. The dux remained bent over the map, achieving an attitude of disinterested disdain. Aelfhere pursed his lips and waited.

"Well? Out with it man! There is no time to waste."

"Indeed, Lord," the ealdorman of Wiht said. "Time is not our friend."

Again he lingered over his words, determined not to be intimidated — the haughty South Seaxe lord would hear him out.

"How so?"

All eyes were on him, and most of them hostile to the outsider with an accent different from their own. Unabashed, he held back his news and stared from man to man before resting a finger on the parchment.

"Caedwalla adds Meonwara warriors to his host. They are set to advance on Kingsham."

The dux stood erect and frowned. "Meonwara? This force, how many does it count?"

"At least twelve hundred."

A clenched fist slammed on the table and the clamour of voices subsided. Beorhthun glared at Aelfhere, voice laden with menace. "Dare you repeat the overripe tale of some startled goatherd?"

"Would it were so, Lord. Six eyes cannot be deceived." No-one missed the bitterness in his words. "My thegn died in bringing the news."

"Twelve hundred," the dux hissed. He stared at the map and placed a finger on the outline representing the upper valley of the Meon. He traced, more or less, the direction Cadan had followed to bring them back here to the stronghold. "Two days…" He straightened once more and turned to his warriors.

Their views and counsel diverged. A grey-bearded warrior, a man of Kingsham and respected adviser to Aethelwahl, said, "The new gate is stout. I say we hold out until Andhun and his host arrive."

"The foe outnumbers us four-to-one. They took this fortress with fewer men. We cannot withstand them —"

"Ay, a craven attack by night! Unawares! This time we'll be ready for them."

The dux tapped two fingers on the edge of the table and the hushed gathering awaited his decision.

"Prepare the defences. Set men to fell trees. Build an outer palisade to protect the gate. We await them at Kingsham! Go!"

Aelfhere shook his head. It was a poor choice but one he half-expected. He turned to leave with the others but the imperious tone of Beorhthun stayed him.

"Wihtwara! A word."

The ealdorman spun round. "Lord?"

"I regret the loss of your thegn. He was a good man. What was his name?"

"Baldwulf, Lord."

Perfunctory, the words of the dux. "Ay, Baldwulf… so you have three men now?"

It was a statement couched as a question.

"Wulflaf, Ewald and Hynsige from Wiht and four with the Briton, Cadan." He stressed the name of each.

With a cold stare along his aquiline nose, his voice glacial, the dux said, "Indeed, and you have proved more than once how you move with stealth in the weald." His ringed finger traced lines on the chart before he slipped off the gold band and passed it to Aelfhere. "Go to Bedingeham, you will find Dux Andhun there. Show this ring so he will know I sent you. Take five horses, make haste, fetch him here! We shall crush Caedwalla in a vice against the walls of Kingsham. Be back within four days, islander."

"Lord, may I speak?"

Beorhthun raised an eyebrow but consented with a nod.

"Is it wise to stay at Kingsham? Why not lead the men to Andhun? Unite with him...and even King Eadric —"

"Dare you challenge my decision? Are you mad?" The frost in the glare of the dux chilled Aelfhere, "Do you suppose I'll leave my lands undefended open to West Seaxe devastation? Go!" The fierce gaze shifted to the door, "Lose no time!"

The Wihtwara turned on his heel, keen to lead his men away from the obdurate South Seaxe lord.

* * *

The band of riders came to the royal burh of Bedingeham, two days' ride to the east of Kingsham and not far from the coast. To the dismay of the local tillers and sowers, the encampment stretched over their fields before the walls of the fortress. Instead of entering the gate, a guard led the Wihtwara to a grub-house located outside the settlement. In part dug into the ground and covered by a turf roof, it blended into the surroundings almost unnoticed. Its unprepossessing exterior cloaked the simple cosiness of a room that contained little more than a bed, table, chairs and a hearth in the middle of a suspended wooden floor. Aelfhere entered alone and found a startling contrast between Dux Andhun and Beorhthun not only in their respective quarters, but also in their bearing. Where one stood tall, arrogant and intimidating the other, stocky in build and the same height as he, set him at ease. The wide-set green eyes in an honest face studied the ring the islander had dropped into his hand. The dux made no comment as he examined the jewel before saying, "What message does Beorhthun send, ealdorman?"

The Wihtwara kept his voice flat, wishing not to betray his true feelings.

"Lord, the dux urges you to come to Kingsham in all haste where he holds the fortress against Caedwalla, the self-proclaimed king of the West Seaxe. With the Meonwara he commands a host of twelve hundred men —"

If the enemy numbers troubled Andhun, he did not show it. "With the warriors at Beorhthun's command the forces are well matched..."

"Were you not informed?" Aelfhere asked. "The dux lost half his men last spring when he drove the war-band of Caedwalla out of the kingdom."

Andhun blew out his cheeks followed by a slow release of breath. "So why does he remain at Kingsham like a quail in a trap?"

The ealdorman shrugged. "Forgive me, Lord, he was deaf to my plea to come here to swell your ranks and to unite with those of my daughter's betrothed...he will not, he insists, leave his lands open to the foe."

"I sent a messenger to Eadric ten days past when we received news of Centwine's 'abdication'," the dux wrinkled his brow, "the King needs more time to muster enough warriors."

Aelfhere wrung his hands in desperation. "Lord, Dux Beorhthun expects aid two sunsets from now! Should you withhold your men, I fear —"

"Ealdorman, the dux is a fool!" Andhun spread his hands in a gesture of apology. "He ignored the good sense of your appeal and chose to stay in Kingsham. Stubbornness is a poor counsellor. Did he suppose I wished to face the might of Caedwalla outnumbered two-to-one? Were he to come here, his six hundred warriors would tip the balance in our favour."

Aelfhere nodded. "True, I tried to tell him —"

"Indeed. To no avail. We shall not change our plan but strike out for the ancient road leading to Lundenwic at once."

Under other circumstances, doubtless, the man standing before him was not unreasonable, but the set of his jaw discouraged the Wihtwara; nonetheless, he protested. "Six hundred warriors entrapped, lord...I beg you to reconsider —"

Andhun glared. "Where is the sense, ealdorman? Tell me, had *you* to choose, in all truth, would you lead six hundred to the slaughterhouse? To toss the land of the Suth Seaxe in the midden as you might a rotten apple? Is that what you ask of me?"

He handed back Beorhthun's ring and his lip curled when the shoulders of the islander sagged. "I thought not! Our scouts have no news of movement around Kingsham — all may not yet be lost." The dux gestured to the guard by the door, "Fetch Osfrid!" He laid a hand on his chest, "My heart aches but the runes are cast. When Beorhthun sees my thegn, he will concede you delivered your message and lead his men east. May the Almighty grant you are not too late! Ah, Osfrid!"

The dux gave swift orders to the well-built warrior whose shrewd eyes belied his youth. They agreed to travel alone to Kingsham with two spare horses to gain time by not riding either mount too hard.

"Return along the ancient road to the bridge over the Ead. We make our encampment there to await the Kentings and the men of Beorhthun —we shall be ready to fight."

* * *

The two men rode until the last glimmer of daylight faded in the forest and set off in the morn with the first feeble light. The nearer they drew to Kingsham the more cautious they became for fear of West Seaxe scouts. At a narrow stream, no more than a brook, they halted to water the horses.

"This dell lies a league from the town," Aelfhere said to Osfrid, "I remember yon rowan with its purple buds. We can ride another two miles with great care but we tether the beasts and approach the fortress on foot."

From the edge of the trees, the ealdorman gazed in puzzlement at the stronghold. The usual calls of birds and rustling of leaves reached their ears, otherwise an ominous silence hung over the settlement. The islander whispered as much to the thegn who nodded in agreement before pointing out, "No smoke. Can it be the dux deserted the fortress?"

"The palisade is new," Aelfhere breathed, "to strengthen the gate, but it blocks sight of the entry."

They waited, unsure of what to do. Long moments passed with no movement to discern and their uncertainty grew.

"You're right," the ealdorman said. "There's no-one in the town. Can Beorhthun have forsaken Kingsham for the ancient hilltop ramparts?"

"Makes sense," Osfrid said. "The first folk dug their earthworks with deep ditches. The dux might hold such a place at length against the West Seaxe force."

"Food and water?" Aelfhere shook his head. "No more than a day or two... but they'd have height in their favour."

They lapsed into quietude, their wordlessness heightening the oppressive stillness.

"Come, it's safe." The Wihtwara nudged his comrade, "We must search for any sign of what has become of the townspeople and Beorhthun's men."

They broke cover at a trot, eyes peeled for the slightest movement. None came.

Where the new palisade curved, earlier hidden from view, they now found several stakes on the ground creating a gap wide enough for two men to pass through. When they entered they were met by a wild flapping of wings as carrion crows rose in raucous protest from the gruesome figures strewn on the blood-soaked earth. The blank death gape and sightless stares of the fallen West Seaxe warriors gave way beyond the broken gates to a heap of Suth Seaxe bodies.

Aelfhere cursed the screeching kites and cawing ravens and spat out a single word: "Caedwalla!"

Stepping over a headless body, he made for a ring of sprawled corpses. In the centre lay Beorhthun, a deep red gash gaping at his throat. The ealdorman swallowed hard. The arrogance of the dux had led to this butchery and the Wihtwara felt no compassion for him. Neither did he wish to dwell on the pathetic remains of the once proud warrior. Instead, he pulled out the gold ring entrusted to him. With no right to keep it and since it was impossible to replace the band on the rigid finger, he tucked it inside the tunic of the fallen nobleman.

Aelfhere turned away letting his gaze stray over the indiscriminate killing and discovered the West Seaxe horde had not spared the women and children of the burh. The ealdorman forced away the numbness enthralling him, fought back impotent rage, to respond to Osfrid's entreaty: "Come, friend! Nothing to be done here. We must hasten to the Dux at Eadhelmsbrigge."

Indeed, the Wihtwara conceded, there was no point in lingering. Two men to bury hundreds of bodies? Futile. They must leave the scavengers to their grisly feast.

They retrieved the horses and headed back east with Aelfhere berating the intransigence of one who had cost so many lives. The thegn endured the outpourings of the man he had grown to respect in a short time. But in practical vein, when the invective ended, Osfrid said, "Do you think we should go on? We failed to sight the West Seaxe horde. Should my Lord ask their whereabouts how can we answer?"

The ealdorman reined in his horse and his companion did likewise. The islander frowned, pondered and said, "Why risk our lives and waste the time needed to locate them? Think on! They destroyed Beorhthun and moved on but not to the east, else we'd have crossed their path. North? No sense, for Caedwalla gathered the Meonwara before the attack on Kingsham —"

"It has to be south!" Osfrid mused. "West is whence he came…but why south?"

"Because there lies Selsea," Aelfhere said, his voice more bitter than before, "and the ram wishes to tup the ewe."

The thegn stared around the oaks, into the bracken, anywhere not to meet the eyes of the islander for fear of what he would find there.

"By the one-armed god, Osfrid," he said, "I swear I will slay the upstart with my own hand. Now, onward! Their diversion to the Seal's Isle gifts us precious days to put to good use."

* * *

The next week, which Aelfhere spent in the spreading encampment, witnessed the sporadic entry of war-bands led by different duces from various parts of Kent. Back in Cantwaraburh, Archbishop Theodore had no difficulty convincing Christian noblemen of the righteousness of the struggle and to unite with their Suth Seaxe brothers against the pagan who led the West Seaxe. Above all, news of the destruction of Kingsham persuaded the most reluctant of the grave threat to their own lands. Seven days after that grievous event, the main force of Cantwara, white horse banner streaming next to King Eadric, crossed the bridge over the river. At the sight of the rising numbers of warriors in the camp, the heart of the ealdorman swelled with hope.

Osfrid sought Aelfhere out within an hour of Eadric's arrival. At the entrance to a huge tent fluttered two banners. To the left fluttered that of the Suth Seaxe with six golden swallows against a deep blue ground. In contrast, on the right, swirled the rearing white horse of the Kenting on its field of blood red.

On entry King Eadric greeted Aelfhere with an embrace. "Father! What doom resides in our meeting — grim foreboding in the stead of merriment." He indicated Andhun, "The Dux tells me you fought the West Seaxe invaders beside Beorhthun but he is dead —"

"Ay," the ealdorman scowled, "he lies ravaged by kites, he, all his men and the women and children…"

The King of the Kenting, surrounded by duces and ealdormen, hung on Aelfhere's every word as he recounted the events leading up to the slaughter at Kingsham. "I believe him to be at Selsea," he said, casting Eadric a mortified glance under lowered brow, "but he will move soon. I reckon he'll take the old road through the weald and when he does we must have a plan to outfox him. Not only does the King of the West Seaxe lead a mighty host, but he is fearless and well-counselled — it is time to slay the wolf from the west!"

Chapter 9

Wilfrith and Cynethryth

Selsea, West Sussex, March 686 AD

'*Ego te baptizo…*'

Waist-deep in the cold water of the font, one hand on the shoulder of Cynethryth and the other in the small of her back, the deaconess immersed the naked noblewoman. Through narrowed eyes, the king's lady marvelled at the submersion bubbles, lit by a slanting beam of sunlight from the high narrow window. Beneath the surface, the events leading up to this moment rushed through her mind: Bishop Wilfrith anointing her forehead, blowing on it to drive away the unclean spirit and speaking in a sonorous language unknown to her, the sensation of a golden stream flowing through her body…

The nun hoisted her and Cynethryth, red-gold hair hanging in rat tails down over her breasts, filled her lungs in time to hear anew from below the surface.

'*…in nomine Patris…*'

resonating as from afar. She had rejected Satan and the nuns had stripped off her clothes and jewels. Her locks loosened, they led her, vulnerable and shivering, down the steps into the marrow-chilling water of the stone receptacle. Up, once more the gasp for breath…

'*…et Fillii…*'

eyes closed tight, she let herself rejoice. What her husband and father would make of this did not trouble her — she was sure of her choice...

Out of the water, under again, denied a moment to glance around,

'...*et Spiritus Sancti...*'

this awesome building — silent, ordered, still, unlike like the hall of her people — noisy with roistering, the reek of smoke and feasting...

The deaconess raised her and smiled into her face, taking her hand and leading her, both dripping, one clothed and one not, up the three steps out of the font. Embarrassed at her nakedness, Cynethryth sighed with relief when a nun wrapped a cloak around her. Only then did she relax to discover a lightness of spirit, as though a hitherto unrecognised weight in her chest had gone. A slave released from her bonds, tears of joy mingled with beads of font water coursing down her cheeks.

Dressed, damp hair clinging to her face, she emerged blinking from the church to a joyous greeting from Bishop Wilfrith.

"A godfather makes a gift at the christening of his godchild. This is for you," smiling with his mouth drawn down at the corners, he showed her a closed fist. "Hold out your hand."

Cynethryth stared at a silver chain threaded through a cross of that precious metal nestling in her palm.

"Wear this to protect you, to recall your promise to the Lord and as testimony to your faith. Remember, pray to the Mother of God for the grace to lead a Christian life." A solemn expression replaced the smile on the lined countenance. "Later we shall speak of the mission the church reserves for you."

The bishop meant in a few days, not imagining he would summon his new convert within the hour.

Cynethryth wished to be alone with her thoughts for a while, so she left the abbey grounds for the woods. The hood of her mantle, she pulled over her damp hair to shield her from the sea breeze of March — the rugged month. She beheld the early spring in its loveliness, the buds of the hawthorn bursting and how they grew, leaves unfolding. A wheatear called from a hazel branch and Cynethryth embraced life. She seized the moment as eternity, seeing herself inside and outside when all living creatures of the Earth opened their eyes wide and stared into her soul. Whence came this grace if not from the Holy Spirit?

The world of her forefathers no longer existed. No more night-times stalked by ghosts or evil spirits lurking in solitary places; no elves dwelling amid the rude stone circles that terrified her in childhood; no fiends and monsters lurking in the marshes. Breathing in the sweet air of the glade, Cynethryth marvelled at the bold yellow of the wild daffodils scattered among the tree trunks. What bliss to admire the beauty of Creation, to glory in the splendour of a babbling woodland stream without fearing the magic of the nicors haunting the water! In the end, the wyrds of fate would not sweep her away beneath the earth to the joyless realm of shades ruled by Hel. Figments of ignorant superstition, Bishop Wilfrith had taught her and she believed it with all her heart: far better eternal life as a reward for virtue. Why not hurry back to the abbey to share this good news with Nelda?

In long years of service, her nurse, latterly maid, never raised her voice — but now she was livid.

"What nonsense have they put into your head, child? How a year away from our isle has changed you! As if a sickle sliced you from your roots —"

"Don't you see, Nelda —"

The servant, red in the face, bit her lip in exasperation and glowered.

"No I do not," she cut in, "nor do I wish to turn my back on what my father and his father before him, and all our folk, ever believed."

The fury in her eyes shocked Cynethryth, who wished to share her joy with her oldest and most trusted companion.

"When you were a babe," the old servant said, "I was your stand-in. I dug a long tunnel in the ground to please Eortha. In your stead, I crawled through it and closed the passage behind with thorns so evil spirits should not follow. Did you not grow healthy under the protection of the goddess? How you —"

"Oh, Nelda! It's so foolish!"

She tried to reach out to her maid but to her astonishment the woman shrank away. In spite of herself, her voice dripped sarcasm.

"Why would *evil spirits* as if they were made of flesh and blood be a-feared to push through brambles..?"

The servant shook her head, electing to remain mute, intent only on braiding her mistress' hair. The occasional sniff behind Cynethryth's back betrayed Nelda crying. The king's lady pursed her lips. Convincing the stubborn nurse of her choice would be a tiresome task — best left for another time.

A few minutes later, a nun fetched Cynethryth to the bishop's quarters. Why did he want to see her so soon? And why did these Christians carry out their orders in such a determined way? The sister said Wilfrith wished to speak with her 'at once', but she would arrive breathless at this pace.

In his presence, Cynethryth placed a hand flat on her chest to recompose herself.

"Forgive this disturbance, my child," the prelate spread his hands, "events have overtaken us. A brother on his way here from the cathedral in Wintanceastre came upon the host of Caedwalla encamped but two leagues distant."

"My husband here? I must go to him!"

The lines at the corners of the bishop's lips deepened. "No need. I expect him to come. And that is why we must deliberate..."

"About?"

The eyes of the clergyman shone with a fierce light. "About the king, your spouse..." he held up a hand to halt the flood of words, "...he and I...we...have an understanding, a sort of pact. The details need not concern you, my dear child. Whilst our faith preaches against killing, at times, as the Holy Book teaches us, slaughter is necessary for a righteous cause." The prelate beckoned her to be seated, but he remained standing, beginning to pace as he warmed to his argument. "Try to imagine the South under one kingship, united in one belief? What do you say to that?"

Cynethryth flushed, were not those her father's words?

'*...United in arms we can stand alone against all comers...worshipping the gods of our forefathers...*'

Her betrayal, manifold, neared completion.

Bishop Wilfrith misinterpreted the glow to her cheeks and nodded, "Indeed, you will be Lady of a Christian South!" The long face tightened in a frown. "There are two problems..." He breathed deeply and his piercing eyes bored into hers. The moment lingered. Would he never enlighten her?

"First, your husband has not embraced our faith and second," he waved over his shoulder, "at our rear the last stronghold of the demon-worshippers threatens our existence." The confusion on her face made him clench his fists. "I refer of course to your homeland, to Wiht. The *last* bastion," he scowled. "In all these isles every other kingdom professed Christianity but not that of Arwald. King Wulfhere of blessed memory brought the faith to the isle, but when he died the populace lapsed into ignorance. The Evil One cast scales over their eyes — the time is ripe to bring the Word and you, my child, are God's chosen vessel."

The wrinkled countenance relaxed and the bishop bestowed on Cynethryth a beatific smile.

"I don't understand."

Wilfrith paused for effect. "...Why, together we must convince Caedwalla to heed the call of the Father." The prelate took the hand of the young woman. "You *will* do your duty?"

She needed no coercion. The thought of spending eternity with the man she loved was sufficient persuasion.

* * *

When Caedwalla at last arrived alone on horseback, the impatient Cynethryth, waiting near the abbey gates, fell into his arms and clung to him wanting never to let go. The warrior, though pressed for time, determined to wring every last sensation from their meeting.

"My love, how long will you stay?" she whispered, her voice urgent.

"Mid-afternoon —"

"So soon?" she broke from his embrace, her expression anguished.

A gentle tug hauled her back against his body whence he caressed the nape of her neck.

"We won a great victory, my brother Mul leads the host along the coast north of the marshes. I must join them before nightfall."

"I know him not," she said, "take me with you!"

Caedwalla stroked her cheek. "The men of the Suth Seaxe muster their men in the east to avenge their cousins. Believe me, the battlefield is no place for a woman! The occasion to greet Mul will come soon enough. I must meet with the cross-bearer, afterwards come with me to speed my farewell."

Inside the dwelling of the bishop, the warrior grinned at the wise man who had seen much of the world.

"Our meetings bring me fortune. The first time I became king and the second, king again."

Wilfrith's piercing stare fixed the warlord. "Then, give thanks to the God of Hosts, whose mighty hand sweeps away those who take up arms against you. Be humble and kneel before the Father who will raise you higher still."

Caedwalla, impassive, outstared the prelate. "In good time. Instead let us talk of what I can give to you..."

Their conversation dealt with the substantial estates of Beorhthun and with the hides the king would alienate to the Church in the case of victory in the forthcoming battle. The King promised treasure to pay for buildings, vestments, books, wine and oil.

More than satisfied, the Bishop pressed for one last concession,. "Arwald is a threat. The whole island is pagan and he has set his face against Christianity. He would unite with the Kentings —"

"Who are Christians..."

"Political expediency, he relies on the blood link between their peoples —"

Caedwalla glared at the clergyman, "I have no quarrel with my wife's folk. It is an isle and as long as Arwald tends to his own affairs..." The rest he left unsaid.

"You may rue this choice. If you'll take counsel from me —"

The warrior advanced two steps, towering over the prelate, menace in his eyes. "Not this time, priest! And be warned, should any harm come to Cynethryth not even your God of Hosts will save your skin." He turned to leave, but spun round and raised a finger. "He must be akin to Tiw this warrior god, so pray to him to lend strength to our arms."

Wilfrith sighed in exasperation at the closed door left by the warlord.

Outside the bishop's quarters Caedwalla found his wife waiting.

"Foam is but a yearling, too young to bear your weight, so you'll ride with me." He lifted her on his horse.

The heart of Cynethryth beat faster, "Did you change your mind? I'll need more clothes if you are taking me with you."

His laugh was deep and raucous, "Where I'm taking you, you'll need fewer clothes!"

Careless of the opinions and sensibilities of the monks and nuns but grateful for their guardianship of his wife, he chose not to offend them by breaking their curious rules of propriety. Given the mildness of the day, the not-too-distant woodland would serve as well.

After a year apart, entwined on his cloak on the ground, Caedwalla and Cynethryth exchanged passionate kisses. His trembling fingers unbuttoned her kirtle to expose her chest, "What's this?" he lifted the silver cross.

She sat up, her voice quavered, "I...I wanted to tell you. I chose to be baptised. Are you angry?"

He placed a finger on her lips, "Hush! Why do you think I sent you to the cross-bearer, Wilfrith? To be safe? More secure with my folk in the west."

Cynethryth gasped, "You mean...but...you do not believe —"

He laughed, "What do you know? Heed me well," he sat up and leant on an elbow, "I spoke at length in the weald with the priest when in exile. These men in their strange dress with their weird language and their sacred books offer much to a king. For them, kingship is ordained by their god…"

She gazed at him open-mouthed. There was so much to learn about this man. Of course, they had spent little time together, no wonder then—

"…their writings deal with law-making and tax-raising. These are all weapons for an overlord to wield."

To his wife in the leafy gloom of the woods, his eyes full of fire and determination appeared a deeper blue, the least of the surprises.

"Then you will be baptised in the faith?" she asked, thrilled.

"Of course, when the time is right, but Wilfrith must not know this."

"Why?"

His mouth turned down in a tight smile, "More use to me this way! While he thinks he needs to convert a king I wrest concessions — our pact works both ways. Not a word of this to him!"

Caedwalla uncovered her breast and they were lost to the world.

Afterwards, lying in his arms, a thigh over his, Cynethryth murmured, "Take care, my love. If ought harms you my heart is pierced."

The warrior laughed, heedless of the augury in his words.

"Fear not, little wren! It takes a wolf to slay a wolf and the Suth Seaxe are but sheep!"

Chapter 10

Aelfhere and Caedwalla

Eadhelmsbrigge, Kent, March 686–May 687 AD

"Curse the toad-head who drew this map — not worth a wart on his slimy skin!" Slamming a fist on the table, Andhun upset a beaker of mead over the object of his wrath and the ink ran. "There! Likely to be of more use now!" the dux said through clenched teeth, glaring around the ealdormen gathered in his tent.

"How am I to choose a battleground when I know nothing of this land? The West Seaxe are nigh on us!"

Folding up the chart, he made to reduce it to shreds.

"Hold, Lord!" One of the ealdormen, a scar from forehead to cheekbone disappearing beneath an eye patch, held up a hand. "This is home to me, leastways the holdings three leagues to the east. Let me," he pointed at the sodden parchment. Ignoring the scowl, he took the document unfolded and laid it down before him. "We are here," he stabbed his forefinger on the rough drawing, adding a smudge to the River Ead. "It flows into the Medweg causing it to swell and flood to the east. From 'bout here to where the narrow ridge runs down to the ferry, here…" at that spot he drummed a finger before lifting it to circle above the map, "…marshland…" He placed heavy stress on the word, paused and stared around noting the puzzled expressions. "Well," he hurried

130

on, "marsh to the south of the river, soft, claggy ground to the north. Consider that, there," he waved the back of his hand, "rises a spur. We call it 'Dryhill' — where we ought to stand and fight."

Aelfhere leant forward in excitement. The fellow had a point. "We hold back our hurling weapons. With height in our favour, we press on them with long spears and drive them down to the marsh…" A glance around the grinning ealdormen reassured him they understood.

For the first time, Andhun lost his frown, "Ay, once they're bogged down we pick them off with javelins and throwing axes! As good a plan as any!"

Eadric turned to the one-eyed man. "How far to this hill?"

"Tunbrycg, Lord? I'd say 'bout three leagues due east."

"Perfect! And is there woodland nearby?"

"On the northern side, there is. Why?"

Aelfhere was asking himself the same question, but the king smiled and in a determined voice, said, "We move in haste. The West Seaxe are two days hence. We can use the time to set up a rough forge, cut staves and make more javelins."

Ever practical, the Wihtwara ealdorman asked, "And the iron, Lord? Where do we get the metal?"

"Ploughshares, spades, wheel-bands, hoops… anything we can seize in the lands around. The tips of the weapons need not be large. Small kills the same — strength of arm counts!"

Disappointed at the quantity of metal collected, Eadric's host still disposed of more than a hundred new throwing spears in addition to many staves whittled to a vicious point. The latter served to thicken the air with missiles, to help wreak destruction on the parrying foe.

From the start, their plan went awry. The guile of Caedwalla, to the dismay of the awaiting force, never failed, with the warlord deploying his scouts well. Thwarting the Suth Seaxe plan to drive the enemy into the wetland to the south, they emerged from the dry woodland to form massed ranks.

Aelfhere surveyed the serried rows of warriors below them and his gaze lingered on the two banners stirring whenever the breeze picked up. Both bore a creature in gold on a red field. The boar of the Meonwara and the wyvern of the West Seax. His pulse quickened for beside it loomed the figure of the man he most hated: Caedwalla.

Today my sword will speed you to Woden's Hall.

The might of the foe did not daunt him. Vast the array ranked below, but expected, and their own host numbered no fewer men. To Eadric by his side, he said, "Change of plan — throwing weapons from the start..."

Distracted, the king did not reply but gestured to the enemy. "What are they doing?"

The Wihtwara wondered the same. Advancing, but instead of coming uphill in the usual flat waves, they pushed forward in long snaking lines three yards apart. The leaders of each file forged ahead. The waste of javelins and throwing axes shocked Aelfhere: many fell to earth in the gaps between the columns, inflicting no harm.

The sly wolf!

The concentration on hurling weapons undid the hilltop defence. Before they had time to snatch up their long spears, the attackers, screaming war cries, fanned out and charged with their own lowered. The iron-tipped poles impaled many of the first line of throwers and pushed on the men behind. Damage wreaked, the onrushing West Seaxe warriors exchanged the awkward poles for battle-axes and swords. The impetus of the onslaught broke the ranks of defenders while more men surged over the brow of the spur to fight at close quarters. Their momentum carried them forward. In spite of the best efforts of Eadric, Andhun and Aelfhere to rally their men around the banners, they were forced over and down the other side of the hill.

Aelfhere, fearless, led his warriors from the front. What he would give to get near the golden dragon emblem fluttering off to his right. This was no common battle for him but a quest, a mission, to heal a festering wound. Using his iron-embossed shield to fend off the raining blows then as a club, he hacked, cudgelled and parried his way in that direction. To no avail, the downhill thrust of the enemy thwarted him. The wyvern and the man he loathed became ever more distant.

To the wonder of those around him, he resembled a feral beast as he groaned in frustrated rage, seeing off one assailant after another.

With a score of Aelfheres in this mood the day might have been won, but the Suth Seaxe and Kentings lost ground down the slope to the spongy footing. Farther back, they began to founder in the mud. A man needs to be nimble in battle but as the enemy drove them nearer the river, they came up to the knee in silt. The cunning of Caedwalla had overturned their plan.

The Wihtwara glanced around in a moment of respite. What he beheld made his heart sink like the white horse banner disappearing among dead bodies into the quag. Over there, no live Cantwara survived to snatch it up. Amid the curses, the clash of steel and tang of blood, it became apparent they were outnumbered. Nearby, corpses hewn beyond recognition lay face down in the mud. The gods grant their number did not include his Wihtwara. But, those fighting were unrecognisable to him, their faces spattered with gore and silt. The brief lull over, three adversaries struggled through the slime to set upon him.

If only his legs were free to help him feint and counterattack! With a desperate lunge, he drove his sword into the throat of the leading assailant. Hot blood spurted into his face, before, in pain and shock he received a deep gash to his shield arm. Had they severed the limb? Falling on his side, with the cunning of an old warrior, he lay still, eyes closed. The half-expected death blow did not come. Unknown to him, as he slipped into unconsciousness, the mire tamped the wound, staunching the bleeding.

His fate had not gone unseen. One of the three Wihtwara, Ewald, fighting next to Dux Andhun, having slain his own adversary, finished off the nobleman's opponent with a seax to the gut. Frantically, he dragged the dux towards his fallen lord. The other two from Wiht and the King of the Kentings all battling nearby formed an arc to protect them.

At the sight of the bloodied wretch in the wolf helm, Andhun spat a curse at having to make a decision. Continue the fight, leaving the valiant ealdorman to die, or save him? The dux chose the latter course of action. With Ewald, heedless of the battle raging behind them, he raised Aelfhere. Seeing the extent of the wound, the dux cut a leather thong from his tunic and tied it tight above the gash. Satisfied, Andhun picked up the wolf-pommelled sword and slid it under his belt next to his own.

Aelfhere drifted in and out of consciousness.

The face of Andhun peering into his, he took for Cynethryth as a young girl, sitting on his knee; but why was she so worried? How he loved her! The image faded, to be replaced by the exposed neck of Caedwalla. One clean strike! Everything went black but the sun lit up his homeland — prosperous, pastoral, in peace.

The dux hoisted the arm of the ealdorman around his shoulder. To Ewald, he said, "Take the place of Eadric. No dead king is a good king! Cover our backs!"

The Wihtwara struggling over the cloying ground, reached the leader of the Kentings to bury his seax into the back of the warrior attacking the Cantwara. Fending a blow from another, Ewald shouted to the king to help the dux.

Understanding the plight of Aelfhere and Andhun, the young ruler sheathed his sword and ducking under the limp arm of the islander, took a share of the dead weight. It was no easy task to drag the ealdorman in haste to more solid ground, knowing the three Wihtwara protecting them had to hold out against greater numbers. The mud became their friend: the enemy unable to rush across to cut off their retreat while none had a throwing weapon. And, the dux meant to reach the drier ridge of land at the ferry, where they would need the luck of Lôgna!

At the river, the welcome sight of the moored ferryboat brought a grim smile to the lips of Eadric, who had assumed himself doomed. Fate decreed the vessel should be tied up on this and not on the opposite bank: the difference between life and death. Almost dropping with fatigue, the king helped lower the ealdorman into the bottom of the boat, the clash of steel ringing in his ears. Collapsing into the craft, he called to the dux, "Jump in!"

"I'll not leave warriors to die for me!"

The sword Andhun drew was not his own. This weapon was lighter and better balanced with a wolf on its pommel. The sheer beauty of the object filled him with joy and renewed energy. Into the fray, he leapt, seven against three — four now, five, for the war cry of Eadric rang in his ears. More of the West Seaxe were slipping and sliding over the treacherous ground striving to reach them. Without delay they needed to rid themselves of their present adversaries.

Desperation and the knowledge the river current would sweep them to safety lent strength to their sinews. A whoop of triumph from Wulflaf mingled with the scream of Hynsige. Andhun drove the borrowed blade under the guard of his attacker into his armpit while taking a mighty axe blow from another on his shield. The force of the strike sent him reeling off balance. As he fell, a backhanded stab with the wolf sword found the thigh of the warrior overpowering Hynsige, wounded in his wielding arm and reduced to mere defence. Faring better, Eadric placed his foot against the stomach of an assailant to free his weapon from deep in his chest. Rising on one knee, the dux was in time to shout a warning to the king, who spun round, but lost his footing on the oozing soil. Eadric slid to one side, regained his balance while the battle-axe flashed past leaving the flank of his enemy exposed. The Cantwara put all his strength into the lunge, driving his blade between the man's ribs and into his heart.

One foeman remained, his seax swinging in his hand, feinting a strike at the dark-haired islander. Beyond them, fifty yards of mire separated them from the oncoming West Seaxe — at least a score, led by a huge warrior with a hawk on his helm. The dux and Eadric sprang at the enemy fighting Wulflaf and Ewald.

"Get in the boat!"

Hynsige staggered away, only too willing to obey the king.

The one-sided contest ended with a slash from Wulflaf to the throat of his adversary. As the man fell, a howl of rage reached them from less than twenty yards away.

"Time to leave!" Eadric grinned at his companions. Skidding the ten paces to the ferryboat, they leapt in. Ewald sliced through the mooring rope with one sweep of his seax. The others looked back to see the tall warrior in front take a battle-axe from the man next to him. Both hands drawn behind his head, he hurled the weapon in a spinning arc towards the boat. The current carried them out of harm's way, the axe leaving a spray of water in their wake.

"Strong of arm!" The dux made no effort to conceal his admiration.

"A cat's whisker between us and death," Wulflaf grimaced, reaching for an oar. Ewald rocked the craft as he made to do the same. "I wonder who he is?" the islander went on. But as they shook their heads, the one man who might have told them lay unconscious in the bottom of the craft.

"You'd have thought," mused the dux as he tried to settle Aelfhere in a more comfortable position, "the ferryman had left his boat on the other bank to flee the battle."

At last, Eadric dragged his eyes from the stricken figure of the ealdorman, "We have the boatman to thank for our lives, but I fear he gave his."

"How so?" asked Hynsige, sat in the prow pulling a bandage tight with his teeth over his bloodied arm.

"What name do you go by, islander?"

"Hynsige, Lord."

"Well, Hynsige, the ceorl who owns this boat fought by our side, I believe. His choice saved us. The cunning of the West Seaxe sent him and all our comrades back there to heaven or to hell."

In sorrowful contemplation, no-one wished to breach the lull in their speech until Eadric addressed the dux. "Any notion of where we are?"

Andhun shook his head. "This is not my land but the river flows to Hrofescaester by the sea. Is it not your realm, Lord?"

"Indeed, but…" he gestured to the prone figure of Aelfhere, "our friend will not survive to see that place. We must seek help in haste to tend his wounds."

They stared from the feverish ealdorman, his forehead beaded with sweat, to the landscape of marsh and woodland with no dwelling in sight.

"Fought like a bear set upon by hounds," the king remarked, his tone admiring, "we cannot let him fade away." Eyes unfocused, he looked downstream. "Ten years ago the Mercians devastated Hrofescaester. Nought for us there…"

In grim silence, they rowed for an hour to where the floodplain gave way to more solid ground its vegetation overhanging the river banks. With no hint of a settlement they feared for Aelfhere, ever more pallid, a groan the only sign of his clinging to life.

"Over there!" Wulflaf rested on his oar and pointed across a pasture cleared from the forest. Smoke curled into the air beyond holm oaks fringing the grassland.

Hynsige, in no state to walk, remained in the boat with Ewald, who held the mooring rope passed around a willow trunk. The others hastened across the springy turf and into the woods in the direction of the swirling wisps.

A swineherd, tending long-legged pigs grubbing for acorns, gaped at the sight of three warriors, spun on his heels and dashed into the trees. Swiftest to react, Eadric charged after the ceorl. Younger, fleeter of foot in spite of his mail shirt, he soon laid hand on the man's bony shoulder. A short-bladed hand seax persuaded the fellow to drop to his knees to plead for his life.

"We mean no harm, but need your help," the king said, hauling the swineherd to his feet. "Is there a village nearby?"

The dux and the islander reached them, causing the man to tremble anew. Dumb with fright, the woodlander nodded and pointed to a track through the trees.

"And is there a healer among them?"

Another nod.

"Lead us to him."

"She be a wench."

"You have a tongue then," Eadric spun the man round and pushed him toward the trail. "No time to lose!"

After no more than five minutes, the air reverberated with the familiar clamour of a settlement: clucking hens, dogs barking, the shrill voices of children and the bleating of a goat. The path led to cleared land where they counted two-score straw-thatched dwellings standing in front of ploughed fields. Their guide, sunken chest now puffed out with self-importance for the benefit of the few women who gawped out from their huts, turned and waved them to follow. Striding next to the swineherd of the soiled tunic, Eadric, in his belted mail shirt, was an awesome sight.

"Where are the men of the village?" the king queried ingenuously.

"Why, the ealdorman took them off to the war. Didn't want me. Too skinny to fight."

At the door of a house, no different from the others, he knocked. A young woman peered out wide-eyed with concern at the unimaginable. Her eyes roved over the crested helm and steel shirt of the king down to his sword. The object of her scrutiny had no time to waste.

"Girl, where is the woman healer? Our comrade lies close to death and her services are needed."

"It...it's me, Lord," she stammered, flushing bright red.

"What! you are no more than a child!"

"I'm seven and ten years, Lord! And my mother's mother taught me all I know. Where is the wounded man?"

Dismayed, Eadric frowned at Andhun. "Can we let one so young tend to the ealdorman?"

The dux studied the maid, fair of face, slight of build with calloused but long-fingered hands. "Have you even seen an axe wound, child? It's all but severed the arm —"

"Where is he?" she repeated.

His lip curled, Andhun turned back to the king. "She'll lose her senses at the sight of gaping flesh," he mocked, we're wasting time here."

"Lying in the bottom of a boat in the river," Eadric said.

"You must bring him here," her voice came over flat and even.

"He can't be moved!" the dux objected. "Death looms over him!"

"Well then, I can't help you," she made to close the door.

"Wait!" the king intervened, "we can make a litter and fetch him to you."

Disappearing indoors, she came back with a sheepskin and thrust it into the arms of the dux. "Lie him on this, make haste!"

The swineherd caught their attention with a cough. "You need poles. I got poles!"

The ceorl set off at a brisk pace into a different part of the forest and despite this Andhun found the breath to repeat himself, "We're wasting time! I say we head downriver in search of another village. That girl stinks of her mother's milk! How can she heal a wounded man?"

"There may be no more villages before Hrofescaester," Eadric protested, "and I told you Aethelred destroyed the place and the land for miles around. The girl is our only hope — an end to it!"

The dux, still voicing doubts with the other two ignoring him, struggled to keep apace along the track after the villager. They came to an enclosure with a rough wooden hut and five stinking pigsties surrounded by a palisade made of stakes and wattle fencing. The man dashed inside and emerged with a coil of cord and two stout poles, each sharpened to a point.

"Spares," he gave them a gap-toothed grin, "I keep them in case of damage."

One he thrust at Wulflaf and kept the other before rushing off down the track, taking a series of forks in the path to lead them at last to the boat.

Aelfhere lay pale and motionless as before.

"He's still breathing," Ewald said, "and I got cramp hanging on here."

The sheepskin lashed to the poles, they turned to stare at the ealdorman.

"Here," Ewald handed the rope to Hynsige, "cling to this with your good arm."

Wulflaf clambered into the craft and with the help of his comrade lifted their lord into the waiting arms of the two men on the bank. Eadric and Andhun laid him on the litter.

"Right," the dux said, "you, what's your... Hynsige, isn't it? Throw me the rope and get out!"

Once they had dragged the bows of the ferryboat up the bank, Andhun cursed and added, "It's too heavy to lift, the ealdorman grows weaker and the day longer. No way to conceal the boat. We have to hope the West Seaxe have no taste to follow us!"

"At least we're on the opposite side of the river from them," Wulflaf said, "and we passed no fords."

Andhun grunted and spoke to the swineherd, "You take one end of that pole. Can't have the king carrying it."

Open-mouthed, the ceorl dropped to his knees in front of Eadric. "The king!"

Hollow and bitter came Eadric's laugh, "One with a kingdom open to the hordes of Caedwalla. The fellow's all skin and bones, I'll take the pole."

Decision made, the four warriors led by the swineherd and followed by Hynsige, bore the litter to the home of the healer. There, they laid it next to a fire snapping and crackling in the middle of the floor. The smoke carried a pleasant herbal scent that permeated the room before it spiralled out of the hole in the thatch. All around, containers and bundles of dried herbs littered the crude wooden tables and benches.

The girl placed a cushion under the head of Aelfhere before cutting through the tight bandage tied to stop the flow of blood and hissed at the silt in the wound.

"As well the blade took the outer side of the limb, else he were dead," she muttered.

Busying herself mixing vinegar and water in a bowl, she murmured, "This filth has to go," before adding, "move him — gentle now — so as his arm rests on the floor. Rinsing out the sludge until, satisfied, she muttered, "shouldn't fester now." Wulflaf, she pushed in the chest, "Out the way, you clutter the place. Hadn't you better get back to your pigs?" she glared at the ceorl.

"Everyone, outside!" Eadric ordered. "Leave the maid unhindered."

The king remained and watched as she poured liquid into the wound.

"What is this?"

"A potion of garlic, wine and ox-gall brewed in yon." She indicated a brass bowl, "it stands for nine days before it's strained..."

"How does it serve?"

"To keep out the evil spirits, so the flesh won't rot."

Aelfhere groaned, his eyes flickered open only for a moment but there was no awareness, as though he were in another world.

The young woman studied the face of the king. "Rest easy, he'll live, his arm'll mend." Rising, she came back with a fine needle and thread. "Lord, nip the wound. Ay, just so. Now, we'll sew him up." Task completed, she wiped her hands on her dress and placed a pot of water over the fire. Next, she made a poultice and spread the contents of a jar over it.

"Before you ask, a salve of lesser centaury...it helps the flesh to heal." Around the moist cloth, she bound a bandage. "There, all done. Come, let's make him more comfortable, take his weight off that pole."

"What is this place?"

"My home, Lord!" She dripped liquid with great care into the ealdorman's mouth. "Takes the fever away."

"I mean the village," the king smiled.

"Maegdan stane, Lord."

"Strange name."

The freckled face and the pale blue eyes lit up, "On account of yon stone. Over in the woods," she nodded her head of short cropped blonde hair. "The folk gather there for meetings."

"And your name?"

"Aetta, Lord."

"I'll not forget these names, nor what you've done."

Aelfhere's head, she laid back down on the cushion, then stoppered the bottle.

"Ain't finished yet. Another's wounded. Bring him in!"

The cut ran across the outer side of the forearm above Hynsige's wrist.

"Severed the sinews," Aetta said, "means you can't move that hand. This is going to hurt…"

"How long will it take?" Eadric wondered.

"Long enough!"

"We must go before night sets in. Hynsige, you stay with your lord until he regains his health. Both of you wait in this village for a messenger. God knows when… the summer… the autumn. Cat and mouse. And we're the mice!" A smile flickered before he confided to their host, "Healer, today you have served your king well. You shall not go unrewarded."

The young woman gaped at his back as the warrior walked out the door. The maid covered her embarrassment by bustling around preparing liquids and salves before setting about the serious task of inspecting the wound.

"You're lucky, you know," she gazed up into the deep blue eyes of Hynsige and her heart beat faster. Too busy and preoccupied, she had not noted his good looks. Flustered, she said, "I didn't mean *lucky*, the blade didn't sever the tendons, see, not quite but they'll need stitching at once or they'll snap. Drink this. It will ease the pain."

When she finished sewing the sinew and the cut, Aetta bound splints so the islander would not move the hand.

"Was it terrible?" she frowned.

"What?"

"The battle."

The warrior stared down at the pallid countenance of Aelfhere and Aetta moved to place a hand on his forehead, "The fever burns less."

"Hundreds of men lost," the Wihtwara said, "maybe some got away through the marsh," he shook his head, "Nought will stop the West Seaxe scourge! We're all right here. But their leader, Caedwalla, will head for Cantwaraburh and destroy whatever stands in his way."

Chapter 11

Wilfrith and Caedwalla

Kingsham, West Sussex, May 686

"Pompous ass!"

The white knuckles of the prelate brandishing a letter and the fury in his eyes, made the affable Abbot Eappa yearn to kneel before the haven of an altar.

"Listen to this!" The bishop read from the missive: *'To the most glorious lord, deserving of every honour and reverence, Bishop Wilfrith, Theodore, by God's gift endowed with pastoral sway over the souls of the Suth Seaxe, and the whole abbey with all the brotherhood of the servants of God in our province who invoke Him ...'* Pah! Long-winded nonsense — "

The abbot clasped his hands and in a conciliatory voice, said, "The tone is respectful—"

"Respectful! Who? The Greek! Was it respectful to drive me into exile? Carve up my diocese in Northumbria? Refuse to honour the decree of the Holy Father in Rome? To glory in my imprisonment!"

The fist of Wilfrith clenched and the parchment crackled. The prelate began to stride around the room, his long vestments flapping at his ankles. "Four score and five winters has he seen — not long enough to rid himself of insincerity..."

Of a sudden thoughtful, he halted his pacing to stare into space. "Insincerity?"

The curiosity of the abbot overcame his prudence.

"Flattery! *'Pastoral sway over the souls of the Suth Seaxe',* indeed! This letter reveals his fears. In it, he informs me a West Seaxe underking named Mul is enthroned at Cantwaraburh: the brother of the conqueror and a pagan. No doubt he feels threatened. The heathen devastated Kent and knocks at the door of his cathedral. Of course, Archbishop Theodore knows of my, how shall we say, *closeness*, to the warlord and implores — ay, *implores* me to convert Caedwalla. He has the effrontery to suggest how I should go about it...as though I were a novice."

Wilfrith, his face contorted with anger, threw the crumpled sheet of vellum on top of far more insignificant documents.

With a discreet cough, Abbot Eappa diverted the glare of the bishop from the letter to himself.

"Is the task possible?"

"What task?"

"That of conversion?"

For the first time, Wilfrith smiled.

"Already half-done, I believe. Caedwalla leads many Christians in his war-band, his wife is baptised and *his* respect I have won." A strange light burned in the eyes of the bishop. "Theodore of Tarsus is an old man. To win his gratitude might be a wise course of action. The incumbent of the see of Cantwaraburh should be a man of vision..." He stopped short, and cast an awkward glance at the monk. "Well, forgive me, I must reply to his letter. Ah, Father, be kind enough to spare me five brothers to accompany me on my journey."

"You are leaving?"

"Off at dawn, proselytising, with the help of the Lord."

* * *

The approach to Kingsham, along a gloomy forest trail in the company of a handful of defenceless monks, tested the most unshakeable faith. At the fringe of the woodland where they emerged, Wilfrith shuddered at the sight of the fresh earth mound, a sombre twin to its grass-covered neighbour. Crossing himself, he muttered a prayer for the souls of departed warriors before announcing their purpose at the gates, whence a guard led them to the mead hall.

In the hearth at the centre of the room, flames changed colour and embers hissed sending up wraiths of smoke caused by fat dripping from a spit. A youth turning the handle of the long rod greeted the brothers with a knowing grin at their savouring the aroma of roasting fowl. From behind them came a deep voice.

"Well met, Bishop. Do you bring tidings of my wife?"

In the doorway, standing with his back to the light, the features of Caedwalla were indiscernible.

Wilfrith peered towards the outline of the tall figure.

"She is well. A willing student, making notable progress in her reading also she will learn to write in time, and they tell me she can ride a horse."

The warrior strode into the hall to tower over the prelate. "This is good news but you did not come from Selsea to tell me about Cynethryth."

"Only in part," the bishop said, "there are important matters we need to discuss."

A deep laugh echoed around the rafters of the near-empty room.

"Not on an empty stomach." He beamed around the expectant faces of the brothers. "Tramping the countryside makes a man hungry. Be my guests at table. After you have broken your fast, cross-bearer, we shall talk."

"I congratulate you on a great victory," Wilfrith said when at last alone with Caedwalla, but his voice betrayed the unease induced by a clash of pride. A bishop above bishops, he brought Roman pride to the encounter, far different from that of the King, born of pagan hills, heath and naked power.

"What is it you seek?"

His shrewd eyes never detached from those of the prelate.

"Chosen One — for the Almighty favours you — other kings will prostrate themselves at your feet or be swept away in a river of blood. My God lends strength to your arm and raises you to glory... and yet you do not bow to his name."

"Hark, priest, who is to say your god strengthens my sinews? More like it be Woden. The flesh of my limbs springs from direct descent. My line is of Cerdric, through Elesa, Elsa, Giwis, Wig, Freawine, Frithgar, Brond, son of Baeldaeg, who was the son of Woden!"

"And who were the parents of Woden?"

"Why, Bor and Bestia — it is well known."

The prelate sat back in his chair, his smile and voice vouching for his pleasure. "Then you admit your gods and goddesses were born after the manner of men? Therefore they had a beginning."

Caedwalla scowled. "Well, and what of it?"

I must spin my web with care.

Wilfrith cupped his chin in thought for a moment, gazed through the smoke hole in the roof to the sky, pointed upwards and said, "What say you, Son of Woden? This universe, did it have a beginning or was it always in existence?"

The warrior poured more ale into his beaker, but the bishop put his hand over his own drinking cup.

Better keep a clear head.

A quaff of his drink and Caedwalla said, "Fire and light, ice and darkness, two realms joined by the world tree. From the frost giant's flesh was the earth made and the seas from his blood —"

The prelate pounced, "So then, who created these places? How did your gods reduce beneath their sway a universe that existed before them? Do you suppose the gods and goddesses still beget others? If they do not, when or why have they ceased? If they do, the number of gods must now be infinite..."

Wilfrith leant an elbow on his chair arm, his chin on his fist, placed a finger across his lips and waited for his rhetoric to take effect.

The warrior, distracted, stared at the bishop and overfilled his cup, froth soaking into his breeches. Unconcerned, he glanced from the damp cloth back to the cleric. "Do you suggest it is your god guiding me from one victory to the next?"

"If your gods are omnipotent, beneficent and just, they will punish those who despise them. Why do they spare those who turn the world away from their worship? Those who overturn their statues! How is it the most mighty kings are Christians?"

Caedwalla levelled a forefinger at the prelate, "The same who sent you into hiding in the weald? Or like Centwine who ill-treated you at his hall?"

"*Errare humanum est.*"

"Eh?"

Wilfrith glared at him. "Men make mistakes. The Almighty allows free will —"

The warrior stood and began a restless pacing to and fro, "Do you want to know *my* will? I desire to rule from the Tamar in the west to the white cliffs in the east and to keep the Mercians at bay —"

I have him! Trussed in a silken trap.

A radiant smile stopped Caedwalla short.

"What?"

"And you will! I repeat, God chose you for this purpose: to create and reign over a powerful *Christian* kingdom in the south ..." After a deliberate pause to lend greater import to his words, he continued, "... but two obstacles exist..."

"Tell me, cross-bearer!"

Rising from his seat, the bishop faced the warrior, "View the raven as a simple bird and consider the wolf a scavenger in the wild. Convert! Follow the example of the mightiest in this land, of the kings over the seas who possess fertile provinces fruitful in wine and olives, and of your own lady. God, the Father will endow you with every blessing and give you 'infants to frisk like lambs, children to dance like deer'. We shall arrange a Christian ceremony to bless your wedding after your baptism. Thereafter, the Lord will fulfil His promise to you of life eternal when at last your soul leaves behind the temple of the flesh."

"Do you swear to these gifts of your God?"

Wilfrith reached for the object resting on his chest. "I give you my word on all I hold precious," and he kissed the silver cross.

"It is a mighty talisman."

The prelate scowled. "Faith in the Lord is the provider of true power."

Pouring another ale, Caedwalla said, "And the second?"

"Second?"

"You said there existed two obstacles, priest."

"Indeed, I did." The bishop tried to keep his voice even. "There is the problem of Wiht —"

"Again you task me with the isle!"

The set of the jaw, the pursed lips and the frown of the bishop spoke louder than his words.

"The last resort of pagans and the stronghold of apostasy festers like a suppurating wound in our flank... *'The lamp of the wicked must be snuffed out'*...Arwald plots with the Kentings —"

Impatient, the warrior said, "The Cantwara are quelled at the moment." He frowned, "Yet reports reach me every day of war-bands gathering north of the Medweg. Others muster near the border with Mercia. Thank the stars, the Mercians have problems of their own to deal with. So, you see, there are more pressing matters than the isle."

Wilfrith glowered under lowered brow. "Excuses! You set your face against invading Wiht because it is the home of your wife!"

The expression of Caedwalla resembled that of a man slapped across the cheek, his eyes narrowed and he hurled the cup in his hand at the wall.

"Make no mention of Cynethryth in these affairs! I did not say I will not conquer Wiht, rather I am mindful of more urgent issues!"

"Then you do not exclude it?"

"It is in my plans, priest."

"I shall pray for the souls of the Wihtwara and that the day of your incursion comes soon so Arwald will *'drink the cup of the wrath of the Almighty'*. The islanders stand in need of purification from the uncleanness and guilt of paganism — as do you, my son. I see no further impediment to your conversion and the surety you will enjoy the favour of the Lord."

"First, I must crush resistance in the south. Then I turn my attention to Wiht."

"In which case, I will pray for the Lord to shield you, in order that you will not die unclean and hence your soul fly to Hell. Come, let us seal the understanding!"

Wilfrith held out his hand.

Caedwalla stared at the bishop. "Invoke with your prayers that all the south and Wiht shall be mine," he said, clasping the hand of the prelate. "If your god grants me this, I swear I will bow to him and be wetted in his name."

Chapter 12

Aelfhere

"Lord Aelfhere! I bear news!"

Hynsige waved and started to run from the house of the healer to the dwelling the ealdorman had made his own. In spite of the yelling, Aelfhere clove another log and tossed it on the growing heap next to the chopping block. Wiping his forehead with the back of a hand, he turned to appraise his comrade. Why the haste? Were there tidings from Andhun? Why carry a basket?

He read the face of the stolid ceorl like the morning sky: rain and sun — worry and joy — competed for dominance. The ealdorman leant on his axe and waited.

Without drawing breath, the self-appointed messenger blurted, "News, my Lord!"

"Might you share it?"

A frown tussled with an awkward grin. "I…I'm not sure it's good…well, of course, it *is!*…But —"

"Aetta is with child?"

The jaw of the warrior dropped. "How…how did you know?"

Amused at the incredulity of the ceorl, Aelfhere said, "It's what happens when a sturdy fellow beds a maid."

"She told me when I found her sick this morning. I'm to the river. Will you come?"

"The river?"

"Aetta wants me to gather mead wort — for the sickness, see?"

"You'd think a healer would have it to hand —"

"Well, the dried stuff, ay, but she says it's better fresh. Anyway, I must be away..." he paused, casting a pleading glance, "... are you coming? I...I need to talk."

The two men strolled along an oak-lined trail under a canopy of vivid green tender leaves.

"So, what troubles you?"

"Three seasons have gone by, winter is passed and the ground is firm underfoot. By now, the king and the dux will have found men. I expect their messenger will come any day —"

The ealdorman grasped his comrade by the arm, "Hush! What's that?"

They stood in silence, but the sudden crashing through the undergrowth nullified the need for cocked heads.

Under his breath, Aelfhere swore, adding, "Hogs! I ought to have brought my spear."

The sound receded and the companions relaxed. "What better practice for wedlock than facing an angry boar with but a sword!" He laughed, clapping his comrade on the back.

"It is about bonds I wish..." Hynsige stalled. "...I am bound to your service, lord...but to leave Aetta alone, defenceless, with child..." his voice trailed off and they fell into a deep silence, each given to his own thoughts.

At last, the older man said, "After your birth, when your father brought you pink and yowling for my blessing, I kissed your brow." His arm wrapped around the ceorl's shoulder. "A brave man, a fine fighter, your father. He died by my side at the battle of Biedanheafde. In those days the men of the West Seaxe were our friends and together we defeated Wulfhere —"

"H-how did my father die?"

"Like a man — in combat. Let it be — fact is, I resolved to care for you, a mere stripling."

With a smile at the memory, he continued. "Do you recall when I fashioned a wooden seax and taught you to wield it ...?" For inspection, he held out his hand. "... I still bear a gnarl where you struck me...the only eight-year-old to best a full-grown Wiht warrior!" The ealdorman halted in front of Hynsige. "There may come no bearer of tidings. What has become of Eadric, we cannot say. In either case, you will be here for Aetta and the babe. When the whelp steals your sleep, you'll wish you were facing the wolf-men from the west!"

"Lord, once more I'm beholden to you, my woman too! When the child is born we will name him after you, if it be your will?"

The sun through the clouds lit the livid scar across the Wihtwara's lips as they curled into a smile, "A hard name to hang on a girl, my friend!" Laughing, they stepped on the meadowland running from the fringe of the woods down to the silver ribbon of water. Treading on the springy turf, Aelfhere said, "Is it not early for mead wort to flower? The bloom is easy enough to spot in summer, but how do we —"

"Aetta told me. Its leaves are like those of an elm and they're dark on top and whitish and downy underneath. What's more, she says chewing the root's a cure for an aching head."

"Yon woman is as steeped in plant lore as the herbs in her liquors!"

Amid idle chatter, the basket filled. Carefree, heading back along the trail, of a sudden Hynsige stopped and sniffed the air. "Smoke! Can you smell it?" They hurried to the fork where they would have turned right, but above the trees in the opposite direction, a plume soared black and dense into the sky.

"This way!" The ealdorman broke into a run, his ceorl close behind. Four hundred strides and he halted. In the clearing with its palisaded dwelling, a body lay on its side, knees drawn up to the chest and arms crossed over the crimson stain seeping over the lurid tunic. Fallen against a thigh, a sickle, a sign of futile defence. Farther back, the hovel was ablaze, flames leaping and sending sparks crackling, bright red against the pitch-hued cloud fouling the woodland air. The same fate had befallen the line of sties, reduced to charred and smouldering heaps.

No mistaking the identity of the corpse: the skinny swineherd. Bent over the pathetic sack of bones, Aelfhere discovered the nature of the fatal wound.

"Still warm..." he said, lifting a forearm masking the point of entry of a blade, "...sliced upwards, looks like a blow from a seax. Forceful enough to take this poor wretch off his feet."

"No trace of the pigs," Hynsige said. "Thieves, then?"

The ealdorman nodded, "By the look of it. No wind today, thank Thunor, yon will burn itself out — it'll not reach the palisade. Come, we can bury him later. Best to raise a hue and cry in the village though it will give us only a handful of men — call them men! Still, taking five youths is better than going after the pillagers alone."

Hastening back to where the path split, they turned sharp left and raced toward the settlement. Once more, they stumbled to a halt in horror and anguish at the sight of a cloud of black smoke rising above the treetops.

A howl tore from the throat of Hynsige, "The village!" He made to dash ahead but his comrade hauled him back. "Not thieves! A warband. Move with stealth!"

At the forest edge, from the undergrowth they peered at the gruesome scene. Bloodied bodies strewn like broken playthings sprawled among the blazing homes, their shroud a billowing pall, pied grey and black.

The ealdorman stared into the tear-filled eyes of his companion and his heart sank. *'When the child is born we will name him after you.'* The words haunted him. No birth, only death.

"Come! All is silent. The raiders are gone."

Hynsige leapt up and raced toward the conflagration, heedless of the searing heat and choking smoke, on towards the torched home of the healer. Following at a steady pace, Aelfhere studied the devastation. Flames springing skyward devoured the roof of his house under his gaze. The fire would die down then he would inspect it. Only one hut at the far side of the village stood as a stark survivor. The straw covering had gone but the wooden shell remained. No time for contemplation, he shook his head, his concern was for the living, one soul alone: his fellow islander. When he joined his comrade, the scene rent his heart. The healer who had saved his life lay, throat cut, eyes staring unseeing to the heavens, dress pulled up as far as her chest. Hynsige cradled the body to his breast, his cheek pressed to hers, his shoulders heaving. The ealdorman knelt to slip an arm under the waist of the young woman and tug her skirt to her ankles, before standing to raise the limp warrior.

"Son, we'll give Aetta a decent burial, but first we must see to the others."

Incredulous, the warrior's tear-streaked stare, his words forced and choking.

"What? We two, bury all these?"

A shake of the head. "See the building that blazes most — the hall — we shall drag them there and let it consume them. Better the flames of Thunor than the ravens of Hel."

A tear rolled down the cheek of the battle-hardened ealdorman. With bile in his craw, he flung the delicate body of a girl, no more than three years old, into the insatiable maw of the fire.

Having completed the harrowing task, he turned to his companion. "How shall we dig the grave without spade or hoe?"

"We will not," Hynsige said, his countenance hard as granite. "Aetta will flare brightest among her folk, so gazing down from Waelheal, where she serves at Woden's table, she will be content."

They went over to her body and Aelfhere made to take the ankles of the woman — but the younger man pushed him away. He raised the healer in his arms and staggering, carried her towards the blistering heat of the hall. The ealdorman followed, intent on aiding his companion to fling the corpse into the greedy flames. Once more, his comrade repulsed him, shaking his head and lowering the body of Aetta. Hynsige embraced her as a lover and kissing her forehead began to walk in a macabre dance, the woman's feet swinging inches above the ground, towards the door of the hall. Aelfhere tensed, would not the warrior thrust the body into the hellish grasp of the fire? The ealdorman started forward. His ceorl must not pass through the flaming remnants of the door! But on he went with measured pace to vanish without sound.

Sinking to his knees, Aelfhere bowed his head and out of sorrow for Hynsige, Aetta and the villagers, for each one now but ashes, a long, uncontrollable howl burst from his lips. His body shuddered and he retched at the stench of burning flesh.

When at last he rose, he did not look back on the grim scene but determined to return in the morning. If he must sleep on the ground, the palisade of the swineherd granted at least refuge from wild beasts.

Unmoved, Aelfhere gazed on the hideous sight of the pigman's skinny body ravaged by scavengers, which he dragged through the trees where the earth was soft. There he used his sword to make a shallow grave.

Later, he retrieved the sickle to gather heaps of fresh fern for a bed under his cloak. Satisfied, he drew from the well, where he rinsed the bitterness from his mouth — if not from his life.

* * *

The lack of wind had saved the stockade from consumption but left the reek of charred wood mingled with the animal stink of the ground around the burnt sties. The ealdorman stared at the night sky and wondered whether the bright stars outnumbered his woes. Alone once more, his sword and cloak for possessions, he considered the direness of his situation. For the company of his own voice, he spoke aloud.

"I cannot depart Maegdan stane, my friends will seek me here — if ever they come. Yet how can I live among those charred remains? Here is the best place. The wooden walls offer protection and I'm near enough to be found. I should leave a sign. Then what? Better think on that too. I can tear down the burnt sties," he covered his nose against the smell, "clear the blackened wood and build a small hut. Water in the well and food in the forest..." He began to feel more cheerful. "…The ground near the pigsties is rich in droppings, I can plant there…tomorrow I'll…" His voice trailed away as he fell into uneasy sleep.

The ealdorman woke with the acrid smell of smoke permeating his clothes and coating his tongue, leaving it dry and sour. Frustration at his helplessness overwhelmed him. "I *will* find Caedwalla and strike him down!" he told the trees as he headed to survey the destruction of the settlement. A sturdy branch lying by the side of the path caught his eye, "It'll serve as a staff," he said, whittling off the twigs.

The pungent, noxious scorched wood assailed him when he picked his way through the shell of his home. Using the stave as a lever, he shifted the debris. The first useful find was his spearhead.

"I'll replace the fragment wedged in the bell end with a fine ash shaft," he decided, tucking it into his belt.

Unexpected joy! His mail shirt lay amid the ruins of a wall corner crushed under a half-consumed roof beam. "Sure, the West Seaxe didn't need it — they'll not lack for one after all their killing and plundering. A good clean and it'll be as new," he said, "but I'll wager they took my helm."

The remnants covering every inch of the floor, he thrust aside, but so it proved.

"When I find it with its golden wolf around the rim, I'll take it back with a head inside!"

By the time the new moon grew into a waning crescent, Aelfhere had cleared the burnt wood from the swineherd's enclosure. From out of the devastation, he dragged the timbers of the surviving shell, to rebuild the home and thatch it in its new location. Only then, weeks later, did he leave a painstaking sign of his presence in the blackened wooden sepulchre of the village: a diamond shape made of small stones with an inlet in the stead of its northern apex; below the southern one, he studded an arrow of pebbles pointing to the trail in the woodland. Any Wihtwara, reasoned the ealdorman, would recognise the form of his isle. This design, he repeated on a smaller scale on the correct path at each fork in the track.

In those languid days of April, he blessed Aetta and the attention he had paid to her words as he lay recovering in her home. Without her chatter about country lore, how would he have known to boil the rootstock and stems of the bulrush, to grub for chicory root or gather clover and burdock? These he supplemented with the flesh of birds and deer, trapped and hunted in the forest. Never had he been healthier — or more alone.

When the face of the white-robed goddess shone full amid the stars, Aelfhere stood in the enclosure arms aloft as his father had taught him. With feeling, he chanted: *'Mother of the night sky, hail to thee, mistress of the hunt, provider of prey for man, guide my aim!'*

The next day, breathing in the rich scent of the creamy haw blossom lining his path, he found Monan had answered his plea. One of his traps had snared a partridge. Wringing the neck of the creature, the ealdorman stiffened.

No, he was not mistaken. Voices! In the direction of the village! Silent, he slunk into the undergrowth, choosing a hollow that hid him while giving a clear view of the track at eye level. Two contrasting figures, in heated discussion, armed warriors, one stocky and the other rangy, approached his hiding place — Ewald and Wulflaf!

A chortle of pleasure caused Ewald to spin round, drawing his sword, while Wulflaf scanned in vain along the trail and among the trees, before they located him by his laughter.

"Hush! You two are making enough noise to wake a bear in hibernation!"

"Lord! We have found you!" Wulflaf grinned at the ealdorman scrambling up towards him. "It is well to see you hale!"

"My strength has returned and I'll take on any man!"

"We knew to come hither by the shape of Wiht in stones. I broke it up, the arrow too, lest another stumble on it."

"You did well."

"West Seaxe raiders!" Ewald said, "They've devastated half of Kent. What of Hynsige?"

The lone survivor of the slaughter shook and lowered his head. In a gruff voice, he said, "The tale will keep. Come, remember the swine-herd? They slew him and torched his home and sties too. I fear there are no pigs for you to tend, Ewald, but I have this," he held up the bird, "and fresh water in the well."

"I'll pluck it as we walk, Lord," Wulflaf said, "the King awaits you at Ottansford where he has gathered a war-band."

"How many warriors?" Aelfhere asked.

"Two score or more. Not a host, but enough to harry the West Seaxe oppressors and rally men to Eadric." A stubborn flight feather resisted but he jerked it free, "We must be off with all haste if we are to reach the encampment before nightfall."

"How far?"

"Six leagues to the west."

After their meal, a forced march brought them before dusk to the camp in a river valley near a ford. In the presence of Dux Andhun, Eadric received Aelfhere with joy, which soon turned to distress at the news of yet another destruction, Maegdan stane.

"Your arrival is well-timed, for you shall avenge their deaths," the King said. "Word reached us from the hall of Aethelred that the Mercians seek recompense for the loss of the Meon territory."

The pale blue eyes of the king dwelt on the countenance of the Wihtwara. "Mul, the brother of Caedwalla agreed to meet them on Kentish soil, but not near the borders with Mercia, we assume for fear of treachery. Neither is there trust from the other party since they insisted on no armed men at the meeting." Eadric's lip curled at the realisation dawning in the visage of the older man. "Quite! We have them at our mercy! Mul is obliged to treat with Aethelred or risk war on another front."

"Where and when is the encounter?"

"Tomorrow. Mul with twelve counsellors is two leagues to the east. The homestead of Wrota, you passed close by on your way to us. Here is my plan: we will split our force and intercept the Mercians. With Andhun, we shall treat to our own advantage before accompanying them, due west, back to the confines of their lands. Take the remaining men and destroy the usurper. In one fell blow, we sever the head from the West Seaxe body. What say you?"

"We leave two hours before dawn to rouse the foe with our wrath."

* * *

The homestead, bathed in the gentle morning light, slumbered unaware of the activity beyond the palisade. The feeble rays of the nascent sun as yet unable to penetrate the foliage, Aelfhere surveyed the heaps of dry brushwood and branches that his men had gathered by torchlight. Satisfied at the quantity, he beckoned Wulflaf, who had a coil of rope wound from waist to shoulder and was the most agile of the band. "Climb the wall and open the gate. Stealth, mind! The geese and dogs will make a clamour, so be swift!" To the nearest four spearmen, he said, "Once it is ajar, race to the hall, wedge the door with your spears. The rest of us will follow with the kindling."

The honking, barking and bleating exceeded the ealdorman's fears. "You five," he said, "leave the wood, draw your seaxes. The sight of the blades should be enough to deter the headstrong. Don't harm anyone from the farmstead unless you have to. They are not our enemy."

From inside the hall came raised voices and curses. While they laid the twigs and branches they had gathered against the walls of the building, battering against the door began, but the stout ash poles of the spears held firm.

Bleary-eyed ceorls, clothes awry, came out of their homes in disarray and alarm. A glance sufficed to understand the intent of the attackers.

A smile of grim satisfaction creased Aelfhere's features when one of them yelled, "Slay the West Seaxe swine!" while others shouted their approval.

"Hand me your torch," the ealdorman said, taking the half-consumed bundle of strips of resinous wood and thrusting it into the heaped brushwood. "Another one!" He strode to the back of the building and rammed another firebrand into a pile of kindling. The last brand, he carried to the side of the hall to finish the task. All three fires crackled and spat and Aelfhere strolled over to Ewald and Wulflaf.

"For Hynsige," he said.

Soon, the pummelling inside the door became frantic. The flames set alight the wooden nogs, so smoke entered the narrow gaps between the joints, causing the captives to cough, swear and threaten. The blaze flared and the assailants drew back from the searing heat. The roof timbers caught, sending the sods of turf crashing down to the room below.

"Aetta, Hynsige," Aelfhere murmured at the first screams. "At last, I strike at the heart of Caedwalla as he pierced mine!"

A ceorl staring at the flames, expression vindictive, attracted the Wihtwara's attention and he sauntered over to him.

"Go to Hel! Let the troll-woman grasp them to her bosom! They slaughtered my brother and our cousin at the river battle," the fellow spat on the ground.

"Who owns this farmstead?"

A tilt of the head indicated a man about the islander's own age but with more white in his beard. As the last agonised scream died away, Aelfhere joined him.

"The deed is well done," the farmer offered his hand.

Clasping it, he frowned. "Friend, this is a mighty blow against the West Seaxe invader, but others will come to seek retribution. You must leave this place!"

The pale grey eyes clouded and the jaw set. "Were my son still alive, I might, but *they*," — he gestured to the blaze — "they killed him and I am alone. Man and boy, this has been my home." He called out, "Whoever wishes to depart, I release from my service. Take your families hence, find a haven!" A hand went to his forehead and he muttered, "God knows, nowhere is safe from the warlords."

The man who had pointed out the farmer came over.

"Master, it pains me to leave you, but we must carry the fight to the enemy." He turned to Aelfhere. "Lord, I am willing to wield arms by your side."

"Ay, me too." A sturdy ceorl stepped forward. "I missed the river battle with a swollen ankle, couldn't walk, and I live with the shame."

"I must fend for my wife and children," another said.

"We'll join you later, Lord," another said, "when we've found refuge for our babes."

"Together we shall drive the West Seaxe out of Kent," said Aelfhere and turned to the farmer. "Will you not lend your sinews to our cause?"

The stubborn expression returned. "I'm old and useless and I'll not leave my land, but fare well friend." He turned and entered his home.

From the edge of the forest, where the path began, Aelfhere looked back at the pall of black smoke rising from the remnants of the hall. In sorrow, he shook his head, not for Mul and his swarm of rats, but for the farmer whose decision to remain was a death wish.

They marched back to Ottansford and remembering the words of Eadric, *'due west'*, the ealdorman led his men towards the afternoon sun. They took the ancient trackway running over the hills to avoid the forest and after two leagues, a scout hailed them. Sent by Andhun and entrusted to lead them to the encampment near the border, the fellow pointed and Aelfhere squinted at a hill. It lay squat, adorned by the halo of the setting sun.

"Other side of the Nokholte, Lord, the Mercians camped down in the valley too."

* * *

The oiled linen of the tent undulated in the evening breeze behind the head of Eadric.

"The cur-dog is slain, so too the pack," the islander said.

The young king clenched his fist.

"The first blow is struck. We must not waste more time with the message bearers of Aethelred."

"Will they not fight alongside us against the West Seaxe?"

"We tried to coax them to our cause." He glanced at Andhun. "The Son of Penda is still in dispute with the king north of the Humber over Lindesse. The East Seaxe challenge his overlordship, hence Mercian reluctance to take up arms over the Meon valley. Aethelred will settle for wergeld."

"Then they must find Caedwalla before my blade does." The lips of the dux twisted into a snarl.

Eadric raised the flap of the tent and stepped outside, gazing at the dying sun, before turning to face the other two, his shoulders slumped.

"Slaying the West Seaxe warlord is a wild hope when we have so few warriors."

Feet planted apart, Aelfhere stood before him and leant forward with a fierce stare, "Not if we move fast to strike the headless wolf in Cantwaraburh. Once the invaders are driven out of Kent, men will join us on our way through the Suth Seaxe lands and our numbers will swell. Today, upon the slaughter of Mul, two warriors joined me."

"Let it be so! We leave at first light!" The voice of Eadric rang like a smith's hammer.

* * *

A three-day march brought them to a hill in the Blean weald to the north of Cantwaraburh. Their advance took them through a series of settlements, where at the news of the death of the West Seaxe leaders, men took up their seaxes and spears to swell their ranks. By the time they reached Fefreham, three leagues from the enemy base, their numbers had doubled.

Aelfhere and Eadric bowed to Andhun's leadership in battle. The vegetation ran down the two sides of the hill, while the centre had been cleared well wide of the trackway running from the town to the north. To the trained eye of the dux, the perfect terrain for a trap. Only a third of the men encamped on the open hillside, the rest he hid in two flanks in the dense woodland. The campfires issued their cheerful challenge to the watchers in the settlement below. Instead, Aelfhere and his men in the forest, with only the warmth of their cloaks to comfort them, tried to swallow their resentment for the good of the greater plan.

At dawn, the ealdorman rose, rubbed his numb arms, before hastening to hush the chatter of his men. The success of their ploy depended on silence.

"Get something between your teeth," he said, "it'll end the prattle and strengthen the thews."

Wulflaf came up to him, "How shall we know whether the foe approaches, Lord? All I can see is the bark of trees!"

"At the blast of a horn, we break cover. Mind, you'll hear the enemy before the signal."

In the woodland, restless for action, the truth of his words became clear to them. The war cries of the West Seaxe force in Cantwaraburh, echoed by Andhun's men, resounded in their leafy hiding place. Convinced of their greater numbers and shorn of the wisdom of their leaders, the invaders surged in a reckless charge up the hill.

At the first clash of steel, the screams of the wounded and the howls of assailants, Aelfhere had to drag back and spin round a warrior intent on dashing into the fray.

"Wait for the signal!"

Even as he glared around the band of men under his command, the horn blast came high and clear. For men who a moment before had desired to plunge into the fighting, there was a strange hesitation. All eyes were on the ealdorman.

"Follow me, we must take them from behind!" And so saying, he dashed through the woodland enclosing the hill like the embrace of two giant arms. When he broke from the vegetation, one glance told him they were in an ideal position to the enemy rear. The sight of Eadric leading a charge from the other flanking woods, a little farther down, but not enough to thwart their plan, thrilled him.

They ran without spears, a decision taken in favour of fleetness of foot. As a result, they came down on the West Seaxe warriors with the advantage of complete surprise. First to strike, Aelfhere took out two men before anyone spun to face him and several of his comrades enjoyed the same luck. Trapped between two lines of swinging axes, the West Seaxe, leaderless as they were, knew not where to rally. Stout-hearted to the last, they fought till not one remained alive.

Ewald, leaning on his axe, chest heaving as he struggled for breath, gazed around. Of a sudden, he staggered forward with a grin, raised his weapon and brought it down clean through the neck of a dead foe. Picking up his prize, he peered around him. Aelfhere? There he was!

"Lord!" he called, shouldering his battle-axe and carrying his grisly trophy in the other hand. "See here!"

He held up a head in a metal helm, a running wolf wrought in gold about the rim.

Wiping blood and sweat out of his eyes, Aelfhere gazed at the fine object.

"By Tiw, I swore I'd take it back with the head inside, but I thought I'd be the one to cut it from the shoulders."

"I did not slay him, Lord."

"All the same, you have my thanks."

The ealdorman slid his sword into his belt and reached out for the spoils, studying the flat, broad face and its lifeless stare.

"Aetta and the villagers are avenged," he sighed, unlacing the helm and shaking it free.

The leather cup under the steel was clean, he wiped around the inside with his hand before fitting the metal cap over his shaggy hair. A part of him had been restored and he walked with a swagger to stand beside Eadric and Andhun, who were deep in conversation.

"...gather such supplies in the town as we can lay our hands on," the dux was saying as he turned to Aelfhere, "...we need more men, though we did not lose many today," and his eyes roamed over the body-strewn field, "at a rough count, we still have two score and ten." To Aelfhere, he said, "Friend, go to Wiht, convince Arwald to throw his forces behind us —"

"Into the lion's maw ... ?" the ealdorman hesitated. "We leave at dawn," he said in haste so no-one should doubt his resolve, "but why not call a moot? Proclaim the death of Mul and the destruction of his men. Announce the push to reclaim the Kentish lands, others will muster to the cause for the thrust on Kingsham and beyond into the wolf's home range."

Chapter 13

Caedwalla and Cynethryth

Selsea, West Sussex, May 687 AD

'Ravished by joy'; thus Cynethryth described her state to Rowena in the days conceded to her by Caedwalla. A dismal morning with fog and drizzle giving way to heavy rain did not dampen her elation. When it subsided, the wind dropped and the immature sun managed to dapple the surroundings of the abbey with sparkling freshness.

Restless, in spite of the sweetness of his 'captivity', Caedwalla needed no coaxing to stroll out of the confines of the religious house with his wife.

"Let's walk down to the coast," she said.

Once through the village, the sea, glimpsed beyond the gorse, appeared flat and calm. The trail led them to a clearing among the yellow-blossomed thorn bushes and Cynethryth pointed.

"That's where the Ring Stone stood."

They approached the hole in the ground, full of clear water, encircled by glimmering feathery ferns, velvet mosses and sword-like grasses.

"It is a sacred place," Caedwalla declared in hushed tones.

"Bishop Wilfrith didn't think so. He had the Rock cast into the marsh. Idle superstition, he called it."

"Is that what you think? Why did you come here?"

"To cure the blackness...I-I feared I'd lose you, husband —"

"Did you heal?"

She bit her lip. "I did. But...oh, between old beliefs and new, I'm so confused!"

"Look!" He indicated the pool. "A spring!"

From the dark earth welled up a crystal-clear fount and on the seaward edge of the hollow, the water flowed away in a tumbling brook that was new to Cynethryth.

"Water sprites have replaced those of the rock."

"There are no spirits," she insisted, "Bishop Wilfrith told me, he taught me the words of the Lord: *'Cleave the tree and you will find me, raise the stone and I am there'.*

"Whatever the truth of it, this is a sacred place. I can sense it. Our people say if two lovers drop a stone into a well, by counting the bubbles that rise to the surface, they learn how many years they will spend together."

He reached down and picked up two pebbles.

Cynethryth gasped. "Let it be!" she pleaded, "husband, I am a-feared!"

"Come, lady, you are of sterner mettle! With me now, drop the stone!"

They released them at the same moment. The eyes of Cynethryth widened and met those of Caedwalla. Neither spoke.

For each pebble, a solitary bubble broke the placid surface of the well.

At last, he said, "Two years! Pah! The cross-bearer is right. Idle superstition! Pay no heed!" He tried to make his tone flippant, but seeing the pale face and taut expression of his wife, he cursed himself for a fool.

"I want...to...go back." Her voice quavered.

Before they reached the village a monk, running, hailed them. When he drew up, his words came breathless. "Lord, Father Abbot sent me. A messenger awaits. Will you come to the abbey?"

"We are on our way. Did he give any indication of his message?"

The novice hesitated, "My Lord, *'grave news'*."

"Grave?" Caedwalla linked arms with his wife, "Make haste! Good news improves with the keeping, the ill worsens."

The postulant led them to the abbot's quarters, but Eappa met them outside to head them off. Unrecognisable in agitation, the rubicund features a-tremble. "Oh my, this is a terrible business. I must advise the Bishop." He made to dash off, but the warlord halted him with a growl.

"Where is the news-bearer?"

The abbot stared at him as if the query were unfathomable, wrung his hands. "In the stables," and surprising for one so robust, he dashed off.

"Abbot Eappa is in a state." Cynethryth took her husband by the arm, "It does not bode well. Come, I'll take you to the horses."

They found a West Seaxe warrior watering his mount at one of the troughs. He bowed to Caedwalla and his lady, saying, "Lord, I am come from Kent with ill tidings …" He paused to gauge the reaction of his king.

"Turned on a slow spit they will taste no better!"

The messenger tilted his head in acquiescence, "Your brother is dead and his men defeated at Cantwaraburh. Eadric grows in strength and repossesses more land with each passing day."

About to speak, at the sound of approaching footsteps Caedwalla spun round to find Bishop Wilfrith hastening towards them with Eappa in his wake.

"Is it true?" the prelate panted.

The King of the West Seaxe, fury in his eyes, ignored him. Addressing the message-bearer, he asked, "How is it Mul lost the battle with greater numbers?"

"He did not, Lord."

"The foe outnumbered him?"

"They did not."

The King took a step towards the warrior, his face a mask of wrath. To his credit, the man did not flinch but in a flat voice, said, "Your brother died before the fight."

Wilfrith gazed, frowning, from Cynethryth to Eappa. Shaking his head in bewilderment he opened his mouth to intervene, but the harsh words of Caedwalla cut him short.

"Cease your riddling man or I'll slice out your tongue. Speak!"

"Lord, Mul perished with his counsellors in an ambush. The foe trapped them in the village hall and burned them alive —"

The King paled, but otherwise showed no emotion.

"Where?"

"A homestead, not far from Ottansford. I saw the burnt-out shell of the building myself. We seized the farmer and sliced the truth out of him."

"What did you learn?"

"Cantwara did not kill them. Before he died, we wrested from him...," he paused, glanced at the king's lady and back at Caedwalla, "...Wihtwara, Lord! He swore they spoke with the accent of the isle and a dying man has no reason to lie. The leader, he told us, bore a sword — a wolf fashioned on the pommel."

Cynethryth gasped and clung to the arm of Bishop Wilfrith, the colour draining from her cheeks. "Father!" she muttered.

"See!" cried the prelate. "It is God's will! If only you had listened to me! The heathen isle sows discord and misery. Had you invaded when I urged you, your brother would still be alive. You can delay no more — destroy the pagan. The wrath of God must be placated!"

Cynethryth released her grip. Pushing the bishop away from her, face white, she rounded on him. "What has become of the God of love and forgiveness of your teachings? Why should my people pay for the act of one man?"

Wilfrith glared at her, "Since when have the affairs of men been decided by a woman?" He turned to Caedwalla. "Your wife is upset. The Evil One clouds her judgement, nipping at the tender shoots of her faith. Arwald plots against you. Crush him and all the enemies of God!"

"You have no proof!" Cynethryth protested, eyes narrowed. "On the contrary, Arwald tried to kill my father and his bondsmen. Whatever act my father may or may not have committed is sure to have been without the involvement of the King of the Isle."

"Enough!" the tone of Caedwalla was peremptory. "The decision will be mine alone!"

He turned and stalked away from the stables. Cynethryth glared at Wilfrith and at the blameless abbot, thought about following her husband, but chose to let his rage cool. Instead, she sought the consoling nuzzles of her white pony.

When at last she joined Caedwalla in the room set aside for them, she found him sitting on the bed, staring at the wall.

"I sorrow for your brother. I never met him."

He did not reply so, respecting his grief, she sat next to him waiting until he chose to speak.

She thought he never would, until at last, he said, "They stole a warrior's death from him — he deserved better. They will pay for what they did."

"Husband, I chose the man I love and will not change, but do not ask me to hate my father or to turn my back on my people. Arwald does not plot against you."

"Need I remind you, he had you betrothed to Eadric?"

"But he wanted to make a strong south against the Mercians and —" she bit her tongue.

"… And the West Seaxe. You see, he is a young king, full of energy and ambition. He will not rest until he achieves his purpose."

"Why did he send men to kill my father?"

"Who knows? He offended him in some way?"

"Or Arwald wished to treat with you?"

She blushed with shame at her pleading tone, but desperation drove her. Caedwalla must not invade her isle.

"Then where are his messengers? Nay, he stands by to gauge which way the wind blows. Whoever holds the south will gain his support. Again, whoever holds it must be a Christian king, Wilfrith is right in that. The kings across the borders will not tolerate any challenge to their *'God-given'* authority."

For the first time, he turned to face her. "Like you, I shall take their faith. For this reason, I will clear Wiht of the heathen."

She took his hand, tears filling her eyes. "I beg of you, they are my people!"

"You have my heart, wife. When we wed, you named yourself Cynethryth of Cerdicsford. I know not the isle. Where is this place?"

Her eyes softened and her voice lost its edge. "Why, it is almost an island within the Isle. It lies to the north-west."

"Your people live there?"

"Ay."

"And the rest of the islanders, you know them not?"

She shook her head, frowning in puzzlement.

"It is settled. Come! We must talk with the cross-bearer."

Curiosity aroused, Cynethryth nonetheless kept silent. Instinct told her that whatever he had conceived in her favour might trickle through her fingers like sand if she intervened. In silence, she hastened to match his stride to the bishop's quarters.

* * *

Wilfrith, ever one of considerable presence, received them with the air of one determined to have his way. Shoulders squared, he bestowed on his guests an imperious gaze. Solemn and bold in tone, he declared, "As a prince of the Church, be aware my words are inspired by the Almighty." Pointing at Caedwalla, he said, "Without His grace, you are as feeble as a shrew by the wayside. When you crossed Him, He turned His face against you and the Cantwara dislodged your hold on Kent."

"Which is why," Caedwalla said, determination hardening his voice, "without further delay, I shall destroy the pagans of Wiht."

Cynethryth gasped. The room seemed to close in on her and her head spun. Had he brought her to hear of the doom of her people?

The eyes of the bishop brightened and an eyebrow raised. "Why this change of heart?"

"It is God's will! You said yourself..." The warrior eyed the clergy-man and added, "One quarter of the islanders I shall spare. Seal this pact! The people of the north-west, those of my wife, you will convert. No harm will come to them unless they refuse your coercion. They will serve you and in return, possess the land and work it for themselves and for their tribute to the Church. The rest I shall destroy, including Arwald and his nest of adders."

He turned to Cynethryth and watched the colour come back to her cheeks. "Wife, will you persuade your people to accept your faith?"

Satisfied, she nodded while he turned to Wilfrith.

"Bishop, do you agree to my terms?"

"Indeed, I do! My Son, God has inspired your choice. Receive my blessing in His name."

He sketched the sign of the cross before the warlord, *'In nomine Patris et Filii et Spiritus Sancte...'*

As the *'...Amen'* died on the lips of the prelate, Caedwalla, staring hard into his eyes, delivered, "Our understanding is thus honoured. I shall count on your support, bishop. Now, I leave to gather my men and a fleet. Wiht, then Kent, will suffer the wrath of the West Seaxe."

Chapter 14

Aelfhere

"Wolf!"

He warned the two Wihtwara behind him, who drew their weapons.

In the evening gloom of the woodland clearing, yellow eyes met those of Aelfhere, but did not burn with ferocity or hunger. The ealdorman read resignation in their dull depths. The beast made no attempt to attack or flee. Its swollen testicles made both impossible.

"The creature is sick," he advanced on the beast, "but a wolf is a wolf and it's mine."

A backhanded slash of his sword sliced into the animal's throat to end its suffering.

"Great brute," Aelfhere murmured, pulling his hand-seax from his belt, cutting through the shorter fur of the underbelly to expose the entrails. "I'll wager he led the pack in his day." With method, he worked to peel back the coat.

"The animal is infected, Lord," Ewald wrinkled his nose in disgust.

"I'm after this," Aelfhere said, redoubling his efforts, "here, over the ribs," he scraped the sharp edge of the seax over the fatty flesh and transferred the grease to his sword. Plucking a frond, he used it to smear the whole length of the blade, repeating the operation on the

174

reverse side. Contented, he threw the ferny leaf to the ground, invoking, "Woden, send the spirit of the wolf into the steel — may the foe feel the fierceness of its bite!"

Ewald knelt over the carcass, greased his seax and remarked, "Let's hope your blade need not serve against Arwald and his men, else this time, I fear we'll not survive."

Wulflaf too daubed his weapon, earning a rebuke from his lord.

"Make haste for we must be at the home of my cousin's husband before nightfall."

"What of the guards at the gate?"

The ealdorman sneered. "I reckon a couple of silver sceattas will buy their silence."

And so it proved.

* * *

The welcome at Siferth's house exceeded the previous visit both in warmth and oddness as his cousin embraced Aelfhere with surprising fervour.

"Easy, Leofe, you'll break my back!"

She seized him by the hand and drew him into the room where a woman was playing on the floor by the hearth with a diffident boy. At the table, sat a monk who eyed the newcomers and their weapons with unease.

"Eabbe! Can it be you? A woman with a child? Last time I saw you, you were 'baking cakes' of mud and pebbles in the street!"

"Remember, you made me cry because you wouldn't try one! I don't blame you now, of course!" She continued, "This is my son, five winters since his birth. Greet your Uncle Aelfhere, Beric."

The boy bestowed a timid smile on him, at which Leofe tugged at the ealdorman's sleeve and drew him apart.

"Careful with your speech, cousin," she whispered. "Eabbe knows nought of your part in the death of her husband. Instead, we shall never be able to thank you enough. Come, lest I arouse curiosity!"

By the fire, Ewald was whittling a piece of wood in the shape of an animal for the child and Wulflaf was talking to Siferth. Rising and stepping over, his niece bestowed a sweet smile on Aelfhere. "And Cynethryth, uncle?"

The sound of her name pierced his heart. Tone harsh, he glared.

"I shall not talk of her."

Breaking off his conversation, Siferth said, "I fear we must. This brother comes from Selsea with a message from your daughter."

Startled, the ealdorman gazed from the monk and back at his host. "From Cynethryth? Why?"

"The content is plain enough," said Siferth, "but what's behind it is harder to understand. She urges me to take the family to Cerdicsford at once, or so the brother says," and he nodded toward the silent figure at the table.

Aelfhere stared in thought at the dancing flames in the hearth. Of a sudden, he crashed his fist into the palm of his hand. "By Thunor! It's as clear as Uurdi's well water! Caedwalla means to invade the isle!" To Ewald and Wulflaf he added, "This strengthens our hand with Arwald! Have I the right of it? Speak, brother!"

The messenger paled. "I know not. The lady came with Father Abbot and charged me to bring the message." A frown creased his brow. "They impressed on me not to talk with anyone, to leave at once, for the bishop had not to know of my errand. One thing I am sure of — Caedwalla left the abbey on the morn before my departure."

Red in the face, the ealdorman addressed his cousin's husband. "Do you see now? When the cur sets foot on the isle, he will attack the fortress first. This is the meaning behind her warning. Versed in the mind of the rabid mongrel, she knows he will slaughter everyone in Wihtgarabyrig."

"Leofe leaves at first light with Eabbe and Beric," Siferth said.

His wife clasped her hands. "Will you not come?"

With a shake of the head, he replied. "I will stay to defend our isle, for Arwald will need every strong arm to repel the West Seaxe."

Pallid, Leofe stayed her tongue. She must take her daughter and grandson to safety and she blessed Cynethryth for her forewarning. For the moment, she had enough to manage with four unexpected guests to feed.

* * *

In the morning, with mutual admonishments, they abandoned the house and headed their separate ways. Setting dread and trepidation aside, Aelfhere clung to the belief that Arwald, rather than slay him on the spot, would hear him out and heed his warning.

Inside the hall of the king, the ealdorman, Ewald, Wulflaf and the Selsea monk stood like prey before the ravening maws of a ferocious pack ready for the kill. Hatred blazed in the coarse inked features of Arwald.

"Are you mad to come here? Do you take me for a fool or a craven?"

The rising flush at the throat accompanied bulging eyes.

"The Dancing Tree awaits you!" The king gestured to a one-eyed thegn, "Truss them like swine for the slaughterhouse! Swing for the crows, carrion!"

With an effort, Aelfhere kept his voice level. "Heed my words, Lord, in days … or indeed hours … the West Seaxe under Caedwalla will land on the isle and we will have a common foe. Set aside past rancour, since we are willing to fight at your side."

A scratch of his matted hair and a sly glance at the expressions of his counsellors to gauge their reactions, then Arwald spoke. "How do we know you tell the truth?"

"Beside me stands a monk from Selsea, sent to warn of the coming invasion."

The eyes of the king, two slits under the russet hawk on his brow, switched to the monk, who nodded in confirmation. A huge fist clenched, "Speak, by Tiw! Or I'll wring it out of you with my bare hands."

The brother, swallowing hard, blurted, "The King's Lady in person and Father Abbot sent me to warn of an imminent attack —"

"Why would she do that? Is she held against her will? Is she still loyal to Wiht?"

Aelfhere seized his chance. "*We* are faithful to Wiht, Lord," he indicated his ceorls with outstretched hands, "ready to shed our blood. There is no time to lose! Muster men from all parts of the isle, gather them here at Wihtgarabyrig!"

Half-rising, a thick vein pulsing at his neck, Arwald shouted. "Dare you presume to tell me what to do?" Enraged, he rounded on his counsellors. "If they speak true, why should we not treat with the West Seaxe?"

A curt exchange ended in concurrence: Caedwalla did not negotiate except with steel.

"My king," Aelfhere tried a placatory tone, "the alliance with Eadric holds. The brother of Caedwalla, the usurper ruling Kent, I slew myself. Later, we destroyed his army." The ealdorman acknowledged his comrades, "We fought beside the Suth Seaxe leaders, duces Andhun and Beorhthun, against the West Seaxe. If the Wihtwara drive the cur back to the sea, our might combined with the Suth Seaxe and the Cantwara will prevail."

Lust for vengeance thwarted for the moment, Arwald spoke through clenched teeth.

"If the West Seaxe fleet comes, we fight together," he growled, "if it does not, you will dance from the oak tree."

* * *

The task as lookouts did not suit the two younger brothers of Arwald. On the hilltop overlooking the haven at Braedynge, they gathered stones and took turns throwing for a wager at a spear planted in the ground thirty paces away. The position the ealdorman had chosen commanded a view of the sea, through a gap in the trees. There the land dropped steeply to a dell. They overlooked the east of the isle, thence across the waves to distant Selsea. The early morning sun, high enough to light the far downs beyond Kingsham, afforded favourable conditions for observation.

In spite of his missing eye, the thegn ordered by the king to bind them the day before, called, "They are coming! See, there! Over toward Portsmutha, that dark patch on the sea."

Ewald nodded, having passed over this stain on the water twice, but on closer inspection, there were white specks in its midst. Realisation dawned but Aelfhere beat him to the words. "Those bright flecks are sails! Come, away to warn Arwald and prepare for battle!"

* * *

Mid-afternoon, on the hilltop of clear land lying before the fortress of Wihtgarabyrig, the Wihtwara formed a shieldwall. From out of the woods below swarmed the West Seaxe warriors. Their grey mail shirts made them look like a wolf pack, ferocious and bonded. From the trees resounded their howling war cry. A hail of missiles, javelins, throwing axes and rocks greeted their slow uphill advance. On they came, relentless, closing the short gap with a rush, shield to shield, using spear and sword, they broke the Wihtwara line.

In the milling mass of men, Aelfhere positioned himself close to his king and his brothers, the two young princes. Together, under the banner of the Isle, they hacked their way toward the golden dragon emblem where Caedwalla and his thegns reaped a harvest of flesh and bone.

Two dragon banners, one white and the other golden, drew closer till they swirled but yards apart. The West Seaxe king advanced toward Arwald, while Aelfhere shouted at the men around them to beware the sudden rush. Caedwalla, foremost, leaped at Arwald who sprang, trusting to his prodigious strength and aiming his battle-axe straight at the head of his West Seaxe foe. The full force of the vicious blow half-severed the parrying shield, cutting through the linden-wood, iron bands and studs. At the same moment, his adversary catching the islander off balance, cut through both the mail shirt and undershirt of leather deep into the flesh between the ribs over the heart of the impetuous enemy. Before Arwald recovered his footing from the overbalance of his violent attack, his assailant chopped again, this time at the bare arm of the Wihtwara, shearing the limb to the bone.

A mighty strike of his axe followed, cleaving through the helm and into the skull of the king of the isle, who sank to the ground, motionless.

The brutal exchange left the shield side of Caedwalla exposed so in the instant he delivered the mortal blow to Arwald, the sword of Aelfhere sliced into the muscle of his upper arm. In the frenzied swirl of battle, West Seaxe thegns crowded round to defend their lord, so to his dismay, circumstances forced the ealdorman far from his quarry. The sight of their fallen chieftain and the seizure and lowering of their banner began the rout of the islanders, who turned and fled downhill.

Mortified and swept along by the retreat, Aelfhere tried in vain to stem the tide of fleeing comrades. Ewald, his beard matted with gore, clutched at his arm, shouting, "Come, Lord, the day is lost. To the woods! To the boat!" Pulling the reluctant ealdorman, he cut across the line of flight, thrusting aside panicked warriors who threatened to knock them down in their blind rush. He led Aelfhere away from the mass of retreating men rushing for the nearest trees, as a result, ensuring no pursuit.

The victors, intent on destroying the bulk of the enemy host, plunged headlong after the bolting men, striking blows at undefended backs. Only the screams of the wounded followed the two islanders.

In spite of the lack of pursuers, they did not slacken their pace until, breathless, they reached the greenwood to the west of the battle ground. Chests heaving, they bent over, hands on knees, gasping air into starved lungs. Safe for the moment, along the trail to Odeton Creek, the ealdorman gave vent to his festering bitterness.

"By the one-armed god, my blade drew blood! And yet the cur-dog lives! What wyrd is this? Once more he evades my wrath!"

"This day is soured and curdled, Lord, but we survive to fight again." Ewald sought to raise their spirits. "The weather is set fair and our vessel will carry us to Andhun."

"Ay, the sun shines, but we stumble in the shadows while the West Seaxe wolves bask in its rays."

No question of leaving the isle with twilight upon them, they settled down for the night in the boat, secure of escape at first light: a fate not shared by many of their fellow islanders.

"What of Wulflaf?" the ealdorman wondered. "And what of the princes?"

"Hard to tell friend from foe in the fury of battle. The mooring is known to Wulflaf; if the gods will it, he may yet join us in the night. As to the princes…" He shrugged.

Raucous gulls and the piping calls of wading birds woke them at dawn. The faint hope of Wulflaf joining them died and with it came the realisation of the extent of the defeat. With heavy hearts, they rowed along the creek to the gentle swell of the open sea. The wind blew from the right quarter to carry them to the land of the Suth Seaxe. The sail stretched taut as Ewald belayed the ropes and Aelfhere called to him from the helm, "Wada tends to his sons! The god gifts us calm water and fair breeze."

The younger man joined his leader aft, who went on, "With the conditions, it might be wiser to set our course beyond Selsea, farther down the coast. The West Seaxe cur lodges Cynethryth in the abbey and will not leave her unguarded."

Agreed on this course of action, as they drew near the mainland, Aelfhere veered the boat to the east. Avoiding the white water of the chalk reefs, they sailed along the shoreline past rolling dunes and reed beds until they came to a suitable inlet seven leagues beyond Selsea. There, they ran the prow on a weed-strewn beach.

"Where now?" Ewald asked, scanning the barren surroundings dominated by the downs.

"Selsea lies to the west, of that we are sure. The sun is high but not overhead. We should keep it in our faces and head inland to higher ground. Remember the plan of the dux is to thrust toward Kingsham —"

"Too soon," his comrade cut in, "Eadric needs to gather men in Kent while Andhun does the same over the confines of his lands."

"Ay, they need to meet to push for the west, so we do the opposite and head north-eastwards."

Heartened by a clear purpose, they struck out in that direction through woodland until with the sun high overhead, they emerged from the trees to find the downs ahead. A strange long spur of land stood stark against the sky, drawing them as a lodestone to its brooding presence.

Halfway up the hillside, Ewald pointed to a group of ruined buildings, ancient in appearance. "Someone's up there. I swear I caught a flash of red."

"Let's find out!"

Circular walls intact to waist height and floors scattered with tumbled stones, roofless, the dilapidated huts bore silent testimony to the distant past.

Before they contemplated their surroundings, a dislodged stone alerted them.

Drawing his sword, Aelfhere rounded the side of the hut in time to glimpse a woman, long yellow hair and swirling scarlet skirt belted at the waist, crouch behind a wall. The ealdorman placed a finger to his lips and urged Ewald to circle in the opposite direction. For his part, he stepped into the open and advanced, enough to startle the woman into ineffective flight. Brandishing his seax, Ewald trapped her between the circular buildings where she sank on her haunches and awaited capture.

They both stared in astonishment and Aelfhere exclaimed, "It's a man!"

Putting up his weapon, he held out a hand to pull their quarry to his feet.

"What brings you to this sacred place?" The pagan priest folded his arms across his chest.

The warrior scrutinised his countenance, the pale skin smudged with lines drawn in charcoal across his cheeks.

"This," Aelfhere gestured to include the ruined huts, "is a sacred place?"

"This is Hearg Hill, where once rose the temple of Ingui, the King of the Elves. Come, see for yourselves."

Leading the islanders up the steep slope to the top where earthworks delineated an ancient square-shaped fort, he showed them the charred remains of wooden columns within its perimeter.

"Destroyed by the dux who abandoned the gods of his fathers! On his head snake venom drips deep in the land of slush and cold mud," the sorcerer hissed, evoking serpent bane with the sibilant sound.

"A dux?" Aelfhere anticipated the reply.

"Beorhthun!" he spat the name, "Cursed forever, he, who defiled the hallowed groves and temples, blinding the people with a cross and promises of eternal bliss. But the gods wreaked their wrath on the unbeliever, weakening his arm in battle!"

"Beorhthun!" The ealdorman frowned. "Ay, he became a Christian, it is true and died sword in hand. I fought beside him at Kingsham."

"Behold! Yonder mound," he pointed to a barrow raised on the hilltop, "there lies a chieftain who refuted the false beliefs and sacrificed his life. The dux slew him for resisting the cross. I brought his body to venerated ground that he might pass over with ease to the hall of Woden."

The long yellow locks trailed behind him on the windswept heights and the priest pointed a gruesome sceptre of bone and crow feathers at Aelfhere.

"You fought with him, but you are not dead! The gods spared you, why? Because you worship them as did our ancestors! Is it not so? They led you to me. Come!" He waved to the ealdorman and his comrade. "Sit! Here — facing north."

The sorcerer sat cross-legged and drew out a leather bag, which he turned over and over, his motion gentle.

"Speak, friend! What burdensome plight leads you to the priest of Ingui?"

"I seek revenge for betrayal," the ealdorman said through gritted teeth.

"Bear it in mind as you draw the runes. Mix them with your hands, now take one at a time, up to six. Lay the first." A finger rested on the ground.

From the bag, he pulled out a stone with a marking and, curious, studied it in his hand before placing it as directed. Five similar stones followed, laid out as instructed, Aelfhere noting the irony of the elongated cross formed by the six runes.

The eyes of the sorcerer glazed as he stared at the figure on the right, its bold white t sign inverted stark against the black stone.

"The past," he mumbled, "your past — defeat and death," he repeated the words twice more as if entranced, adding, "it's over!" A finger hovered above another symbol in the near centre of the layout, marked with n. "This represents the present," the priest explained, "what constrains you now." His features clouded and, rocking backwards and forwards, he moaned. Ewald looked at Aelfhere in alarm, but the ealdorman, with the slightest movement of his hand up and down, insisted on calmness. "A wolf! A wolf in the forest with a hawk on its head! The beast holds you amid the trees, you cannot pass!"

The young islander made to speak, but a choking rumble deep in the throat of the priest halted his words. "What lies ahead," said the sorcerer, his finger shifting to the leftmost rune bearing r on its shiny surface. "The way you follow takes you afar...," the blue eyes rolled, disappearing in white orbs, "...far over the seas, into the earth, down, down, down! To where the cross speaks in tongues."

Bewildered, the ealdorman frowned but he had no time to reflect as the sorcerer touched the nearest stone.

"Aaaaagh!" he howled and withdrew his hand as if scorched by the rune, uncovering o.

"What is it?" Aelfhere cried.

"Slaughter, desecration and ravaging! The land overrun by grey coats! Crosses springing up behind their paws!" The priest groped blindly for his feathered bone and with violence rammed it into the turf beside him in defiance. With a sigh of relief, he handed the far centre rune to the ealdorman, who, mystified, took it in his hand and studied the white v.

"The challenge. The wolf with the hawk on its head lies wounded, its strength waxes and wanes as the moon. Hunt the beast! Far and wide! At last, it fails and dies! Take its mate…"

Aelfhere sat upright. Dare he hope? Or was this another trick of the Lord of Mischief?

Again, the words of the sorcerer cut across his thoughts, "the outcome," he muttered, pointing at the farthest stone, marked x, "upside down, see! Be guided by the opposite — not revenge, not loathing — to overcome, *love* must guide you."

The shoulders of the priest sagged, the energy drained from his body.

* * *

Two leagues into their march away from the seer, following an ancient chalk ridgeway, Aelfhere broke his silence. Used to the thoughtfulness of his lord, Ewald had respected his need for reflection. In truth, the weird appearance and utterances of the sorcerer had awed him less than the unseen energy of the sacred site. Under the influence of the priest's words, he had half-expected the earth spirit to manifest itself in apparitions, spirits of the dead or the elves of Ingui. The stolid islander was happy to put distance between themselves and Hearg Hill.

"Not by chance, brother, did we meet the priest. The gods guided me to heed his words. What did you make of them, Ewald?"

"Not much. But the wolf with a hawk on its head is Caedwalla — the helm he bears is wrought with a falcon."

"Ay, the soothsayer spoke of the wound I meted him, saying the curdog weakens though the land be overrun by grey coats — the West Seaxe host. But he also speaks of talking crosses under the ground and my path leading over the seas…"

"Never much good at riddles," Ewald said.

Their exchanges brought them to a gap in the chalk hills where a settlement lay in the valley below.

"We should seek food and a place to sleep." Aelfhere pointed at the houses huddled by a river. On the far side of the sparkling silver band, the steep rise in the land led to the continuation of the ridgeway. "Were we able to *soar* up yon hill on wings it would be a great comfort to my *sore* legs!" The ealdorman lightened the mood. "But the day draws to a close. Come!"

A trail wound down the hillside and as they marched, he took up the skewed words of the sorcerer.

"The rune showed Caedwalla failing and dying, am I right?" He did not wait for a reply. "The priest bade me to take his mate —"

"Cynethryth!"

"Ay, and when I do I'll slay her!"

Ewald halted, staring at the back of the lord he served and loved as a father. Conscious of the lack of companion at his side, Aelfhere turned.

"What ails you?"

"Slay her? Your own daughter?"

"The viper betrayed the isle — us all. Father, relatives, friends—"

The ceorl drew three steps nearer. "Your own flesh and blood! Lord, back there, the wise man told you to set aside loathing —"

"Enough!" he spat. "Cynethryth..! I rue the day my seed bred her, but my blade will right that wrong. Come, night closes in!"

* * *

A warm welcome awaited them in the town named Laew, food and a bed, but not the news they sought of the whereabouts of Andhun and his men. At their query, their hosts told them the lack of men of fighting age in the settlement was owing to a plea from a messenger sent by the dux. His tidings of victory gained the keen response of the townsmen. Sons and husbands had taken the ridgeway to the north to drive the West Seaxe war-band from their lands. But as to where to find them, no-one knew, the ealdorman and his friend must follow the ridge to where it crossed another. Taking the left fork would set them on the heels of their menfolk.

A three-day march brought them to the Suth Seaxe encampment, where the swollen ranks heartened them in spite of their weariness. A force to be reckoned with stretched before them.

"These alone can drive the West Seaxe invaders beyond their confines and the Cantwara must yet join." Aelfhere raised a hand in the direction of the camp. "A good night's sleep, Eadric, and we'll be in fettle to lend our sinews to the cause. But the news from Wiht cannot wait, let's seek out Dux Andhun!"

* * *

"What tidings of Arwald?" the dux beamed at Aelfhere, but his smile of greeting faded, changing to a disdainful expression at the words of the islander. "An invasion? Defeat?"

"Caedwalla is wounded, I struck the blow myself. We would have fought to the end but wished to bear this precious information. The West Seaxe must still quell the isle so if we move at once, we can be ready to pen the returning foe on the shore. When his warriors wade through the waves they will be hit by a hail of steel —"

"We must wait for Ealric to unite his host to ours." The dux raised his chin.

"What? Loss of time means they will land and we must face them on the field of battle."

"Indeed, but with greater numbers —" his tone was resolute.

The ealdorman looked around at the unconvinced faces of the Suth Seaxe thegns and made one last attempt.

"Their numbers will be fewer after they drop in the sea —"

Andhun softened his voice. "Friend, your judgement is clouded by the hard days that tested your mettle. Rest, for tomorrow you will see the wisdom of our decision. The Cantwara are on the way and together we shall overwhelm Caedwalla."

Sullen, Aelfhere left the tent of the dux and trudged with Ewald to a campfire where the Suth Seaxe warriors welcomed them.

"With that decree," he said in a voice so low that Ewald was pressed to catch the words, "Andhun may hand the south to Caedwalla. Three times he bested us on the battlefield. What makes the dux believe the wolf will not succeed again?"

Chapter 15

Wulflaf

Wiht, July 687 AD

The barking and snarling of his two hounds in the mid-night woke Deorman. Raiders, he assumed or worse, warriors of Arwald, seeking able-bodied men throughout the land against the threat of invasion. Impossible! Not at night? A distinct but faint knocking, not a battering, came at the door. The unexpected and the unexplained left the woodsman motionless with fear. His hounds might not be adequate protection against armed intruders, so he thrust his seax into his belt, kicked the animals quiet and lingered at the door reluctant to open without identification of the prowlers. The dogs' menacing raised hackles and bared teeth confirmed a presence outside his dwelling. Again, someone knocked.

"W-who goes there? Who are you?' Deorman called, hesitancy in his voice betraying his apprehension. In the silence, he repeated "Speak! Who is it out there?"

No noise alerted him so he lifted the bar and inched the door open — wide enough to view the threshold, his body rigid to prevent any sudden attempt to enter. The pallid moonlight revealed no living soul, until lowering his gaze, he made out the gore-encrusted shape of a wounded warrior. Satisfied the crumpled heap did not pose a threat, he woke his wife to help him haul the hideous man inside.

"Bring fresh straw, woman, and be quick! Set a pot over the fire...we need hot water...the man is scarcely alive." His woman obeyed his orders without uttering a word, knowing her place when it concerned fighting men. Once the fellow lay unconscious on the improvised pallet, however, she assumed the role of nurse, removing his helm and ordering her husband to take off the mail shirt. With great care, she cut back the breeches to reveal the extent of the leg wound. Her eyes met those of her man, confirming the miracle that the stranger yet lived. He had suffered a deep cut to his shoulder, a gaping slash to his leg and lesions across his face. A mixture of congealed blood and mud from the battlefield sealed them, disguising his features.

Deorman sat at a wooden table scrutinising his wife clean away the filth obscuring the man's countenance with swatches of white linen torn from a threadbare under-garment. Satisfied, she poured vinegar into the wounds before, with great patience, using a needle and thread to sew up the gashes in his leg and shoulder.

"Will he live?"

"He is sore hurt and much blood lost but he looks like a strong brute...we'd best pray..." and she paused, "...to whichever god Arwald has chosen this time of year for—"

Before she ended her slur on his King, Deorman leapt from his bench to deliver a slap that sent her reeling.

"Do *not* mock our King! We have much to thank him for and you better remember it! He will protect us to the end." But his voice carried little conviction. "I fear there is war and we'll find out...if the strength of this wretch prevails."

Glowering, rubbing her reddened cheek and about to mutter an unwise retort, instead, distracted, the woman answered. "And so he will! See, he stirs!"

The warrior groaned, his eyelids flickered a moment before he blinked and surveyed his surroundings. The effort required to sit up exceeded his strength and he fell back again, his mumbling incoherent.

The woman raised his head, succeeding in forcing a little water between his lips, enough for him to mutter, "Where…where am I…it isn't…" But he lapsed into unconsciousness once more.

She studied the face, cleaned of the filth of battle, and exclaimed, "Deorman! Deorman! I know him…I've seen him at market with a woman. We engaged in idle talk while you settled on a price — the day you set up stall with the ox yokes you fashioned. Remember?"

"Ay, the face is familiar. Who is he? Speak!"

"He goes by Wulflaf, a ceorl of the ealdorman across the estuary at Cerdicsford and their homestead is north-east one day hence…the woman told me…sure, he is Wulflaf!"

"I know not what brings him here but he will have news of battle and of our king and thus of our future. Now get you off to bed. I'll lie down by the hearth in case he wakes." So saying, he unhooked his cloak from a nail to wrap around himself, heaved away a sullen hound and took its place by the smouldering embers."

Wulflaf revived the following morning, enough to offer thanks for his refuge and to sip warm milk and honey prepared by Myldryde. Deorman, by now impatient, sat on the straw beside the wounded Wihtwara and, in almost a whisper, said, "My wife tells me you are Wulflaf of Cerdicsford — is that so?"

"It is so…I am Wulflaf," he replied, though his head was heavy and his eyes strained to focus.

"What brings you here into the forest?"

"Flee!"

"Flee? What, now?" Deorman fair spat out the word, "Flee! What do you mean?"

"Broken the battle-hedge of shields…destroyed by darts…slain, fell to the ground…"

Again he slipped into oblivion.

The forester gaped at the warrior in disbelief and fear. He turned to his wife. "It *is* war!" He twisted back to the ceorl, gripping his shoulder and shaking him, "We *will* hear you! On the instant!"

Myldryde sprang to her feet. "Stay, Deorman, leave him be! Give him time! He scarce escaped his death day... give him time, I say...!" she implored.

When the warrior at last sat up, Deorman and his wife stared at him, agog, anticipating the intruder's account. After a while, head rolling from side to side and eyes glazed, he began in faltering tone, but talking in delirium as if in a different time, "Alhmund! Alhmund! See! He lies on the bloodied earth...no comrade to staunch his wounds...smitten...! His day of destiny...to doleful battle with brave heart...honed sword high..." he paused, gathering thoughts and spirit, "Bothelm! How goes the fight? We stand in gore among cadavers. Flinch not from the weapon-wrestle...!" Sweat beaded the fevered brow of the sick man and he moaned, "Ah, Bothelm with swords hewn...the black-mantled raven with hard beak of horn, wings to the slaughter-bed..."

The strain of reliving the catastrophic conflict overwhelmed Wulflaf for the moment and he swooned insensible once more.

"Can this be true?" Myldryde stared at her husband. "All lost to the invader?"

"Woman! Do not heed the ramblings of a fevered mind! He dreams! Arwald the bear-grappler will never surrender to the violators of our isle, never! I have better things to do than listen to his ravings." Deorman seized his cloak and slammed the door, determined to set about his work. His wife dabbed the face of the warrior with a damp clout before stepping outside to begin her daily chores by milking the goat.

In the afternoon, Wulflaf regained his awareness and as Myldryde was putting fresh dressings on his wounds, he mumbled, "Goodwife...what do...why...?"

"Hush now, you are with friends. Do you not recall telling us of the battle?"

His eyes shone with an unnatural brightness, "I remember nought...but I must away with my men to seize victory...Alhmund! Bothelm! Gather the others!"

Again, the fever in his mind overcame his brief respite and hallucinations prevailed, until he cried, "The ring-locked mail pierced...with spear stung...no longer to hold hard blade nor axe to wield..." He groaned and his eyes rolled back as Myldryde pulled the blanket over his senseless body.

After some time, her husband returned with a pheasant hanging limply at his belt. He set to plucking and gutting the bird before he passed it to her. "Take this, wife and do with it as you will."

She de-boned it and busied herself making a broth. A while later, she stroked the damp hair of the warrior. "Wulflaf! Pray, awaken! You must take nourishment to aid your recovery," she said, holding a cup to his lips.

"I thank you, goodwife. You and your husband have saved my body if not my spirit. On the morrow, I must away. My relatives are in sore need of protection."

Deorman, hearing the man's intentions, gave a bitter laugh. "You are in no condition to protect anyone. It is here you stay until your strength returns!"

Myldryde hushed the warrior's protests and ensured, sip by sip, that he drained the cup of broth. The beads of sweat on his brow and the flush to his face indicated the fever burning within and the words of the warrior began to ramble once more, "...the King is severed from his kin...the blade run through his soul-house...the golden dragon sweeps all before...flee...and fleeing felled from behind...into the woods...the fastness of the forest..."

Aghast, Myldryde mopped the forehead of the wounded man. "Husband, can it be true, is Arwald slain?"

"Never!" the forester cried, "these are but the babblings of sickness! Eventide is upon us and as you well know, fever worsens at day's end. In the morn, away to the village. Seek feverfew from the crone, Seledryth, she's sure to have herbs for balm to tend his wounds. Wife, let's be off to bed, for there's another man in need of tender care!"

In the morning, they found the warrior awake but restless and feeble. When they emerged from behind the awning, he used all his strength to greet them once more with the word, "Flee!" before closing his eyes to breathe in shallow gasps.

"The fever ravages him, wife. Break your fast and then off with you to rouse Seledryth from her idle slumber!"

Myldryde again mixed milk and honey, carrying it over to the wounded man. With unsuspected strength, the warrior gripped her wrist. "Arwald is slain," he hissed, "flee! Caedwalla spares no-one." He shook her arm, his urgency causing liquid to slop on the bedcover, before he slumped back, fatigued by the effort.

The woman shot an appealing glance at her husband.

"Heed him not, for he knows not what he says," Deorman said, "Make haste, he is in need of feverfew."

"B-but he spoke clear enough —"

"Less of your prattle, wife! Feed him the milk then be on your way!"

Deorman slammed the door behind him and began sawing at a tree trunk, hauled back the day before, destined to a new sty.

"Good woman, heed me well," her patient said when he finished his drink, his speech lucid. "Make haste, find the words to make your man leave. It is not safe here!" He breathed hard, gathering his strength, and again the fierce grip made her wince, "Head for the marsh and thence the coast. Warn the folk at Cerdicsford to depart the isle," he moaned and released his hold. While she rubbed her wrist, he sagged back and in a feeble voice, added, "they have boats to carry you over to the land of the Suth Seaxe. Go, abandon me!" He closed his eyes and murmured, "Tiw help me! I am as weak as a babe."

Wrapping a shawl around her shoulders, Myldryde took a wicker basket and, determined to speak to her husband, approached him at his saw horse.

"Still here, woman?" he said, ceasing his toil and wiping his brow with his forearm, "what is it?"

His wife pointed back at the house, "Wulflaf, he told me we must leave him and hasten to the marsh thence to Cerdicsford. We ought to depart the isle, he says —"

Deorman took a menacing step forward. "Are you mad? Leave our home and all we have, on the word of a fever-wracked coward!"

"Coward, Wulflaf?" Her mouth dropped open.

"Ay, you heard him, didn't you? He fled the battlefield, leaving our King alone to sweep the invaders into the sea."

"Deorman! How can you know King Arwald won the day? Wulflaf says he's slain!"

The forester raised his fist and his wife, fearing his temper, hurried away.

"Ay, he would, the craven!" he taunted her, "Now get those herbs afore you feel the flat of my hand."

Resentful, fearful and anxious, she set off into the forest along a trail through elder shrubs and sycamore. The dew of the early summer morning lent a fresh sheen to the foliage and made the air heavy, resonant with the insistent hammering of a woodpecker. A red squirrel shot up a trunk and peered down at her with beaded eye. Myldryde began to calm and enjoy her walk until, of a sudden, a cricket flew into her hair. With a cry, she brushed it away and it clattered off into the shrubbery. Overcome with dark foreboding, she stood still for a moment. Of what did the conehead wish to warn her? Sorcerers kept them in miniscule cages to hear their advice yet heedless, she had swept the insect away. She scolded herself for her foolish anxiety that, her good sense insisted, was born not of a harmless winged creature but of the gruesome wounds she had tended. Still, the flittering blue butterflies and the lush green moss shining in the sunlight failed to restore her calmness.

Near the village, where the undergrowth became criss-crossed by the distinctive paths of badgers, Myldryde froze. The alarm call of a redstart, an abrupt silence following distinct crashing in the scrub, and she gasped, putting a hand over her mouth. Hearing strained, she caught a sniffing or rather, a snivelling: the unmistakeable whimper of a child.

Locating the lament, she pushed through the hazel scrub to find the cowering form of a young girl, each grimy cheek whitened by a runnel of tears. "Come my sweet, you can't stay here! You can't wander off into the forest. You don't want wolves to find you, do you? They gobble up little ones, like you..." she stretched out her hand but to her surprise, the girl cringed deeper into the leaves.

Myldryde squatted down, face level with the infant, "Where is your mother? What is your name?"

In stubborn silence, the girl curled like a hedgehog in defence. The woman reached for her but found her rigid and unyielding. Trying to be as gentle as possible, she hauled the youngster out of the shrubbery to the woodland track.

The sunlight that did not penetrate the bushes lit up the features of the waif. "You're Nerienda's child, aren't you?" Myldryde asked in a gentle voice. "Did she chide you? Is that it? Well, now she'll be worried, beside herself to know where you are!" She tugged at the tiny hand but the child dug in her heels, shook her head and burst into tears.

The woman set down her basket and gathered the infant into her arms. How she weighed for such a slight creature! Then again, she must have seen five summers. The girl snuggled into her breast and Myldryde marvelled at the pounding of the little one's heart. The chit was terrified. With difficulty, the woman bent at the knees to retrieve her basket and with determined step set off for the village. Still the child said not a word, but her tears soaked into the woman's dress as she nuzzled closer.

Where the trail opened out into fields stretching before the village, the woman slowed to a halt. Something was wrong. No movement captured her attention and an eerie silence hung over the settlement. No beat of the smith's hammer, no voices, no crying babes. Where was the sense in it? Had they fled as Wulflaf had urged her and her man to do? Had the child's family lost her in the confusion? She walked along the banked ditch of the wheat field, the swaying green ears beginning to turn to gold and from a distance studied the nearest house. Like all the others no smoke rose from the roof and no sound of animal, not even a dog's bark disturbed the stillness. One detail caught her notice and she lowered the girl to the ground for she must take her no farther if what she suspected was right.

"Stay here, sweetness, look after my basket while I go see what your mother's doing."

The child's eyes filled with tears and she clung to the wickerwork as though it were a shield.

Drawing near to the dwelling, Myldryde's suspicion proved well founded. What she had glimpsed from afar was indeed a booted foot protruding beyond the threshold. Pushing the door back, she screamed when two huge black birds winged cawing past her face. Dozy, heavy blow flies rose and settled again. The stench of death assailed her and she covered her mouth and nose with her shawl. Blood lay sticky in pools next to three corpses, the third that of a child. Sickened, she staggered into the clean air and forced one foot ahead of the other to take her towards the next homes set farther back from the fields. No need to enter these houses since bodies lay outdoors, strewn in unnatural positions with gaping wounds, gore-matted hair and the white of exposed bone. Scavenging raptors screeched at her approach, ravens cawed and flapped, rats scurried and Myldryde collapsed on her hands and knees, her gorge heaving. The sight of a headless body destroyed the last of her resistance. Women and children had met the fate of the menfolk or worse, judging by the clothing ripped from the indecent bodies. Her back heaved in soundless sobs and her first tears splashed to the ground. With an effort, she stood. Think of the child and get back to warn Deorman, she told herself. There was no point in enduring anguish at the sight of further atrocities deeper in the village. No-one had been spared, Wulflaf spoke true about the West Seaxe. Thoughts of feverfew distant from her mind, the woman hoisted her dress above her knees and ran back to Nerienda's daughter. By what miracle had she been saved? Poor mite! She must have hidden in some cranny to evade the reavers before emerging to witness the horror inflicted on her village. No wonder she refused to speak. "I must not show her my distress," she muttered aloud and hastened back to the field where the child, still clinging to the basket, had not moved.

She offered her hand, "Come, we'll go to my home where you will be safe. Are you hungry?"

At last, she gained the reaction of wide open eyes and a nod of the head. The girl made no effort to give back the basket, too big for her arm, but placing a hand in the woman's, she let herself be led along the woodland trail.

The sound of sawing from their clearing carried to Myldryde at the end of the track. A warm feeling of affection suffused her, Deorman, so strong of arm, was a hard-working man, hasty-tempered but on the whole a loving husband. Coming out from the trees, she determined to make him understand, but for the moment he had his back to them, concentrating on his cutting. So much the better, she took advantage of this to care for the child, leading her over to the goat, exchanging the basket for a milk pail. The little one must not hear the words she would speak to her man.

"You know how to milk, don't you?"

Keen, the girl nodded.

"Rub your hands to warm them first, that's right!"

Myldryde hurried over to her husband who slowed his sawing at her footfall, before halting.

He straightened but at his wife's expression he stifled his words before her pale, taut distressed face.

"Slaughtered!" she said, "the whole village, babes and all." He stared beyond her at the child milking the nanny goat and she explained, "Nerienda's youngest — she hid from them. I found her in the forest..."

Tense, Deorman set his saw down. "It's true then, Arwald is dead!" He stood for a moment, crestfallen, unsure of what to do, then said, "Come, gather a bundle of clothes. Not many, we ought to travel light! We'll take the goat."

The child walked towards them with studied step, carrying the pail, holding the handle in front of her with both hands, careful not to spill the milk. Myldryde took it, leading her into the house where she poured a cup of the warm liquid and gave it with an oatcake to her famished helper.

Groaning, Wulflaf pulled himself into a sitting position but Deorman interrupted as the lips pursed to pronounce *'flee'*.

"Ay, we must flee and we're taking you with us, so get up and I'll help you into yon metal-ringed shirt."

The warrior shook his head, "Leave without me. Go! I'll slow you down."

"I know the forest like my own hand," Deorman said, "there are places the West Seaxe can never find."

Wulflaf, in pain, swung his legs clear of the pallet and rose unsteadily to his feet. He reached for his tunic, "Help me with this, but no mail shirt — too weak to bear it." Deorman slipped the clothing up the limp arm and over the warrior's head. Wulflaf had no trouble putting his other arm through and drawing the cloth below his waist. The freshly stitched wound showed raw and speckled with blood through the hole in his breeches, indicating they would make slow progress. Determined not to forsake the ceorl, the forester fastened his belt for him and struggled to force the man's feet into his boots, "Here! Myldryde, lend a hand! Fasten the thongs, will you?"

She knelt to do his bidding while all the time the village girl looked on wide-eyed, nibbling like a timid mouse at her cake.

At last, they were ready to leave. The woman seized her bundle and took the hand of the girl, Wulflaf grasped his sword and Deorman took the warrior's weight to steer him towards the door. "We'll have to leave the goat," he said with a sigh.

"Not so," Myldryde said, "the girl can cling on to my dress, I can manage the animal and the pack." And she began to untether the creature from its post.

As she did so, a band of mail-shirted men burst out of the woodland. Myldryde screamed, her first thought for the girl who she dragged over to her husband. Letting go of Wulflaf, he gathered his wife and the child to him.

A west country voice rang out loud with relish, "We stumbled on a fair prize! A fine ewe for the tupping!"

Deorman shielded his wife but even as he did so a spear thudded into him and he fell in agony to the ground. Myldryde wailed and tore at her hair. The onrushing West Seaxe warriors, intent on seizing and defiling the woman, had ignored the smitten Wihtwara, seeing him as no threat. A violent upward slash of the wounded man's sword and the woman's neck gushed blood, the light of life in her eyes fading to nought as she buckled to the ground. That he had saved her from pain, shame, humiliation and a lingering death was Wulflaf's last thought as the impact of three spears took him off his feet and sent him to Waelheal.

The small child, still clinging to her oatcake and unnoticed at first, scampered towards the house but a javelin transfixed her. The spearhead buried into the wooden wall of the building and pinned the pathetic body like a grotesque ward among the other fetishes by the doorpost. Charms effective against evil spirits maybe — but of no avail against earthbound fiends.

Chapter 16

Caedwalla

Day speared by night bled crimson across the sky: the heavens mirroring blood seeping into the earth below. Fury of bloodletting sated, Caedwalla leant on his axe and surveyed the carnage. His chest heaved and his upper arm throbbed where a blade had sliced into his muscle — a small price to pay for such a victory, he supposed. His eye swept over the heaped corpses seeking the bodies of Arwald's younger brothers and one particular Wihtwara. No sign of them, so he stared down the slope to the fringe of trees and observed his men returning towards the fluttering golden dragon lording the hilltop. The decision of his ealdormen not to pursue the defeated islanders into the forest, he considered wise. Elated, the king brandished his battle-axe in a guttural howl of triumph and summoned his thegns.

"Brothers, this day we regained the isle and righted the wrong inflicted on Cenwalh by the Mercian dog, Wulfhere, when I wauled, a babe in arms. Men will sing of this day when we are long gone." A mighty cheer hailed his words. "Yonder stands the stronghold of Wihtgarabyrig. On the morrow, we take it and slay those who dared oppose us. Spare no-one, nor woman nor child. Take what possessions

you find," he called out to the accompaniment of a deep growl of satisfaction, "but do not burn the houses. They will serve for our folk when
we settle this fertile land." The King paused and searched the expectant
faces until he found Guthred. "Ealdorman," he commanded, "gather
your men! At dawn, divide them into bands to seek out and slay those
who fled the field of battle…" again he halted, "…and every other
dweller of the isle you chance upon. Do not venture beyond the creek
to the west but scour the rest of the island. Remember, the woodland,
marsh and heath are enemies more fearsome than any man. Be wary!"

The West Seaxe chose to burn their dead, leaving Wihtwara corpses
as carrion. At nightfall, the victors encamped at the bottom of the steep
embankment encircling Wihtgarabyrig.

At dawn, after little rest, Caedwalla inspected his wound. Removal
of the blood-stained cloth revealed why the throbbing worsened: red
streaks radiated from the swollen suppurating cut.

"It is infected, Lord…" said Guthred, who had slept on the ground
beside his king, "…a tainted blade. Fetch water," he ordered.

They swilled the gash and bound it. "It needs the fermented juice
of apple to clean the poison —"

"We'll find it in the stronghold. What say you, Guthred, breach by
burrowing or by fire?"

"The palisade is of oak and will resist flame the day long…"

"Well then, like moles —"

"Unless —"

"Unless?"

"Unless you call on them to open the gate in exchange for their
lives…"

Caedwalla snorted and folded his arms. "My orders are to spare no-
one. Would you have me fickle as a maid? Away! Rake through the
land," he placed a hand on the ealdorman's shoulder, "cut out the blight
that the plant may grow in vigour and in health. Find Arwald's brothers and destroy them. Return in ten days and you will find us seated
in his hall."

The morning witnessed the mining operations interrupted by an anvil launched from above. To the glee of two greybeards peering over the palisade, it crushed the head of one of the diggers. This proved to be the only serious damage the defenders inflicted on those below. The burrowing prowess of the West Seaxe attackers dismayed the besieged Wihtwara and long before the danger of the oak piles toppling, the gate opened.

Caedwalla, weapon in hand, led his men through the entry and without hesitation or mercy swung it at the defender foolish enough to unbar the barrier. The kneeling posture of the man, head bowed, served to expedite the beheading. The victim's furious hound launched itself teeth bared at the chieftain and to the taunts of the assailants, met the same fate.

At this, the few misguided inhabitants, gathered in hope of surrender near the way into the town, fled in terror but spears pierced their backs, cutting short their flight. Inexorable, the West Seaxe warriors moved from house to house slaughtering men too aged, and youths and boys too young, to fight in the battle. They murdered infants and babes, raped women and girls before plundering the few objects of value to be found.

Caedwalla, impassive, spurned the massacre, deeming such feeble resistance beneath his dignity. Rather, his concern dwelt on the pounding in his shoulder. Making for the lair of Arwald in the centre of the settlement and intent on seeking an acidic rinse for his wound, he found three armed greybeards barring entry. Two of them had the bearing of one-time warriors prepared to fight to the death. Too experienced to underestimate a man on account of his years, Caedwalla set his guard.

"By Tiw!" he cried, "never too old to lose hope of embracing the wælcyrie —"

But they charged as one to cut short the mockery of one with his shield arm hanging useless by his side. A weaker man could not have wielded a weighty two-handed weapon in one hand but Caedwalla made light of his handicap. The ferocious arc of his battle-axe held them at bay but the least warrior-like of the three, reckless, rushed in to deliver a blow to the chieftain's unprotected flank. A simple spin proved sufficient for such an untrained adversary. The honed steel of the axe-head clove into his arm, the might of the strike severing the limb above the elbow. Nimble on his feet, Caedwalla sprang aside to avoid a lunging blade, burying his axe into the spine of his off-balance opponent. With no time to free the weapon from the body, in the face of the oncoming Wihtwara, he spun away from the sharp edge aimed at his neck. In an instant, he seized his attacker by the wrist and used all his might to dislocate the shoulder joint of the weaker man. With a vicious butt of his helm to the face, he watched the greybeard crumple senseless to the ground. Full of respect for a valiant foe but devoid of mercy, he picked up the sword, running it through the man's heart. For a fleeting moment, he wondered whether he had dispatched his victim's soul to Woden's Hall or to the Heaven of the new God. However, the pressing matter of his wound did not induce reflection, urging him instead into the building.

In Arwald's chamber, his by conquest now, he found an earthenware flagon of wine.

"Ah, this is better than sour apple juice," he said aloud, "and it serves a dual purpose!" He raised the vessel as he searched for a clean cloth to use as a bandage. Wiping his mouth with his sleeve, he murmured, "Fear not, friend Arwald, your kingdom and all its bounties are in good hands! But the fairest of your gifts awaits me across the sea — ah, that bites!" He winced as the red liquid coursed out of the gash and down his arm. Binding it, knotting it with his teeth, he thought no more of the cut but drank another beaker of wine before lying on Arwald's bed and falling into battle-weary sleep.

A messenger hesitated to disturb him — the wound did not. In his slumbering, he rolled on his side and the sharp pain woke him. Cursing, he shook his head and lurched to his feet intent on finding water to splash on his face. In the hall, the waiting ceorl rose from a bench saying, "Lord, five ships sailed from the isle —"

"When?"

"About the time we entered the town."

"Fetch Ealdorman Hwitred at once. Ah, and find a smith. Tell him to bring a hammer and chisel."

Caedwalla rinsed the fatigue from his face and pondered. Five vessels meant at most two hundred Wihtwara had fled the isle. What chance Arwald's brothers lurked among them? Or, Guthred's men might have hunted them down. A discreet cough interrupted his thoughts.

"Lord, you sent for me?"

"Friend Hwitred, once more, I need your seafaring skills. Gather a crew and hasten to Selsea to alert Bealdred at Kingsham — that the Wihtwara have landed thereabouts. Should the whelps from Arwald's litter have reached the Suth Seaxe lands seek them out. They must not escape!" The King locked eyes with his ealdorman. "Capture them, ealdorman, you will find me a grateful lord."

The warrior was about to bow out but Caedwalla held up a hand when a burly figure wearing a leather apron appeared, hesitating in the doorway.

"Come!" Caedwalla ushered in the smith, "I have need of your deftness." He addressed the ealdorman, "Wait here! If it pleases the gods, I will have a further task for you."

The King led the smith behind a heavy curtain and into the bedroom where a wood-planked strongbox banded with iron stood beside the bedhead.

"We do not have the key. Set about it!"

The smith held up a lump hammer and the tempered chisel, "It will take a while but these'll persuade it, Lord."

After constant striking on the same spot, the band ceded, then repeating the operation on the other side, the smith at last forced the box open. Caedwalla, strewing coins and jewellery on the bed, picked up five silver pieces and passed them to the smith.

"For your efforts," he said, "and to repair the strongbox. Put in a new lock and make two keys."

Delighted with his reward, the craftsman bowed his way out while his king turned his attention to the jewels. He hesitated, he was tempted to choose a gold and amber girdle hanger for Cynethryth but opted for a gold necklace with alternate garnet and rock crystal pendant beads.

"Why keep such workmanship in a wooden box!" he murmured, exchanging his own ring for a heavier and better-crafted one.

Thrusting his way past the dusty drape and into the hall, he handed the discarded ring to Hwitred "A gift in friendship, and take these coins. Use them to loosen tongues — a man will sell his brother for less. Find the brood of vipers!"

The ealdorman slipped the gold band on his finger and admired it. "It shall be done, Lord!"

"Take this necklace to my wife. Tell her to wear it against my return."

His patient wait over, the warrior hurried off to assemble a crew.

During the following days, Caedwalla settled the hidage of the isle among his landless thegns. But the stubborn wound did not heal and towards the end of the week, he began to complain of aches and pains in his back, arms and legs. A febrile state confined him to his bed for fourteen days and nights. Guthred, his murderous assignment at an end, waited with growing concern and impatience for his lord to recover.

On the twelfth day of his illness, Caedwalla swept the drape aside, entering the hall pale but free of fever.

"Lord, it is good to see you on your feet!" Guthred greeted him.

The warlord touched his arm. "This wound, with its foul bane, will not let me be."

Guthred weighed his words. "We should leave for Selsea, my King, among the monks is one skilled in healing —"

The deep laugh of Caedwalla boomed around the rafters. "Ay, and one skilled in loving!"

Guthred smiled. "We both have one such awaiting us!"

With the weather set fair, they agreed on departure the following morning and by mid-afternoon of the next day Caedwalla sat bare-chested in the infirmary of Selsea Abbey.

The grey tonsured head of the infirmarian bent over a bowl suspended above a candle where the monk heated and stirred a salve for the third time. Beside the wooden tripod lay a discarded eggshell, used to measure the quantity of honey in the mixture, and a dish of clean butter. The brother's prayer ended, an orison to render the unguent efficacious followed, but the eyes of the King narrowed at the words of the infirmarian addressed to his listless young assistant.

"There can be little doubt. It is a case of the flying venom and as a rule I'd balance the humours by bleeding. Now, Brother, tell me why do I not follow my instincts!"

The apprentice flushed, looking uncomfortable, he muttered an incoherent reply.

A testiness came into the monk's voice. "For Heaven's sake, have you learnt nothing? Look out of the window!"

Hastening to stare outside, the youth said, "I see Brother Medwin tending the herb garden."

"And what pray have in common Brother Medwin and bleeding a patient?"

A shrug of the shoulders from the sullen pupil and, exasperated, the monk lost his temper.

"St Telemachus grant me patience! May he, the patron of idiots, aid your learning. See, the day is hot! We do not let blood in the heat: it worsens the infection."

His tone became gentler as he turned to the king. "The youth serves when he need not use his own mind. He carries out my instructions to the letter," he allowed himself a thin smile, "from the stream, he fetched fresh roots of water dock — those that float. From the herb garden he gathered a handful of maythe, one of waybroad and one of hammerwort. He took them to the altar where the brothers sang mass over the worts before I wrought up the salve —"

Little interested in the method, more in the ailment, Caedwalla interrupted. "Let be the simpleton! This flying venom that you talk of…?"

"Ay, Lord it entered the wound from the air and thence the blood. The salve of worts I melted thrice and prayed over the flame."

"Not a tainted blade, then?"

The monk scratched the nape of his neck. "The flying venom and a tainted blade might well have similar effects —"

"Will this balm heal me?"

"The maythe reduces the swelling and pain; the waybroad fights back the inflammation and the hammerwort brings fresh blood to the area of the wound. The whole soothes and mends. Now, it is time to clean and treat the seat of the infection. But in the end, it is God's will and we can only pray for His aid…"

The gash bound, the chieftain returned to his wife and found her sewing with Rowena. She looked up and the love and concern on her face warmed his heart. The necklace he sent with Hwitred sparkled at her chest and increased his pleasure.

"Husband, did the infirmarian cure you?"

He placed his hand over the binding and flexed his arm, "It is but a stubborn scratch, but the brother says if God so chooses, it will heal."

"Then I must add my prayers —"

Caedwalla interrupted, "Where is Guthred? I'd speak with him."

He glanced from one woman to the other.

Rowena said, "He's away to the smithy, Lord, to have the edge of his battle-axe ground fine."

"I will join him there with matters of my own to attend to."

The two women watched the sturdy figure leave the room, and Cynethryth whispered to her friend, "Happiness will elude me until the south is in peace, settled and under his sway."

The leader of the West Seaxe had this same thought on his mind when he coaxed his ealdorman away from the forge and his precious axe.

"Remember, Guthred, when we defeated Aethelwalh at Kingsham and sought the corpse of my wife's father among the bodies?"

"Ay, Lord."

"And we found it not."

"We did not."

"How were we to recognise the body?"

"By the sword and helm bearing the image of a wolf."

Caedwalla raised his injured arm, grimacing in discomfort.

"He who struck this blow wore a helm with the image of a wolf around the brim. I cannot speak for the sword, so keen of bite. I saw it not in the swirl of battle."

"You suppose your wifefather fought under the helm?"

"Ay, the islander fought beside Arwald. Hark, brother, I thought long on it. For love of my wife, I cannot hunt the cur and slay him, but you have no such bonds..."

"Lord, I will find him and end his wretched life."

A grim smile greeted these words, "I expected no less, friend. Now, ask yourself, why a man famed for his bravery would flee from the battle? Not once, but twice."

Guthred frowned, "There is no sense in it, for as a man boasts and sings of his deeds so does he enhance his fame with a proper death."

Caedwalla spat as if to remove a bad taste from his mouth.

"Like a lone wolf, he roams. He craves to unite the Suth Seaxe to Wiht and Kent."

"All the more reason to slay him."

The chieftain pulled his friend into an embrace and spoke close, "I consented to spare Cerdicsford and the holdings around the settlement. Since your wife and mine are as close as sisters, I name you Lord of the land from the ocean to the great estuary —"

A cry cut across his words. "Over there...!"

The King released Guthred and spun round. A small band of men led by Hwitred hauled two captives, young men of noble bearing, on ropes tied at the wrists. Struggling to keep pace with them hobbled a ragged figure with long white hair and straggling beard contrasting with the fine array of Bishop Wilfrith.

The King turned to his ealdorman, "To the smithy, fetch your axe! I'll test its keenness on their necks." He strode to meet the oncoming group, pointing at the bound men, one a strapping man of eighteen and the other younger, darker and of slighter build. "On your knees!" Caedwalla roared.

Wilfrith stepped forward, his familiar haughty expression directed at the Lord of the West Seaxe. "What is your intention?"

"I mean to take off their heads," Caedwalla said, "as soon as Guthred comes with his axe."

The bishop pursed his lips. "See, here is a holy man, Cynebert, a saint on Earth," he stretched a hand towards the fellow in tatters, "a hermit. They sought refuge in his cell near the Ford of Reeds not far from the Great Ytene Forest but your men found them. In his distress at the seizure of the princes he attached himself to the captives as a limpet to a rock —"

"Cross-bearer, let me remind you who drove me to invade the isle. Alive, they are a threat to *our* plans."

The prelate took a step forward, a frown creasing his deep-lined face.

"It is so. I do not say to spare them, but since you have God's favour and sustainment, as we see from your supremacy on the field of battle, do not send them to Hell. If they die as pagans, you must answer for their eternal souls to the Lord."

"What? I killed hundreds of pagans on the battlefield of Wiht!"

Unflappable, Wilfrith replied, "Ah, *that* is different. Your noble purpose was to bring the Word to the isle and rid it of the heathen. A high moral stance indeed! Showing restraint now will gain you favour with the Father."

The King looked in confusion at Guthred who had arrived with his battle-axe and in spite of the words of the venerable priest, took the weapon.

"Stay, hear me out!" the bishop implored. "Of course they must die! But concede me six months to lead them to Christ. This holy man agreed to instruct them."

The rotten-toothed ascetic nodded his head with vigour to show his accord.

"They're all mad!" Caedwalla said to Guthred out of the corner of his mouth. "They die!" he said to Wilfrith and, smug, watched consternation appear on the prelate's face, "in four moons, not a day longer and the first moon is three days hence," he added with relish. "Hwitred, make sure they finish in a cell fit for the purpose and when you are done, come to my quarters."

The ancient recluse followed the captors and, the King, handing the battle-axe to its owner, remained facing the bishop.

"My son, you grow daily in wisdom. We must begin to think of your induction into the Faith. Think on this, the Lord God favours one who is not His own. What blessings must accrue when you learn to worship Him!"

Wilfrith did not wait for an answer, but walking away called, "Come to me when the spirit moves you!"

Caedwalla turned to his ealdorman, "Friend, the cross-bearer does not admit of strength in battle. Our success, he believes is the will of his God. Yet, to the priest I must go in the end, for once we have secured the south my kingship must be as blessed as those of other kings. Hence the immersion needs be held before a crowd —"

A rider, interrupting these considerations, galloped into the abbey courtyard, stirring the dust of the dry ground. He leapt off his horse and bowed before his king.

"Lord, I am sent by Bealdred. Word reached him the Kentings led by Eadric march forth. They follow the Medweg to gather men at Tunbrycg, they learned you — *er* —"

"Speak, man!"

The messenger lowered his head, his tone apologetic.

"Forgive me, Lord, they learnt the Wihtwara wounded you and say you are laid low. They believe it is propitious to strike."

The King laughed, contempt in his voice, "They do? They share my own thought on the matter, friend. See first to your horse, when you are rested hie you to Bealdred. Bear the message that Caedwalla is well and follows you forthwith. He is to send a messenger to Cenred in Witan-caestre to raise and dispatch men to Kingsham by the waning crescent to crush the Kentings once and for all. Tell him to work the smiths for javelin points, spearheads and throwing axes."

The rider repeated the three items of the message before leading his horse away.

Two days later, Caedwalla stood in the hall at Kingsham, pleased at the activity in the two smithies and more so at the progress of his wound. The infirmarian at Selsea had given him an unguent before he left. Now as he bound a cloth over it, he murmured to himself, "These men of God have many skills, so I hope their Almighty, as they name him, will smile on us when we meet the foe."

Not that he indulged in prayer, his murmurings directed at the deity were more the passing on of a thought: the destruction of the Cant-wara would speed Wilfrith's plans to unite the south in one large dio-cese. The arrival of Cenred's men to swell their numbers some time later heightened his mood as he led his host across the border into the land of Kent.

In the same spirit, a week on, he surveyed the foe ranked below them, seeking in vain near the enemy banner for a helm with a running wolf. To Guthred, he said, "Do you see the Wihtwara? I do not."

The ealdorman narrowed his eyes, "Nor I, Lord."

The West Seaxe host advanced to fierce battle, weapons raised, shields to defence, and stepped towards the swirling banner boasting its rearing white horse. Resolute they drew closer, from ealdorman to the lowest ceorl, intent on harm for the enemy. The slope in their favour, javelins, throwing axes and rocks descended on the enemy like a swarm of angry hornets.

In the clash of shield-walls, a spear cut through the linked rings of Guthred's shirt; he thrust with his shield so the spear shaft broke and the spear-head freed as it sprang back. Enraged, Caedwalla, next to him, swung his battle-axe at the warrior, a Briton clad in West Seaxe mail, who had delivered the blow, ending his life on the instant. At the same moment, he glimpsed the impressive figure of his rival, Eadric. The formidable young king hewed linden shields, hacked helms and slashed exposed limbs.

Caedwalla roared, more in frustration than in aggression, with Guthred tottering beside him.

How can I leave your side, friend, when you need me most?

He fended another blow aimed at his ealdorman and glanced towards the red emblem.

It is farther away, my men are gaining on the Cantwara!

The battle raged, valiant foes the men of Kent and their Suth Seaxe comrades, but the greater numbers of Caedwalla told. At last, the clash of metal, cries and screams ending — the West Seaxe howled in triumph.

The King leant on his battle-axe next to his fallen friend. Guthred breathed and sure that he would not die, he turned his attention to more pressing matters.

"Cenred, Bealdred, Hwitred…!" he bellowed summoning the under-kings and the ealdorman. "Over here!"

Three figures, begrimed enough to scare Hel herself, emerged from the milling ranks picking over the corpses. They grinned at their King and at each other, knowing the south of the land to be in their hands and Kent lying open to plunder.

"What news of Eadric?" Caedwalla asked.

Bealdred of Sumerseate spoke. "He fought like a demon but, thank the Creator for this day's work, when the might of our blows brought us close, his ealdormen and thegns gathered round —"

"Did you see one with a golden wolf on his helm?" Caedwalla cut in, his voice was as keen as a blade.

Confusion on the face of the underking provided answer. He shook his head and went on, "…they cried to him to flee, but the worthy warrior, stern and determined, refused."

"Then Eadric lies with his accursed banner in the mire!"

"Nay, Lord," Hwitred cut in. "Twenty men dragged him against his will. He spat and cursed like a lynx from yon forest," he pointed down-hill, "where they hustled him away in all haste."

"He shall not elude us! It must not be!" Caedwalla roared. "Hwitred, stay with Guthred who lies sore wounded. I'll take two score men into the woodland, have them gather three javelins each, we'll hunt the cur until he lies bloodied on the ground!"

"I am with you, Lord," Cenred exclaimed.

"I too!" Bealdred added.

It was no hard task to follow the trail of fleeing men through the forest, their way betrayed by the scuffed leaves, tracks in the mud, broken twigs or bark rubbed off a fallen log by boots. The pursuit took them to a stream running down to a narrow steep-sided gorge.

"Lord, we cannot go forward," Cenred said.

"Here, see, the stones are scraped back and others pressed into the mud," one warrior cried, "they headed uphill along the edge of the defile."

"Likely they seek a place to cross," Caedwalla muttered. "This way!"

Soon, ahead of the others, Bealdred raised a hand.

"Someone stepped on a chunk of rock and mud here," he jabbed a finger, "it broke beneath his feet and separated from the soil then it pitched the cur into the gorge! There are marks on the bank where he fell." He pointed eight yards below. "Look! The bushes broke his fall, see how they bend into the stream bed."

"And here," said Cenred, "is where he struggled back up. Beware! The signs are fresh!"

No sooner had the words left his lips than the enemy rose out of the land above them, shields presented and battle-axes or swords bran-dished — no more running.

A growl of satisfaction rumbled in the throat of Caedwalla. "We have him!" He sensed the defiance beneath the wrought faceplate of the helm — Eadric of Kent!

The King of the West Seaxe pushed past Bealdred, unslung his axe and shouted orders to his men. "Advance up to ten paces and release all three javelins!" A grim smile accompanied his words in the knowledge his foe had no missiles to launch. A wildcat stalking a vole, Caedwalla approached. Over his head, high in the air, the death-laden hail arced down on the quarry. The enemy squatted, shields above their heads, to parry the darts. Four men, impaled, would take no further part in the skirmish. At the sight of the Cantwara rising, Caedwalla leapt forward with a harsh battle cry, closing the distance in a few bounds.

Three men rushed to meet him to protect their sworn lord, well aware fate chose this ground for their doom, but determined to sell their life at great cost. Parrying a blow to his left, Caedwalla spun round, his axe biting deep into the linden shield of a warrior, wrenching it broken, from the man's grasp. Beside him, Cenred's sword pierced the throat of another and the greater numbers of the West Seaxe penned the men of Kent in a horseshoe of death. In their midst, Eadric stepped over a fallen defender and, lithe and muscular, killed two of his enemies before he came face-to-face with Caedwalla, Cenred and Bealdred.

For the briefest moment, the young king, visage concealed behind the metal countenance of his helm, paused and scrutinised his attackers. Not one of the three imagined fear delineated beneath the mask. Their respect for a worthy foeman involved no mercy. Alive, Eadric proved a threat to them and he must die. Few remained in the fight and outnumbered, they bore death in their hearts. The three kings charged, the battle-axe haft of Caedwalla met that of the King of Kent and the clash shook both men, causing them to stagger. Cenred's sword glanced off the short mail sleeve of Eadric's shirt as he stumbled backwards. They rushed him and once more he blocked the lethal arc of the battle-axe but in doing so exposed his side. Swift as an adder upon its prey, Bealdred drove the point of his sword through the ringed mail and, sore afflicted, Eadric lurched. Ready for this, Caedwalla swung his axe in a sweeping blow of savage might, taking the axe arm off at the elbow. Cenred's sword cut short the howl of pain by passing through the throat of the young king whose body slumped at their feet.

In the eerie silence of ceased battle, the West Seaxe gathered around their King, who laid down his battle-axe and bent to unlace the helm of his foe. The throes of death had distorted the handsome face.

"A worthy end," Caedwalla said through clenched teeth, "prepare a litter that he may be honoured in death as in life." He tossed the helm aside, where it rolled in the grass before slipping over the edge of the gorge to fall into the undergrowth. This was not the head protection that occupied the King: he brooded on finding one with a gilded wolf around its rim and on having its wearer lie dead at his feet like King Eadric of Kent.

Chapter 17

Aelfhere

Tomwordig, July–August 687 AD

"Why ought we heed the words of a boy-king? One unwise enough to send as a mouthpiece a *Wihtwara*?"

Aethelred of Mercia allowed the scorn in this last word to linger as he smirked at his counsellors and ealdormen.

"Was not Arwald slain and were not the islanders slaughtered by the West Seaxe?"

The mocking tone of the King irked Aelfhere, but he was wise enough to hide his feelings.

"Lord, I am indeed a Wihtwara and have fought many battles. My daughter is betrothed to Eadric of Kent and —"

" — married to Caedwalla…" the ruler of Mercia corrected, to the amusement of those within earshot.

The ealdorman of Cerdicsford seethed inside but otherwise did not react to the laughter.

"Lord, the same usurper is ailing, he lies with a fever in the Abbey of Selsea, ill of a wound inflicted by my own blade. Caedwalla at their head, the West Seaxe are a force to be reckoned with — without him is another matter. Should the men of Mercia unite with the Cantwara, the south of the land would be saved from the invaders."

The subtle change to an air of appraisement did not escape Aelfhere and the tall, hollow-cheeked ruler stroked his beard, his tone growing dour. "These are serious affairs to discuss among ourselves." Turning to a younger man by his side, he said, "Alhfrith, see that our guest is comfortable then hasten back, we need your counsel." Addressing Aelfhere, he said, less a question, more a dismissive command, "Wiht-wara, you will share our food tonight."

Ewald, who with his ealdorman had made the ten-day journey to where the river Tame meets the Anker, joined them outside. He arrived in time to hear, "Be not wrathful, friend, I am the King's wifebrother, hence I know him well. To measure a man, he tests patience to the limit." The pleasant smile and Northumbrian intonation of the noble-man eased Aelfhere's rancour. "He will consider your petition. Come," he waved them into his own home, snapped his finger and thumb and a maid appeared. "See our friends have food and rest. Until the evening," he said with a disarming grin.

Once alone, Ewald asked in a low voice, "How is this Aethelred?"

"The son of Penda? A man of two-score years and more. I like him not. Though men say he is more famed for his piety than his skills in war, remember he devastated Hrofescaester in his first year of king-ship." With a frown, he added, "Later he defeated Ecgfrith at the Trent. If he has the mind to do so, he can raise a mighty host."

The ealdorman savoured the cheese and ale the maid left them but with a faraway expression.

"What troubles you, Lord?"

"Eadric. He is young and headstrong. The mission he sent us on is well-judged but when I pleaded with him not to make a move until our return, I trusted not the wariness in his eye. He did not pledge to it and I doubt his steadiness."

"But he must fear the strength of the West Seaxe. Sound sense will have him wait to unite his force with the might of the Mercians."

"Ay, *your* sense, friend Ewald, but will Eadric curb his boldness?"

Each deep in thought, they ate and drank in silence. The weariness of the long journey told and they dozed until Alhfrith roused them for the evening meal.

The sultry summer air hung heavy around the bow-shaped walls of the hall. The shutters of the three windows facing their approach were thrown back to combat the smoke from the central firepit. Along the wall upon a raised step were ranked Aethelred, his thegns, ealdormen and lords in their high seats while on either side ran benches for their bondsmen. Younger men sat on the far side of the open fire opposite them, adding to the din of spirited laughter as they passed round the ale.

The King, noting the newcomers enter the hall, beckoned to his wifebrother and gestured to the empty places near him. Three vessels, froth brimming, arrived and Aethelred raised his huge silver-gilt auroch horn in greeting.

A scop struck up a tune on his hearpe but Aelfhere had difficulty understanding the tongue he sang in, not helped the rowdy clamour of voices drowning the song. From the nearby kitchen came serving women bearing platters of mixed roast beef, pork, venison and fowl. Small wicker baskets held chunks of chopped eel and wooden bowls, parsnips, cabbage, onions, beans, barley and peas flavoured with mint. The two Wihtwara reached for the rye bread and relished their first solid meal in many days.

The drink flowed but Aelfhere and Ewald determined to keep a clear head and avoid any rashness, drinking only when the King or one of his thegns lifted a horn in friendship.

Aethelred licked his fingers and said, "Earlier, you told us Caedwalla lies ill at Selsea."

Aelfhere set down his food. "It is so, Lord."

"I have a friend at the abbey," the King said, his tone casual, but the Wihtwara suspected that behind the simple statement lay a purpose, obliging him to show interest.

"I visited there, Lord, not many moons past."

The King stared at the ealdorman and waited, revelling in the daunting effect of his power.

For his part, Aelfhere, knowing the King of Mercia to be a pious Christian, hoped to evade the issue of beliefs. He settled for a neutral reply.

"Abbot Eappa is a good man."

"But not *my* friend," Aethelred said, lifting his frothing vessel to the islander thus forcing him to drink. Mind racing, Aelfhere opted for jest. With a discreet laugh, he said, "Caedwalla, then?"

The King roared his appreciation of the witticism and those seated around their King, most of them unaware of the exchange, bellowed ingratiating laughter in unison.

When the mirth subsided, the Lord of the Mercians said, "I speak of the bishop. After Wilfrith's imprisonment by Ecgfrith and exile from Northumbria, he stayed here under my protection. We sent him to convert the Suth Seaxe." The King smiled at the Wihtwara, called for more ale thus forcing Aelfhere to sup again. The ealdorman wondered where this was leading but Aethelred continued, "My informants tell me Wilfrith is close to Caedwalla, so why, islander, ought we to fight a friend of a friend?"

"The King of the Suth Seaxe was also patron to Bishop Wilfrith," he replied without hesitation, watching the King's eyes narrow, "the same Aethelwalh who served as underking to you, Lord. Caedwalla slaughtered him and seized his throne. Can it be that Wilfrith is no ally to the usurper but forced to tread with delicate step?"

Aelfhere yearned to add to this, but waited, not wishing to show disrespect.

"The West Seaxe warlord is a heathen which makes him a strange comrade to the priest," the King conceded. In a firmer voice, he added, "The islanders are pagan too."

He glared at the ealdorman, who seized the moment not to lose all, "True, Lord, but King Wulfhere befriended Wilfrith and he, your brother, gave the island to Aethelwalh. In turn, the Bishop supported Eadric as King of Kent against his uncle. Now is the time to strike at the other usurper, Caedwalla, before the West Seaxe come to menace the borders of Mercia."

The effect of the ealdorman's words on the King showed for a moment in a thoughtful frown.

"Enough of weighty matters! Let us drink," said the Lord of the Mercians offering a toast to his visitors, "and listen to sweet music." He waved the hearpist to approach, "Come, sing to us of *Widsith, the Far Traveller*," and he clapped his hands for silence, crying, "fetch fruit and nuts!" To Aelfhere, he said, "We shall give you our decision after due and considered deliberation."

* * *

For Aelfhere, time crept like a lengthening shadow.

"We've lingered here five days," Aelfhere said, his tone bitter, "Still no message from Aethelred. Eadric is an impatient youth, imagine how he champs at the bit!"

"What shall we do, Lord?"

"There is little we can do. Let's seek out Alhfrith, he is well-disposed towards us and better-placed for a word with the King."

They found the Northumbrian in the company of two thegns and, begging his leave, Aelfhere drew him aside to confide his worries. The nobleman sighed. "The King will not disclose his concerns to an outsider. Heaven knows he would move against Caedwalla on the morrow for the slaughter of his underking rankles as does the betrayal of the Meonwara. I have heard him say they *'threw off the Mercian mantle in exchange for the West Seaxe yoke'* — but it is not so easy." He frowned and said, "The problem of keeping our neighbours, the Hwiccas, stable preoccupies him. Their King, Oshere, died two years past and his three sons contend to take the throne while across the Severn, Mercia is in dispute with Powys over Pengwern and there is talk of war." Alhfrith raised his hands in resignation. "When I judge it right to tax my King, I may wrest a response but I fear the reply might not be such as you wish."

The ealdorman shrugged. "One way or the other, we must know, for Eadric awaits our return."

In spite of Alhfrith's assurances, the day came and went but the next morning a messenger arrived on horseback at the court of Aethelred. This, a regular occurrence, did not arouse their interest until a ceorl hurried over saying the King required the presence of Aelfhere.

The hall, its carved columns painted in gay colours, contrasted with the grim expression on the countenance of the Lord of Mercia and it did not bode well.

"Wihtwara," he said, his voice not unkind, "we have news from Tunbrycg in Kent. The Cantwara are defeated and Eadric is dead at the hand of Caedwalla. The West Seaxe thus gain dominion over the South."

Aelfhere gasped in dismay, for a moment the floor seemed to sway under his feet.

'Eadric dead! All hope is gone!'

The thought, insistent, left him reeling unable to grasp the words of Aethelred.

"The illness of Caedwalla cannot be so grave if he can lead his host to crushing victory and destroy Eadric with the might of his sinews."

The King scrutinised the ealdorman, whose pallor and spent mien induced him to continue.

"The gains of the West Seaxe please us not, but friend, with problems on our borders the time is not meet for conflict. Our affairs change with the slaughter of the Cantwara but you may stay for as long as you wish.

Aelfhere nodded and bowed. "Lord, your kindness is as great as your name but we must depart. My mission is over and my grudge personal; thus, to remain in Mercia has no sense although the thought is pleasing, and I thank you for hearing me and may God grant you health and long life." But the ealdorman's speaking disguised the truth of his paganism.

King Aethelred inclined his head in acknowledgement and clapped his hands. A servant entered. "Escort our friend to the kitchen and ensure he has all he needs for his journey. Take him and his bondsman to the horse thegn. My gift is a pair of ponies to ease your travels."

Pleasantries exchanged, provisions and mounts consigned, Aelfhere and Ewald left the court at Tomwordig, sorrowful and bewildered concerning their wyrd.

* * *

In their overnight camp, they strained to come to terms with their situation.

"All I believe in and all I strove for is in vain," Aelfhere said. "Caedwalla prospers, Cynethryth betrays me, her own father, yet she is Lady of all the South. I am worthless and feeble! My land and home seized by invaders, King and friends all dead," he sighed, staring into the embers of their fire, "what is there to live for, except revenge?"

"Lord, it is not too late! Ought you not make peace with your daughter and —"

"Never! I will slay her and her contemptible husband —"

"But she is your flesh! Your very being! Without a wife you raised her —"

"And a poor effort I made of it!"

"Untrue, Lord! Think on this! Did the priest of Ingui not read the rune you cast? What were his utterances? *'You must be guided not by revenge nor loathing but the opposite, by love to overcome.'*"

"Priests! What did they ever do for me? Ewald, a way must be found. With my bare hands, I will choke the life out of the serpent, Cynethryth, and this blade having sipped, thirsts to drink its fill of the usurper's blood."

Chapter 18

Cynethryth, Caedwalla and Wilfrith

Kingsham, August 687–November 688 AD

Rowena hesitated in the doorway, unsure whether to offer comfort or to leave Cynethryth alone in her distress. Compassion for the figure curled on her pallet, shoulders heaving, led her to cross the room to the edge of the bed, there to stroke the red-golden hair, entreating, "Tush! Sweet lady, shedding tears will not heal your husband."

The weeping ceased and she turned, eyes red-rimmed, cheeks drawn and wet, expression so anguished that Rowena embraced and rocked her as she would a child.

"Hush, hush! All will be well."

Cynethryth, as ever, delicate in her movement, detached herself from the consoling grasp and straightened.

"It's cruel," she wiped an eye with her sleeve, "the wound closed, seemed cured and four moons passed since his fever, only for it to return."

"Do not distress yourself so, my angel, Caedwalla is in good hands. Did not the infirmarian come from Selsea? What says he?"

"He talks of *flying fever* and bloodletting, but my husband gainsays him and will not be bled."

"How so?" the sage-green eyes conveyed tender concern.

"He insists a tainted blade cut him and his body must combat the poison as in battle. Oh, Rowena, I fear it is a fight he will lose!" She took her friend by the hand. "He is fatigued and complains of aching in his head and back. Nor will he eat. If he is right, how can his body overcome the bane when it lacks nourishment?"

Rowena squeezed the hand. "Does the brother healer not give him sustenance?"

"Ay, draughts and potions but my lord has no appetite. Fourteen nights he lies like this and I dread he will die! Why must it happen so? Just when I have the sickness every morning."

Rowena's eyes opened wide. "You are with child?"

Cynethryth smiled through the tears and nodded.

Her companion embraced her anew, holding her tight and murmuring soothing words but in her heart she too shared her friend's dismay.

To their surprise and delight, Caedwalla rose from his bed within seven days and to the relief of his wife, his appetite returned with desire for red meat and wine. After a while, to regain his strength, he set about any opponent willing to trade blows with wooden practice swords. He chopped logs, hurled spears and raced his comrades, not satisfied until he won every race. Guthred organised a feast to celebrate his lord's regained health.

At table that night, Cenred brought up the matter of the two princes.

"While you lay ill, Lord, the moon shone full, the fourth since we took the brothers of the Wihtwara king."

A sudden silence fell in the hall, everyone wishing to hear the fate due to befall the noble captives. Setting down his drinking horn with care, Caedwalla frowned and declared, "On the morrow we leave for Selsea to dispatch the last of Arwald's brood."

These words brought rousing cheers and cups beaten on the table. The West Seaxe warriors expected no mercy from their foes and harboured none for their captives. They pretended no less from their chosen lord.

The carved peg of the sundial of the abbey church cast a short shadow at the hour of Sext as Caedwalla stood before the kneeling Wihtwara.

Bishop Wilfrith, a small bottle in one hand, indicated the prisoners with the other and addressed the King of the West Seaxe, "Their preparation is complete. They have prayed and fasted," he raised the glass vessel, "they are baptised, sins remitted, to be numbered among the faithful. The rite of unction remains for admission into paradise."

Caedwalla did not fail to notice the serene acceptance, the fearlessness and the light of spiritual joy in the eyes of the princes and he marvelled at it. No less, did he wonder at the devotion of the scrawny, bent hermit, hands clasped to his breast, his mouth moving in silent prayer.

Wilfrith stepped forward, taking exorcised salt from within his tunic and placing it in the mouths of the royal brothers. Signing with the cross, he poured oil from the bottle on his hand, touched it on their ears, eyes, nostrils, lips, hands and groin.

"Through this unction and His own most tender mercy may the Lord pardon you whatever sins or faults you have committed by hearing, sight, smell, taste, touch, or carnal delectation."

Impassive, the bishop turned to the King, "Proceed as you see fit, their souls are ready to fly to the bosom of Christ."

With a gesture of his hand, Caedwalla summoned a bystander, "Unbind their hair." He watched unmoved as the man completed the task. "Entwine the withy in his hair and hold it tight," he glared at the younger captive.

The prince looked up and smiled, "That is not necessary, Lord. I shall not flinch if you strike true."

The crowd of on-looking warriors grew restless, murmuring, for they had hoped for the sport of cries and laments, not the sheer courage of a noble youth.

"You die as a king should," Caedwalla said in admiration, raising his axe and measuring the distance.

"Bless you, Lord, for releasing my soul," the boy uttered his last words.

The weapon swung and the head fell two paces from the body, the dull thud the only sound to break the expectant silence.

"Be swift, Lord. You have my forgiveness," the elder brother said, without a quaver.

Enraged and troubled, Caedwalla struck with equal swiftness, then turning to the praying bishop, interrupting his invocation, "Father," the title rang strange off his tongue, "we must speak." He took the prelate's arm, without respect, hauling him toward the bishop's quarters from the sullen onlookers, their entertainment thwarted if not their bloodlust.

Inside the chamber, he asked, "What do you teach captives that they face death with such calm?"

Wilfrith smiled, gazing at the Cross hanging on the wall. "Their end came merciful, brief and unwilling; His was cruel, lingering and *willing*. He gave His life for us that we may all accede to paradise, as we taught the princes — they died content to live in splendour for all eternity. It is the gift of Faith."

Caedwalla stared at the Cross, after a long silence in which, with increasing interest, the prelate watched the emotions change on the king's face. "This gift you speak of... it must be mine! You must teach me what you taught my enemies."

"When we met, each in exile, in the Andredes weald, you called me *'holy father'* and vowed you would be an obedient son. I promised to be a faithful father to you in teaching and in aid."

The bishop studied the warlord, the long visage taking on a graven sternness. "God was our witness but, Caedwalla, have we not both disappointed Him?"

"Did I not give your Church a quarter of Wiht as I swore on my oath? In exchange, you offer me your counsel."

The prelate shook his head, "The Almighty favours you because you are an instrument to destroy the pagan. Yet it is your soul He cherishes. He is a demanding Father and His spirit has entered your breast so that now, He summons you and you must become a catechumen and I your catechist."

"Cross-bearer, speak with words I understand!"

Wilfrith laughed, "You need mental and moral preparation and I shall be your guide. You must stay at Selsea to learn day by day."

"Impossible!" Caedwalla roared, "I leave to destroy the Kentings once and for all!"

Wilfrith clicked his tongue, "What happened to the *'obedient son'*? Send your thegns in your stead to ravage Kent. The Cantwara are weakened in defeat and no match for the West Seaxe host. Bid your ealdorman seize what riches they can and dedicate a portion to the Church of God."

The King paced the chamber like an entrapped beast. At last, he halted and declared, "Very well, I shall send my men to Kent and order one-tenth of our gains to be delivered unto you."

"The Almighty will raise you above all others, my son!"

The next morning, standing next to his wife, Caedwalla oversaw the departure of his men.

"I should be at their head," he murmured through clenched teeth, "but the time has come to accept your religion."

Cynethryth, exuberant with joy, seized her husband by the hand.

"You will see how the Holy Spirit, once entered your heart, changes even the way you see a bird," she enthused. She drew his attention to a thrush alighting on the top of the standing cross to flute forth its song.

Equally, she yearned to pour out her feelings, to speak of her gladness he was safe in the abbey with her, for once not a day snatched between campaigns. They would worship together and in the future when God chose to take them to His bosom, they would share in His boundless love. None of this she revealed, judging his mood unreceptive as he stared narrow-eyed at his men off in the distance. Little did she think in that moment of contentment it would be *her* faith, not his, put to the test in the months to come.

For the moment, her life proved full of contrasting emotions. While she enjoyed the bliss of married life, once in a while, she thought with sorrow of her father whose love she missed and wondered what fate had befallen him. Prayers for his wellbeing uplifted and consoled her and assuaged her guilt at what she knew he believed to be her betrayal. Conversely, her blossoming friendship with Rowena and their daily rides outside the abbey grounds amid the beauty of the countryside made her heart sing. It pleased her when Caedwalla shared his new knowledge in discussion and to learn of her husband's fine intellect.

As a catechumen, the priest allowed him to attend the first part of the Mass to the end of the sermon but then dismissed him. Unlike his lady wife, Caedwalla was not yet considered one of the faithful. Cynethryth's patience, she knew, would be rewarded at his baptism. Meanwhile, she marvelled at the droves of animals arriving at the abbey, sent by the pillaging West Seaxe. It troubled her that the folk of Selsea would prosper in the forthcoming winter while those of Kent would struggle to survive depredation. Were not the Cantwara Christians too? Why, she wondered, did God not intervene to end these torments.

When she pursued Bishop Wilfrith, he replied, "Without sin, suffering or evil in the world, Jesus had not been nailed to the Cross. So, suffering in the world is needed to attain the Cross, which in turn reveals to us the great and awesome love of God."

In the night, Cynethryth turned these words over as she lay sleepless. However, they did not drive away her imaginings of starving babes and mothers with breasts dry of milk. But the greatest test of her fledgling faith came in the days before Christ's Mass, when Caedwalla fell ill for the third time, not long after Guthred and the others returned with plunder.

On this occasion, as the fever raged, she believed he would die. Her prayers seemed in vain and she questioned how God chose to inflict this upon one embracing His commandments to the full. In moments of lucidity, Caedwalla complained of acute pains in his joints and, fatigued, he fell into a deep depression that threatened to undermine his will to live.

The illness lasted three weeks but after Epiphany he recovered and once more began to build up his strength. Cynethryth noticed the King's deepening faith with curiosity and Wilfrith with satisfaction. It seemed Caedwalla's brush with death had touched a profound chord within his being. His daily contact with the bishop stretched longer and in the early spring they travelled together to Kent. In that land, Caedwalla, distressed by the devastation of the kingdom he had ordered, drew the prelate aside.

"What can I do to make amends, Father? How can I put this right?"

"My son, if you are willing to be generous, your legacy can be such that generations will pray for your soul henceforth and to the end of days."

"How so? Guide me, Father."

"Soon we meet with Archbishop Theodore of Tarsus in Cantwaraburh, he who rules over the Church. We quarrelled, thereafter he deposed and expelled me but with your ascendancy in the South and our close friendship, the time is ripe for reconciliation."

* * *

Wilfrith's judgment proved astute. A priest led the bishop and the King into the presence of Theodore and Eorcenwald, bishop of Lundenwic. Theodore, stood tall and straight for a man of five and four-score years. With his white hair and long nose, he cut a dignified figure while his olive skin and dark eyes announced his Byzantine Greek origins. Behind the formal polite words of circumstance, Caedwalla detected animosity towards his companion. This sentiment did not extend to himself — indeed, the archbishop clasped his hand with sincere warmth and introduced the other man, a former abbot of royal descent. The blond Eorcenwald's curly hair and beard were shot with grey, but the bearing of a younger man belied his sixty years.

"I believe you are preparing to embrace the true Faith," the archbishop remarked. "These ten years past, the Bishop," he gestured to Eorcenwald, "converted another King, the noble Sebba of the East Seaxe. Now," he directed a tight smile at Wilfrith, "it appears you will match his achievement."

Wilfrith bowed, otherwise making no comment. Instead, he raised the matter underlying their visit.

"The King seeks guidance for he wishes to manifest his gratitude to God for benefits received in acts of munificence and piety."

The two high clergymen exchanged glances although neither spoke. At last, the archbishop, choosing his words carefully, said, "After recent — *er* — upheavals, the Church in Kent is destitute. The need for an abbey at Hoo is most pressing. Abbot Ecgbald needs a grant of land," he stretched out his hands in a gesture of helplessness, "and God knows, there is no coin to build the walls..."

"In the diocese of Wintanceastre," said the Bishop of Lundenwic, taking advantage of the sudden silence, "there is sore need of a religious house near Fearnhamme. If the spirit were to move the King to grant land there, I am most willing to draft the charter."

"This is a fine beginning," Caedwalla smiled, directing a shrewd glance at the archbishop, "two monks' houses there shall be... as long as..." he paused for effect, enough for Theodore to wave an impatient hand, "... prayers are offered for my soul at Mass in both abbeys."

Ready acceptance of these terms led to the four men spending the next days in profitable discussions from which each gained. In private, Wilfrith suggested strengthening ties by sending West Seaxe witnesses to the land concession of the King of the East Seaxe to Abbess Aethelburh at Berecingas. Caedwalla added territory nearby falling within his gift, to the noblewoman, sister of the Bishop of Lundenwic. As Wilfrith observed, this new political and military order might prove resilient to any future Mercian attack. To extend West Seaxe influence north of the River Temese, he granted land for an abbey on Badrices ieg amid the marshes.

On the return journey to Selsea, a highly satisfied Bishop Wilfrith confided to the King, "Theodore expressed the wish that I succeed him at Cantwaraburh. See how God smiles upon our pact!" The eyes of the prelate shone with the bright glow of ambition. "May His will be done — that we both, King and Archbishop, shall hold sway over the souls of the South!"

It seemed the well-laid plans of Wilfrith would come to complete fruition with the aid of Divine Providence, but it was not to be.

Once more, Caedwalla fell ill and as on the previous occasions each bout, lasting three weeks, struck graver than the one before. A pattern became clear: the disease recurred every four months leaving him weaker and wasted. The first appearance of grey strands in his hair shocked Cynethryth, for her husband had not yet reached his thirtieth year. She cursed the man whose blade had sliced the arm of Caedwalla. In disobedience to her Christian precepts, she wished all the torments of Job upon him, knowing not her own father was the object of her malediction.

As the King, face as grey as the wolf pelt under which he lay, sipped broth Cynethryth held to his lips, Guthred begged urgent admittance.

Standing awkward by the bedside, he said, "Lord, bad news! The Mercians have seized the land to the north of the Temese."

"By the gods!" Caedwalla dashed the bowl out of his wife's hand, spilling its contents over the floor. The King struggled to raise himself on one elbow.

"Out!" he shouted at Cynethryth, who bent to retrieve the vessel. "Leave us!"

Not accustomed to such behaviour from her loving husband, she hesitated, but only for a moment. Disobedience must not follow a severe displeasure, for in his feeble state, it might harm him.

Left alone, Caedwalla drew his ealdorman to sit on the edge of the bed. His hand grasped the wolf pelt covering until the knuckles showed white.

"The Mercian spies did their work well. Their royal master struck safe in the knowledge I lie here powerless." His grip on the wrist of

Guthred tightened with surprising force for one so haggard, "I am dying —"

"Nay, Lord! Do not speak so...!"

The eyes of the King flashed. "Hush! Do not make me waste what little strength I have in pointless discussion! Heed me well! Take a horse to Wintanceastre, seek Ine, son of Cenred, my cousin in second. My mind is made up, he is young but has the vigour and character to lead the West Seaxe in my stead." Caedwalla shook the arm of his ealdorman, "No-one must hear of this, neither Bealdred nor Cenred, the two underkings must swear fealty to Ine, or all my work is undone."

"Lord, sickness laid you low before and —"

Rage flared in the febrile eyes, but the King released his grasp and fell back on his bolster.

"You know nought, friend Guthred," he said in a tired and frail voice, "be gone and not a word to your wife, lest mine get to hear of this!" Summoning the warrior nearer, he said, "Before you depart, send a messenger to Selsea, have the Bishop brought to me."

Caedwalla closed his eyes and gave a heavy sigh. In sorrow, Guthred gazed at the drawn visage, his lord had aged twenty years in but six months. Despondent and sorrowful, he turned to fulfil his orders.

* * *

After two days, Bishop Wilfrith entered, trailing Cynethryth behind him. Impatient, Caedwalla's intended bellow resembled a puny bleat, "You again, woman! Out!"

The Wihtwara woman stood her ground and, glaring, retorted. "If you were well, husband, I would beat some manners into you...!"

The King's lip curled, "If I were well, you would be beating in this bed with me!" He looked towards the prelate. "Forgive me, Father! Wife," he pleaded, "we have grave matters to discuss; prepare food for your unworthy lord."

Cynethryth pursed her lips, shook her head and pushing the drape aside, made for the kitchen.

Caedwalla waited to gather his thoughts. "Be seated, Father, I have much to tell and I am weak." Everything he had told Guthred, he repeated, ending, "I mean to abdicate and Ine is my choice." Weary of voice, he added, "His sister Cuthburh is wed to King Aldfrith of Northumbria —"

"Ha! You are an able student. I have taught you well!"

The King snickered, "The Mercians will be thwarted. Let them keep the northern stretch of the Temese. It's marsh for the most part and the river forms a natural barrier…" Caedwalla closed his eyes, the effort of speech too great.

Wilfrith leant forward in his chair, "You overtax yourself, my son. Rest now and tomorrow we shall speak again of the wisdom of your decision and the benefits it may accrue."

The Bishop, convinced of Caedwalla's imminent death by the King's words and appearance, resolved to anticipate his baptism. This idea pleased the invalid and surely would have been brought to a conclusion but for the strange order of the ailment. Once more, Caedwalla rose from his sick bed and exchanged it for the invigorating spring air of Kingsham.

When Ine arrived accompanied by Guthred and a well-armed force at his back, the King welcomed him and ordered a feast to be prepared. In the evening, he pulled a heavy ring from his finger and placed it on the hand of Ine, declaring his abdication and departure forthwith to the Abbey of Selsea.

The underkings swore loyalty to Ine and Caedwalla rode unburdened of affairs of kingship with his lady, Rowena and Guthred to Selsea.

For a few days, his wife and companions saw little of him as he spent most of his time with Bishop Wilfrith. When he judged the moment right he went to that close assembly to make a declaration.

"Cynethryth and I," he imparted, to his wife's astonishment, "will board a ship across the sea to Rome, for I wish to obtain the cleansing of baptism at the shrine of the apostle. Since I am a king, no one but the keeper of the keys to Heaven will baptise me. Guthred, go to Cerdicsford, take up your lordship. Rowena, await Cynethryth there."

"Only Cynethryth?" Rowena asked, startled.

"Ay, lady, for I shall not return from Rome."

Chapter 19

Aelfhere

"Ewald! What tidings of Lord Aelfhere?"

The greeting of the Wihtwara ceorl betrayed avidity for news of his former life. "I never thought to see you again in this world!"

"Well, I'm no wraith," said Ewald, detaching his regard from the excited face to the ploughed field then beyond to the palisade enclosing Selsea Abbey, to ensure his presence had gone unobserved.

"Aelfhere has made a homestead many leagues hence hidden deep in the wooded land of the Cantwara. In body, he is well but his heart, set on vengeance, frets."

"Revenge?" said the labourer, tossing down the sickle used to clear away the briars and weeds invading the ditch, tone suspicious: "Ay, he lost his farmstead at Cerdicsford, right enough, but those of us as came over here wi' him can't complain. The soil suits growin' and Abbot Eappa treats us well. If one of us falls sick, the monks treat the ailment —"

"Hark! Medwin, I came not to disturb settled lives, but for news of Cynethryth and her husband. Know you of their whereabouts?"

Relieved, the ceorl laughed, "Ay, sure! Did you not hear? The country being agog wi' it, like!"

Ewald snarled, "I heard nought and nor will I if you don't spit it out!"

Another chortle and the pause of one who has the power to withhold news before he caught the glint in the warrior's eye, and in haste added, "Caedwalla stood down."

"Stood down? How can that be?"

The ceorl shrugged, "What them high and mighty choose has nought to do wi' us until it comes to givin' and takin'…"

Ewald bunched his fist. "You're making no sense, man! Out with it afore I beat it from you!"

"No need to take that tone!" Medwin grumbled, "No patience some folk," and he spat in the ditch. "Caedwalla, he upped and went. We got a new King now. They say he be young wi' an old head but he's still one of them West Seaxe scum."

"Gone? Where? And Cynethryth?"

"Gone wi' him, like as not. A brother from yon abbey told us he's off to Rome to do *pen…* something or the other…whatever they call it…for his sins. Anyhow, we all had to furnish his voyage, as if we don't work our hands to the bone as it is." The labourer gazed to the hills in the distance and continued, "They say he took all the sheep from the Downs. Took their fleece too, and all the wheat in the clay steadings of the Weald, coin and iron and the monk's gave him wine. Upped and left wi' the last moon, he did, took a company of monks, nuns and priests an' the sheep…did I tell you that..?"

Refusing the Wihtwara's insistent offer of food and drink, Ewald, wishing his visit to pass unnoticed, pledged Medwin to silence. Near Maegdan stane, weary, he entered the enclosure of the late swineherd and slumped into a seat across the table from his lord. The weakness of the ale did not bother him as he slaked the thirst of his six-day journey.

While Ewald drank, Aelfhere studied the face of the one man he counted a friend. Pushing back his chair, he crossed the small room to fetch fresh-churned butter and bread, carrying them over on a wooden platter. Though yearning to hear his news, Aelfhere said nothing, recognising silence as the best way to show his gratitude for the fatigue he had caused his bondsman. After all, he had sent him many leagues on foot.

Ewald ate heartily, but paused. "Remember Medwin, Lord?"

"The bandy-legged fellow? Ay, a hard worker, what of him?"

"I found him clearing a ditch and he told me Caedwalla stood down."

Aelfhere, leaning on the table, stared at the warrior. A while passed before he spoke.

"Abdicate? Why would he do that?"

"Seems he took ship for the tombs of the Apostles..."

"Rome!"

The ealdorman slammed down a fist and cursed.

"Medwin said he took Cynethryth with him, Lord."

Ewald clutched his beaker of ale as the fist came crashing down again and grimaced when his lord leapt up sending his heavy wooden seat crashing to the floor.

"I shall slay them if I must follow them to the very end of the world!"

"Let them be, Lord!" Ewald kept his voice respectful, "We can find women for wives, have sons and make a good homestead here. As you say, Rome is the other side —"

"You are young, so make *your* home here! I leave for the land of the Haestingas at dawn."

Aelfhere dropped on his pallet, pulled a blanket over his head and soon his snoring revealed to his sleepless bondsman that, unlike himself, he had no doubts to torment him into wakefulness. Cursing the ealdorman for an old fool, Ewald accepted he'd not abandon him. Instead, he swore to use the long journey to Rome to dissuade the vengeful father from taking his daughter's life.

* * *

"When we head south to the coast," said Aelfhere, the next morning, "we need to find the White Rock headland. A port lies in its lee whence traders leave for the land of the Franks. We can buy passage and glean word of how to reach Rome."

They drove the few yearling animals they had reared to the hut of the nearest ceorl who blessed the gods for his good fortune. From him, they accepted a meagre supply of cheese and dried meat for sustenance on their journey to the coast.

On the quay in the shadow of the white cliff, Aelfhere, seeking passage, spoke to a fisherman sorting his catch. After a few polite exchanges, the man straightened, "Wihtwara by yer speech?"

"Ay."

"Rare as a cockle's tooth, you be!"

Aelfhere stared into the weather-beaten face. "How so?"

"Speakin' to one o' yer kind o'er at Selsea o'ny yesterday. Them's fled from the isle. Bare got out and saved them's skin, them did! All dead — them poor folk!"

The blood drained from the ealdorman's face and he clutched the fisher's arm. "Who did this deed?"

"Why, the Seaxe from the west — word is, them's led by the Son of Woden!"

Vengeance devouring his soul, Aelfhere's resolve to reach Rome redoubled.

Silver sceattas made it a simple matter to find a willing boat owner prepared to cross the Channel, especially given the favourable calm conditions. The uneventful voyage completed, the solidity of the wooden quay at the bustling port of Quentovic was a matter of indifference to the two islanders. Accustomed to the motion of the waves, they grinned at the sight of a band of queasy Saxon pilgrims. Chuckling, Aelfhere nudged his companion. "Not used to sailing! As well it's flat calm! Who do you think is in charge?"

"One way to find out," Ewald said, wandering over to the travellers.

The ealdorman watched as a man pointed out a black-cloaked figure, grey hood pulled over his head, leaving his face completely hidden. They exchanged words before Ewald strode back.

"Their leader is an abbot," he told Aelfhere, "goes by the name of Aldhelm. They're monks and nuns for the most part, on pilgrimage."

"Christians!" Aelfhere spat into the dock. "Had to be!...On their way to visit the Pope. We'd best gain passage, come on."

He went over to tap the grey-cowled monk on the shoulder. The abbot unmasked his face to reveal a forceful countenance illuminated by questing brown eyes. The ealdorman judged him to have seen fifty summers.

"Our destination is Rome and we are willing to pay if you have two berths...we're not Christians though," Aelfhere warned.

The monk brightened, his handsome face shedding years, "We have saints and martyrs who were not Christians till the holy Spirit touched their hearts." He looked the two men over, "Our party counts but five warriors, so two sturdy fellows like you are most welcome." The shrewd stare bored into the islander, "Why go to the Holy City if you do not share our faith?"

"To seek my daughter," Aelfhere replied with murder in his heart and was startled to see the abbot tense and frown.

Have I betrayed my thoughts? How?

The moment passed and before clasping hands, the Wihtwara paid a contribution to the passage as far, said the monk, as the mouth of the great River Rhône near the Mediterranean. The names meant nothing to him.

With the wind set fair, the square-sailed craft cut well down the stream.

Mid-afternoon, the abbot sauntered over to Aelfhere and leant on the gunwale beside him with a friendly nod.

"This waterway is the Canche, some say its name is from the Cant-wara who go on pilgrimage in droves. Soon, we leave the ship and the guides will lead us into the forest where we will walk across country to another river."

That night they slept under the trees in a secure enclosure, its palisade protection against howling, grunting wild beasts.

Not yet dawn, Aelfhere, an early riser, found Aldhelm sitting by one of the fires he had revived. By the light of the flames, he strained to read a parchment from which his eyes then strayed over the treetops to a lone star in the lightening sky.

Curious, the ealdorman approached. "You're up before the lark, monk," he said in a hushed voice, not wishing to wake the others. "Do I disturb you?"

"Well enough to stop my poor mind from yielding!"

"What is it you do?"

"Trying to do," the abbot corrected, with a gentle smile. "I'm riddling but the metric is not right."

'*Metric*' meant nothing to Aelfhere but he loved a teasing rhyme. "Is that the puzzle in your hand? Will you read it out?"

Aldhelm turned the vellum toward the flickering light and recited the first line, "*Nitorem ante lucem semper fero...*" he began.

The ealdorman growled, annoyed, "I know not the language of Christians. Tell it in our tongue."

"It's crude in Latin," the abbot chuckled, "so it won't scan in Saxon, but if you desire...for what it's worth, it's rough, mind," he repeated before reading:

> '*Ever I bring lustre before the daylight*
> *Splendid, sign the wakening sunlight,*
> *Side-tracked, I become low in the skies*
> *In Orient, where my resplendence vies*
> *O'er far Byzantium with early gleams*
> *While sleepers lie in gentle dreams;*
> *Listener, time behoves thee to proclaim*
> *To all and sundry, what's my name?*'

The monk shook his head in frustration, "it needs working on, but it's better in Latin."

"Recite it again," Aelfhere said. "I might have an inkling!"

The abbot obliged but as he finished his attention drifted to the heavens again, the islander glanced in the same direction toward the bright star.

"You'll have to try harder than that, friend!" Aelfhere chortled, "Look to the east! Daybreak and the answer is the *Morning Star*," he pointed over the trees.

"Ha-ha! You have bested me on this occasion, but be warned, I have a hundred and more rhymes. They improve the Latin of the novices and the journey is still long to test your cunning. Come sit and talk!"

An unlikely companionship arose between the two men, in spite of the unease the abbot induced in the ealdorman. The sensation of having his innermost thoughts read persisted. Yet, the force of Aldhelm's personality drew him back to seek out his company. The monk spoke of the love of his God and the beauty of Creation. Unperturbed, Aelfhere countered with tales of Woden, Thunor and other gods but the intangible power of the doctrine of love and sacrifice began to breach the islander's certainties. Nonetheless, it failed to overcome the shield the ealdorman had erected around his heart. Behind its protection crouched the dark warrior of revenge, sword in hand, ready to strike.

The shimmering Marne carried them upstream beyond Catalauns whence they marched overland to the Saône to take a flat-bottomed barge along the river and thence into the wider Rhône. The fast-flowing, muddy watercourse taxed the skills of the crew with its shifting sandbars, most of all where it narrowed. On those occasions, the Wihtwara manned poles and oars to help make headway amid the unpredictable currents. These dangers made travelling by night impossible so the sailors moored the boat during the hours of darkness. This meant six weeks passed from leaving Quentovic to rowing into the coastal delta and disembarking at Fos where all river traffic ceased.

Aelfhere smelt Marseilles before he sighted its huge defensive walls. The hot mid-June sun heightened the mingling stench of narrow streets, fish and the aroma of imported spices. The governor of this Western Mediterranean emporium ruled trade to Frankia with an iron fist, his officials overseeing the loading and unloading of countless vessels. Sailors both, Aelfhere and Ewald gaped at the number and order of craft lashed side by side in the port. The *cellaria fisci,* the enormous royal warehouses swallowed up amphorae of oil and grain and goods of every kind — papyri, spices, skins, silver plate and slaves passed before their bewildered eyes.

"Come!" Aldhelm tugged at Aelfhere's arm, "the guides call us. Make haste to the ship. We follow the coast to the port of Ostia."

"We must pay," the ealdorman said.

"Ay, on board, come!"

A favourable wind from the Rhône valley carried them into the Ligurian Sea but when they changed course southward the stiff breeze and current obliged the captain to tack or use his oars.

At last, they moored in the once noble Ostia where people lived, for the most part, in hovels among the ancient ruins. The travellers were relieved to put the squalor behind them and to head inland the six leagues to Rome.

The perimeter wall of huge stone blocks faced with red brick stretched eleven unbroken miles around the city. They entered between the twin round towers of the Porta Ostiense.

"We shall stay in the Abbey of St Vincent in the Borgo," Aldhelm said, "I'm sure there will be room for two more if you wish to join us."

Aelfhere looked around the teeming streets at the innumerable churches and the strange religious figures hurrying in and out of their doors.

"I thank you," he said, "I never thought to make a friend of a Christian, a monk, to boot. But to sleep in an abbey is one step too far! We shall find an inn…" and he hesitated as he had an idea, "…we'll find it near your lodgings."

Later, when he and Ewald settled into their room, he explained.

"If travellers from our homeland come to this part of the city, there's a chance that the wanton and her consort are skulking hereabouts. A tavern is a likely place to begin our search!"

Discreet inquiries and generous offers of wine in the hostelries did not elicit the response they sought. Nobody recognised the descriptions the ealdorman gave of his daughter and of Caedwalla. Neither did scouring the Borgo produce results in the following days; but they by chance encountered Aldhelm.

"Ah, Ealdorman," he said, "I had hoped to cross your path before the morrow. Come with me, there's a matter of interest to you...but I'll say no more! Trust me, what say you?"

The monk smiled engagingly and Aelfhere found himself agreeing to a meeting the next morning outside the abbey.

When he had gone, the perplexed ealdorman turned to Ewald and asked, "How is it that fellow gets me to do his will?"

The next day Aelfhere in the company of the abbot, two monks and Ewald trod the monumental paving stones of the Appian Way. To their right he noticed people converging on an entrance leading underground.

"Are we going there?" he asked.

In reply, Aldhelm took his arm and steered him behind those shuffling along into the gap in the rock. They followed the steep downward slope and soon, the ealdorman's eyes adjusted to the darkness. Startled, he brushed against walls encrusted with sepulchral niches.

"This feels like you are leading me into the kingdom of Hel, monk, or do I err?"

By the flickering light of the smoky oil lamps, the shadowed countenance of Aldhelm indeed took on a diabolical appearance.

"On the contrary, my friend, this is a holy place of saints and martyrs and we are going to where lie the mortal remains of nine popes, interred many lifetimes ago. But, even more, you will be in the living presence of Pope Sergius — the Holy Father will conduct mass here in these catacombs, a privilege granted to few."

Aelfhere did not reply. His head spun. He, an unbeliever, had let himself be led docile as a goat to sacrifice before the master of the religion he hated. It made no sense: the abbot had the powers of a sorcerer! Resigned and walking on, he ran his eyes over repeated images painted or etched on the walls: a dove with a branch in its beak, fishes, anchors or strange birds amid flames.

They arrived at a narrow crypt with a high arched roof in red brick-work. Taller than most of the congregation, Aelfhere gazed over to a man standing before an altar. With his back to the people, he wore on his head a white mitre, cloth of gold at its base, shaped like a warrior's helm.

The assembly fell into a profound silence as the Pope began to speak in a tongue the ealdorman did not understand. His chanting evoked short responses from the participants in the same language. Awed, the hairs on the arms of Aelfhere stood on end while from the corner of his eye, he glanced at Ewald bringing a shaky hand to his forehead.

Sergius turned round and making the sign of the cross, no longer chanting he addressed the people again, in Latin. The swarthy-skinned Pope with a full dark beard, the ealdorman guessed, was communicating with his followers.

Afterwards, grateful to be outside in the fresh air, Aelfhere turned to Aldhelm, "What was the instruction your priest gave to the gathering?"

"Instruction? Ah, the sermon! The Holy Father was giving us a lesson from the scriptures — our sacred writings."

"And what did he say?"

"He spoke to us from the Gospel of St Matthew." Aldhelm quoted from memory, " '*Or what man is there of you, whom if his son ask bread, will he give him a stone?...If you then, being evil, know how to give good gifts unto your children, how much more shall your Father...give good things to them that ask him?*'" The abbot smiled at the ealdorman. "Those are the words of Christ."

Ewald leant close, gripped Aelfhere by the arm and whispered, "The same message as the sorcerer's: you ought not to defy the will of the gods!

Chapter 20

Cynethryth and Aelfhere

Rome, April 689 AD

Pope Sergius leant forward on his throne, his gaze passing over Cynethryth to fix Caedwalla standing beside her.

"I hear," he said, addressing him in an even tone, "you would be accepted into the Faith."

"Holy Father, I have defeated many enemies and shed much blood. My past, I cannot change but I have travelled over foreign lands to crave baptism at your hands."

"There is no special treatment for kings. All are equal before God, the rich, the poor, the master and the slave. Bishop Wilfrith writes to say you are willing to stand barefoot, humble among others."

"It is so."

The countenance of the Pope softened. "The *festum festorum* approaches and with it, the solemn baptism of Easter Eve. From today, observe continence and do not partake of food for forty hours before the feast of Easter. Go, don the white robes of the *electi* and you may not put them off until Low Sunday."

"Before I lose the white garments, death will take me," Caedwalla said, voice flat.

Cynethryth gasped, her eyes filling with tears and she laid a hand over her swollen womb.

After the audience with the Pope, outside the Apostolic Palace of the Lateran, she clutched his arm. "Why did you say you will die? This is not so!"

Caedwalla halted to turn and face her. "Because, wife, it is true. The sickness festers inside me, I am weak and tired." He dropped to one knee, circling her thighs, drawing her to him, kissing the slight swelling of her belly, "Think of the little warrior in your womb; raise him to be a better man than his father whose sins by count and nature may doom him forever to Hell."

As he rose, the drawn greyness of his visage gnawed at her heart.

"Not so, husband! You have founded abbeys in Kent and on our way to Rome you bestowed money for the church foundation in Samer." She smiled. "Here in the city you give to the beggars on the street and did not Bishop Wilfrith teach us the words of Christ? *'In truth I tell you, in so far as you did this to one of the least of these brothers of mine, you did it to me.'* Have faith! Baptism will cleanse your sins but I beg, no more such talk! Defeat the illness as you swept aside your foes!"

Seven days later, they stepped out into the night of joy that had begun with the blessing of the fire, the lighting of lamps and candles. The Angelic Night in Rome shone as bright as day where torches blazed outside the houses, in the streets and squares resplendent with the light symbolic of the Risen Christ. The gay mood of the swirling crowd anticipated the morrow's feast. Raised voices and laughter contrasted with the silence and sorrow of the day before when the fervour of the Passion pierced the hearts of the faithful with thorns.

Swept along and jostled with Cynethryth on his arm, Caedwalla spotted others dressed like himself in white robes, their number increasing as they drew near the baptistery adjoining the basilica.

Inside the building and sheltered from the hectic bustle of hurrying citizens, Cynethryth cast an anxious glance at her husband. Suffering had etched deep lines around his mouth: the shell of the muscular warrior whose presence not long ago exuded menace. For the first time, in this sacred place, she recognised the inevitable and closing her tearful eyes, she prayed for his redemption.

A young man in priestly garb led her away to be seated amid the congregation surrounding the baptismal font. She judged the sunken octagonal pool to stretch nine yards. Hundreds of *competentes*, men and women of all ages, dressed in white, stood barefoot on goatskins. With difficulty, Cynethryth located her husband among them and, heart a-tremble, identified the figure of the Pope before him, head uncovered, like the other priests.

A succession of events, familiar to her from her own baptism, passed in a mist, made hazier by a tumult of conflicting emotions. The stark reality of impending loss, the new life she bore within her, the thought of eternity with Caedwalla, joy at his salvation and fear of an uncertain future mingled with the sentiments evoked by the rituals and the Latin pronouncements. *'Ergo, maledicte diabole'*, she heard as the Pope and the other clergymen, in the rite of exorcism, laid hands on the convert; the chanting of Psalm 139, *'Erue me Domine ab homine malo a viris iniquis serva me'* — 'Deliver me, O Lord, from the evil man: rescue me from the unjust'; the reception of the creed and banner of the cross for protection against the *'diabolical adversary'*; the renunciation of the devil, his pomp and his angels and the inscription as a *'soldier of Christ'*.

Cynethryth sighed, clasping her hands as the Pope, amid all the other participants, stepped into the font and wading waist deep, plunged Caedwalla three times under the water. Pope Sergius enunciated the ritual words of baptism.

The ensuing days, such as Cynethryth hoped never to have known, were marked by the ebb and flow of doctors, infirmarians and priests. Delirious and wasted with fever, Caedwalla did not recognise her any more and the bloodletting and potions proved to be of no avail as he grew weaker and more pallid. She understood the considerable effort he had made to achieve baptism and once attained, he relinquished whatever weapons he had brandished to ward off the invisible foe.

Instead, he had placed his trust in his initiation to peace and sacrificial love.

Seven days after his immersion, still in his baptismal robes and nearing his thirtieth summer, Caedwalla breathed his last. Distraught, Cynethryth, unable to share a final farewell with the man she loved, allowed herself to be escorted into the presence of the Holy Father.

Sergius, in the company of the Archbishop of Milan, gazed with compassion at the tear-stained visage of the young widow.

"Be not sad, Lady," he said, "your husband died in the grace of God and is in bliss at the bosom of Our Saviour. Console yourself with the new life the Father has granted you. Bring up your child in righteousness so that when the Almighty summons you, all three will be reunited in Paradise."

The Pope, in his wisdom, seized the opportunity of Caedwalla's death to glorify the Church. With outstretched hand he indicated the prelate by his side.

"This is my brother in Christ, Crispus, Archbishop of Milan," he said to Cynethryth, "the Almighty raised your husband high and he served the Father well. With your consent, my child, we shall erect a magnificent tomb worthy of him in the basilica of St Peter, whose name he chose for baptism. My venerable brother will create his epitaph."

Red-eyed, Cynethryth looked at the Pontiff, sighed and said, "Holy Father, I must leave my husband here, for I cannot take him to the isle of my birth. I know not how to undertake the journey home," her tears welled up once more.

The Pope reached for a silver bell. A secretary entered the chamber and bowed.

"Accompany our Lady Cynethryth to the Abbey of St Vincent. Find Abbot Aldhelm and instruct him to include the lady among those due to return to their homeland. Ensure she has enough coin for the journey."

Sergius rose, blessed Cynethryth and wished her God speed: the audience at an end.

Dazed, Cynethryth followed the young priest through the teeming streets of Rome, past the ancient temple of the Pantheon and over a bridge across the river. They entered the Borgo on the far bank. Occupied with sorrow and oblivious to her surroundings, the widow walked behind her guide in silence, head bowed.

Aelfhere, passing the Abbey of St Vincent, recognised the red-golden hair of his daughter well before she saw him. With deadly intent, he drew his sword and pushed the helpless priest into the pinioning arms of Ewald who, in dismay, watched Cynethryth gasp and raise a hand to her mouth.

"Father! Here?"

"Viper!" the ealdorman spat the word, "Under which rock slithers your husband?"

Face contorted with rage, he approached his daughter, placing his blade under her chin, "Lead me to him, else I'll end your life where you stand."

The tears coursed down the cheeks of Cynethryth. What further emotions must tear at her heart this day?

"Caedwalla is dead," the words choked from her throat but Aelfhere, though he understood, had no desire to believe them.

"Dead?" he said, "you lie, serpent!"

"It is true, in the name of Christ!" the priest exclaimed, "he died this hour past."

"How so?" He retracted the weapon.

Woeful, Cynethryth gazed at her father, "He never recovered from a wound he took in battle on Wiht," she sobbed, "the blade tainted his blood."

"*My blade*," Aelfhere breathed, unheard by those around him. In effect, he had killed his enemy. Revenge was his! He studied the woman before him. "Then, you are alone!" he growled, fury in his voice. "You will wish to join your husband in the Land of Hel! And I shall oblige you."

With menace, he raised the wolf-pommelled sword.

"Nay, Lord, I beg you!" cried Ewald, "Not your only child!"

"Slay me!" Cynethryth hissed, "and with me destroy your grand-child."

"Child?" Aelfhere lowered the blade, eyes dropping to the slight but noticeable roundness of her belly. In confusion, he replaced the weapon at his belt. He closed his eyes and saw the face of Caedwalla, back in the battle, it faded into that of the priest of Ingui eschewing revenge then changed again into Sergius, the Pope, preaching Christ's speech of — *good gifts* — to one's child. Last, the clearest image of all, that of a red-golden-haired girl of ten hauling her drowning friend to the safety of the beach. Tearful, Aelfhere, overwhelmed by tenderness, took a step forward and held Cynethryth tight.

'*Be guided not by revenge nor loathing but the opposite. . . to overcome.*'

As a smith forge-welds two metals, beating them into a blade, Aelfhere melded the words of the sorcerer with those of Christ. The life within his daughter's womb promised a fresh beginning, but where to start?

Cynethryth breathed into his ear: "Father, we must go to Cerdics-ford, our lives are changed for ever, but..." she quoted what Bishop Wilfrith had taught her: '*... if anyone is in Christ, he is a new creation. The old has passed away; behold, the new has come.*'"

"Ay," murmured Aelfhere, "I've had my fill of the old world and bloodthirsty gods! Daughter, let's embrace the Spring."

Appendix

The epitaph on the tomb of Caedwalla written by Crispus, Archbishop of Milan:

"High estate, wealth, offspring, a mighty kingdom, triumphs, spoils, chieftains, strongholds, the camp, a home; whatsoever the valour of his sires, whatsoever himself had won, Caedwal, mighty in war, left for the love of God, that, a pilgrim king, he might behold, Peter and Peter's seat, receive at his font pure waters of life, and in bright draughts drink of the shining radiance whence a quickening glory streams through all the world. And even as he gained with eager soul the prize of the new life, he laid aside barbaric rage, and, changed in heart, he changed his name with joy. Sergius the Pope bade him be called Peter, himself his father, when he rose born anew from the font, and the grace of Christ, cleansing him, bore him forthwith clothed in white raiment to the heights of Heaven. Wondrous faith of the king, but greatest of all the mercy of Christ, into whose counsels none may enter! For he came in safety from the ends of the earth, even from Britain, through many a nation, over many a sea, by many a path, and saw the city of Romulus and looked upon Peter's sanctuary revered, bearing mystic gifts. He shall walk in white among the sheep of Christ in fellowship with them; for his body is in the tomb, but his soul on high. Thou mightest deem he did but change an earthly for a heavenly sceptre, whom thou seest attain to the kingdom of Christ."

"Here was buried Caedwalla, called also Peter, king of the Saxons, on the twentieth day of April, in the second indiction, aged about thirty years, in the reign of our most pious lord, the Emperor Justinian, in the fourth year of his consulship, in the second year of the pontificate of our Apostolic lord, Pope Sergius."

Historical Notes

Whereas it is known that the wife of Caedwalla was called Cynethryth, historians know nothing of her origins. For purposes of my novel, and with considerable literary license, I chose to have her born on the Isle of Wight. Aelfhere is a creation of mine.

Regarding the isle and concerning to the massacre to which the Venerable Bede [4, 16] refers '…also took the Isle of Wight…and by cruel slaughter endeavoured to destroy all the inhabitants thereof, and to place in their stead people from his own province…' could be interpreted in different ways. Had Bede been thinking in a typical Dark Age Christian manner of the warrior class? In which case the massacre would not have involved farmers, elderly men, women and children as in 'Wyrd of the Wolf'. Bede also refers to the two princes '[…]conducted to a place called At the Stone as they thought to be concealed from the victorious king, they were betrayed and ordered to be killed. This being made known to a certain abbot and priest, whose name was Cynebert, who had a monastery not far from thence, at a place called Reodford, that is, the Ford of Reeds, he came to the king, who then lay privately in those parts, to be cured of the wounds which he had received whilst he was fighting on the Isle of Wight, and begged of him, that if the lads must inevitably be killed, he might be allowed first to instruct them in the mysteries of the faith. […]' Now having restored dignity to the maligned (by me) Cynebert who was not a ragged hermit, it should also be added that usually more than the four months I conceded to the instruction in the mysteries of the faith would be required.

The Anglo-Saxon Chronicle notes under 685 that Caedwalla 'began to contend for the kingdom' and notes that Caedwalla was the son of King Cenberht who died in 661 after being granted royal authority by Cenwealh. It may be that Caedwalla was disappointed not to be confirmed by Cenwealh in his father's position, thus leading to him contesting the kingship with Cenwealh's brother Centwine. It is not be excluded that Centwine was forced into a monastery after this struggle and did not retire voluntarily.

The relationship between the Christian Wilfrith (aka Wilfrid) and the heathen Caedwalla has also been subject of much speculation. Caedwalla is spoken highly of in Stephen's Life of Bishop Wilfrid (Chapter 42), noting that Caedwalla sought out Wilfrid and that Wilfrid supported him in his exile. This murky pagan-Christian relationship becomes clearer upon reading that Wilfrid was badly treated at the court of Caedwalla's rival Centwine, as noted in the Chronicle under 676.

Bede also mentions the granting of a quarter of Wight to the Church under Wilfrith. That this part should have been the area of Cerdicsford is attributable to my imagination.

The curious nature of Caedwalla's illness intrigued me because while documentation tells us that he was ill of his wounds, this does not account for how he was able to conduct the all the events in the last years of his life. It appears that the malady was recurrent. This made me think of human brucellosis which manifests in the same symptoms described in the novel.

There is no evidence that Caedwalla met Ine in person to consign to him his kingdom.

Finally, Pope Sergius often conducted Mass in the catacombs to feel spiritually nearer the Church Fathers. when Caedwalla died the Pope ordered him to be buried in St. Peter's, and a laudatory epitaph to he inscribed on his tomb. When the new Basilica was erected, the relics of

Caedwalla were translated to the Crypt. He is recognised as the patron saint of (reformed) serial killers and his feast day is April 20.

Dear reader,

We hope you enjoyed reading *Wyrd Of The Wolf.* Please take a moment to leave a review, even if it's a short one. Your opinion is important to us.

Discover more books by John Broughton at
https://www.nextchapter.pub/authors/john-broughton

Want to know when one of our books is free or discounted for Kindle? Join the newsletter at http://eepurl.com/bqqB3H

Best regards,

John Broughton and the Next Chapter Team

You could also like:

In The Name Of The Mother by John Broughton

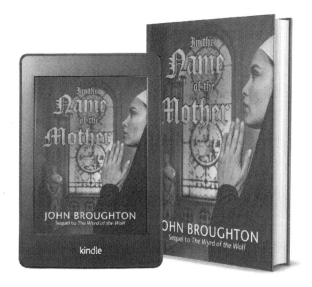

To read the first chapter for free, please head to:
https://www.nextchapter.pub/books/in-the-name-of-the-mother

About the Author

If you wish to find out more about the author, please visit his Facebook page at www.facebook.com/caedwalla/ or his blog at http://www.saxonquill.com/.

You may also be interested to check out his first novel, also published by Endeavour Press, *The Purple Thread,* which deals with the (mis)adventures of Begiloc, a British warrior forced to conduct Saxon missionaries to Thuringia in the eighth century.

Printed in Great Britain
by Amazon